EVA STONE'S SWEET ROMANCE

SHORT STORY COLLECTION 1

Contents

The Sunshine's Grumpy Protector

ACTION & SUSPENSE SWEET ROMANCE SHORT STORIES COLLECTION

EVA STONE

Contents

The Man Sleeping on a Bench

The New York University's purple flag trembles in the winter wind as if it's shivering from the cold just like I am. With my collar turned against the brisk air, I walk Buddy, my Golden Retriever, after class. The streets are almost empty. They only have a few students heading home and some last-minute shoppers.

In the soft glow of a streetlamp, I catch sight of something that makes me stop in my tracks. A man is lying on a bench. The trees' shadows almost conceal him entirely, but I can barely make out his outline.

Why would someone sleep outside in this cold?

Concerned, I approach him cautiously.

"Hey, sir," I begin, hesitating, "it's too cold to sleep here."

He stirs, slowly sitting up and looking at me with a weary gaze. His voice comes out gruff and cold. "What's it to you?"

Taken aback, I try to respond gently, "I just thought... well, you might get sick."

He sighs, irritated. "Look, girl, I appreciate the concern, but I've been through worse."

I remove my long coat, feeling the icy wind cut through my sweater. "Here, take this. I live just around the corner. I can run home and grab another one."

The man glances at the coat, then back at me. His voice is softer but still firm. "No need. Thanks, though."

I am figuring out what to do next. I decide to walk away. But as I go on with my walk, an idea strikes me. I take out my phone and dial the number of a nearby shelter. The old lady who answers the call promises to send someone over.

Time flies as I meander through the streets with my Buddy. When I return to the bench, I notice a van with the shelter's logo parked nearby. Two men are helping the one from the bench into the vehicle.

As the man climbs in, our eyes meet. It's the first time I have seen his face clearly. He is a handsome man in his early thirties. There's no gratitude in his gaze, no anger either. Just a deep, unreadable emotionlessness. It's like looking into a frozen lake, clear but cold.

He doesn't say anything. Neither do I.

As the van pulls away, I can't shake the feeling that I may have intruded more into his life than I should have.

Did I do the right thing?

With snowflakes beginning to dance down from the darkened sky, I look up and let out a long sigh. The man might not be happy with what I did, but at least tonight, he'll be safe and warm.

The next few days are a blur of classes, home-work, and the typical bustle of student life. But I can't shake off the memory of that night. Whenever I pass that bench, my thoughts wander to the man and our fleeting interaction.

One evening, while grabbing a coffee from a nearby café, I spot the man again. This time, he's not on the bench but standing near it, feeding some birds with scraps of bread. He is tall and well-built. He must be in a better mood.

Hesitating, I approach him, clutching my cup for warmth. "Hey, it's you again," I begin, unsure.

He looks at me, his face still unreadable, but he recognizes me. "The girl with the coat," he says in that same gruff voice.

I nod a bit awkwardly. "I'm Julia. How have you been?"

He shrugs. "Been better. But it has also been worse. Thanks for that call to the shelter, I guess. Oh, by the way, my name is Robert." I'll remember this name. There's a pause, and he adds, "I wasn't thrilled about it. But... it was kind."

I smile, relief washing over me. "I'm glad you're okay. I just... didn't want to see you freeze out here."

Robert chuckles, a sound I don't expect from him. "I've been through a lot. But it's rare for strangers to care. So, thank you."

Robert turns and looks into my eyes. His gaze is so sharp that it appears as though he is looking into the depths of my heart.

We chat a little more. But, Robert doesn't talk about anything personal.

Before we part, Robert looks at me with a hint of warmth. "Sometimes, it's not the big gestures but the small acts of kindness that make a difference. Remember that."

I'll remember that, along with his deep voice and beautiful eyes.

I nod, taking his words to heart. "I will, Robert. Take care."

Days turned into weeks, and I have never seen him again. It's intriguing how you can cross paths with some men daily without giving them a second thought. Yet, others you might meet just briefly, but they leave an indelible mark on your memory. Robert is one such man I'll never forget.

Spring breathes life into the city. Trees flaunt their fresh green leaves. Walking home, I feel guilty about Buddy. Whenever he brings me his leash, I can't look into his hopeful eyes. Working two part-time jobs and going to class keeps me super busy. Paying for school is tough, and I miss our long walks outside. But having Coco as my new roommate helps. Her laugh always makes me smile.

"Hola! You look tired," Coco comments as I drag my feet into our apartment. She has sun-kissed skin. Her curly black hair cascades down her shoulders. Her eyes sparkle with mischief. She's a burst of sunshine.

I nod. "Yeah, I had a double shift today and then an evening lecture."

She pats the spot next to her, her eyes twinkling. "Come, sit. I made tacos. Authentic Mexican style."

Gratefully, I dig in. Between bites, I tease her, "Hey, Coco, thanks for bringing the Mexican sunshine to cold NYC."

Coco giggles, cheeks rosy. "Well, someone needed to do it!"

In moments like these, we bond, and within just a few days, it feels like we've known each other for years.

But it's not just me Coco bonds with. She falls head over heels for Buddy. Buddy has a wagging tail and gives endless licks. He seems to feel the same. When my class or work schedules get too tight, Coco steps in. She takes Buddy for walks and spoils him with treats.

This evening, I came home a little earlier than usual. The apartment is quiet. But as I tiptoe to my bedroom, a soft sound stops me. It's Coco's melodic laughter, interspersed with Buddy's playful barks.

Pushing the door gently, I see them. Coco lies on the carpet. Buddy is sprawled beside her. They are both in a tug-of-war with his favorite toy. She catches my eye and waves, her face beaming. "Hey! We're just playing a little. Hope you don't mind."

It is the first time Buddy does not run to me.

I lean against the doorframe, a smile tugging at my lips. "Mind? No. But I think Buddy has found his new favorite human."

She chuckles, "Oh, come on! He still loves you the most."

I sit down beside them, ruffling Buddy's fur. He looks at Coco with his tail wagging and his tongue hanging out. I can't help but wonder if he has betrayed me for this bundle of sunshine.

Before I fall asleep that night, I see Buddy's eyes shine in the dark.

"Hey, Buddy. Are you still mine?"

The following day, I need to buy Safe Haven, the bestselling romance novel of 2010. It's a lovely spring evening as I walk to the bookstore. Everything feels fresh and new. I'm enjoying the moment when I suddenly bump into Robert just outside the bookstore.

Still surprised, I look up to find Robert's familiar eyes smiling at me. "Oh! Hey there," I stammer, brushing a loose strand of hair behind my ear.

"Hey! What a coincidence," Robert says with a chuckle. "Are you looking for a book?"

I nod, still a bit flustered from our unexpected meeting. "Yeah, just needed to pick up this book for a class project. How about you?"

Robert shrugs, looking a bit awkward. "Actually, I had plans to have dinner with a client. I'd reserved a table at that Italian place around the corner. But he just called and had to cancel because of a family emergency."

"Oh, that's too bad," I reply, trying to sound sympathetic.

He hesitates for a moment, then with a teasing glint in his eyes, he says, "Now I have a table for two and no one to share it with. Would you be interested in joining me? I promise the food is great."

I blink, surprised by his offer. I've never seen this playful side of Robert before. "Really? I mean, I don't want to intrude on your plans...."

"You wouldn't be intruding at all," he reassures, his tone light and humorous. "It would save me from the pitying looks of the waitstaff. Plus, I've always thought food tastes better with company."

The restaurant's interior is more luxurious than anything I've experienced. The ceiling holds golden chandeliers. They give the space a warm, inviting glow. Soft notes from a piano in the corner fill the room, adding to the ambiance.

Robert looks around with an amused grin. "It's almost like stepping into a Fitzgerald novel, don't you think?"

I laugh. "I just started my literature major, and you're already testing my knowledge?"

He raises an eyebrow playfully. "Well, surprise! Fitzgerald's not part of the curriculum. But his works... ah, they paint life so vividly."

We continue our talk about literature. I'm truly amazed by his knowledge and insights. "You might know more than some of my professors," I comment, genuinely impressed.

As our food arrives, Robert's demeanor turns sincere. "I wanted to thank you," he says, looking directly into my eyes. "For that night at the bench."

I tilt my head, a burning question on my lips, but I hesitate. It's his private moment, and I shouldn't pry.

Seeing my struggle, Robert chuckles softly. "You're wondering why I was there, right?" I nod, and he takes a deep breath. "I came back from a business trip early, and let's just say I found out my marriage wasn't as solid as I believed."

I'm taken aback. "Oh, Robert, I'm so sorry."

He waves me off, a small smile playing on his lips. "Don't be. That's life. I could've gone to a hotel, but I needed some air, some space to think."

I wonder aloud, "Who could ever hurt someone like you?"

He chuckles. "Life's strange. But that chapter's closed. I'm free now." As he pours more wine into my glass, I notice that his finger does not have a wedding ring.

The music from the piano calls out to him. He walks to the pianist, whispering something before taking his place at the keys. The room goes quiet as he starts to play, and it feels like the world stands still. The melody he produces is hauntingly beautiful.

As the last note fades, I realize the feelings bubbling inside me are unfamiliar yet welcome.

There's a warmth in my chest, a sweetness that wasn't there before.

We leave the restaurant, and the night sky sparkles more than usual. The stars, shining faintly overhead, celebrate the unexpected connection between two souls.

When we say goodbye, Robert smiles at me. "Life's like a piano. Whether it's happy or sad depends on how you play it."

I may be falling in love with Robert.

When I return to my apartment, the quiet street is alive with flashing blue and red lights. They cast an eerie glow on the building's front. My heart races as I approach, panic gripping me. Why are the police here?

To my horror, my apartment unit's door stands ajar.

Is Buddy okay?

Taking a deep breath, I cautiously step inside. The scene before me shocks me. Four policemen are in the living room. Two others are coming out of my room.

Buddy looks distressed with a muzzle around his snout and chained up in the kitchen. His eyes meet mine, full of confusion and sadness. I approach Buddy, gently stroking him to calm his distress.

A tall policeman with sharp gray eyes and a stern demeanor walks out of my room. "Ma'am, is this your room?" His voice is harsh, demanding attention.

I swallow, my voice trembling, "Yes. What's going on?"

He points to a table displaying many small plastic bags with a white substance. "We found these drugs in your closet. Care to explain?"

I stare, my eyes wide. "I... I have no idea how those got there. I've never seen them, let alone touched drugs in my life."

His gaze is piercing. "We've received tips that someone in this unit has been selling drugs to the community kids. Is that you?"

"No! That's not me! I don't even know how those got into my closet." My voice cracks, and my emotions overwhelm me.

I look desperately towards Coco, searching for some support. But she's different tonight. There is no laughter, no friendly banter, just a stoic calmness. She's sitting on the couch, observing everything, but her silence is deafening.

"Do you have any visitors or anyone with access to your room?" the policeman continues, his voice sharp, and without missing detail.

"Just Coco," I mutter, "and some friends occasionally, but I trust them."

"We will need to question everyone," he states firmly.

Coco finally speaks. Her voice is clear, "Officer, I've lived here for a short time. But, I've never seen anything suspicious.""

I nod in agreement. "Please, Officer. I don't know how those ended up in my closet. You have to believe me."

The tension builds as the policeman's gaze shifts between Coco and me. "Given the circumstances, both of you must come with us," he declares. His finality allows no argument.

Coco stands up abruptly, her voice edgy, "Why me? Those were found in her closet, not mine!"

The sharp-eyed policeman narrows his gaze at her. "Until we get everything sorted, everyone present will be considered a suspect. Unless one person can take responsibility."

"But, Officer," Coco argues, pointing to Buddy, who's still agitated, "she's the dog's owner. If I'm free, I can take care of the dog. What will happen to him if we're both gone?"

"The dog will be sent to a shelter. Unfortunately, the shelter can only hold the dog for a short while."

"Take me." I can't let Buddy go to a shelter.

There's a brief pause. The Officer considers the situation, then finally nods, "Fine. "Then he turns to Coco. "But don't think this means you're completely off the hook. We might need you to answer further questions."

Coco nods, relief evident on her face.

I feel betrayed and confused. "Coco, please make sure Buddy's okay. I... I don't understand what's happening."

Coco avoids my gaze, "Just... sort things out quickly."

The handcuffs close around my wrists. I'm led out of my own apartment. The weight of the situation presses down on me. Coco's words ring in my ears. But, I'm focused on Buddy's whines. They pierce through the hum of the unfamiliar and intimidating atmosphere.

The cold metal of the handcuff bites into my wrists as I'm led away from my apartment. My heart aches as I catch one last glimpse of Buddy's pleading eyes. How did we get to this point? Can I ever trust Coco after this?

The car ride to the police station is a blur of flashing lights and the distant hum of city life. It's strange how life outside usually continues, unaware of my turmoil. Once inside, a policewoman steps forward, her expression unreadable. "You have the right to remain silent..." she begins. The Miranda Rights echo in my ears, but my mind races elsewhere.

"I need an attorney," I interrupt her, my voice shaky. "I don't have money for one, so I'll need the court to appoint me one."

The policewoman nods and proceeds to remove my personal belongings. The weight of reality hits me hard as she takes away my cell phone. "No jewelry, money, just a phone, it's simple." She says as my cell is sealed in a bag. But, it is more complicated on my side. "It'll be returned to you upon your release." She put the zip bag into a box. At that moment, the gesture feels like I'm being stripped of a part of myself.

The policewoman leads me to the front desk and then stands beside me.

A young, good-looking policeman sits across the desk and looks at his computer screen. "I need some details from you," he says calmly. His ten fingers move smoothly as if he is playing the piano. I feel ashamed as he records my name, date of birth, and address in the system. Why is he involved in this? Why am I?

"Do you know why you were arrested?" he asks without looking up.

"The drugs," I mumble, "but they weren't mine."

He enters the details. These are the drug's type and amount, the arrest's location, and the arresting officer's name. Then, he runs a criminal history search about me. Unexpectedly, he smiles and adds, "You have a clean record."

I meet his eyes. "I'm still clean."

Without much delay, the policewoman escorts me to the fingerprinting area. My fingers are covered in dark ink, each pressed firmly onto paper. I cringe inwardly, knowing this might tie me to any unsolved case, anywhere. My prints could be shared far and wide, a brand of my alleged crime.

The young policeman from earlier returns, a camera in hand. "Time for your photos," he says.

I feel a surge of anger. This is not how I envisioned my life. But there's no escape now. Click.

The front image is captured.

Click.

The side profile. My mugshots are added to a database of criminals. I am sure these are the ugliest pictures I have taken since birth.

After the invasive procedures, I'm led to the holding cell. The metallic clang of the bars reverberates in the dim corridor. Inside, it's cold and sterile. I huddle on the bench, my thoughts racing. Tears prick my eyes as I replay the evening's events. The betrayal was confusing and scary. There's also the paperwork due tomorrow at school.

Hours drag by. I toss and turn on the hard bench, unable to find solace. Every time I close my eyes, Buddy's face fills my vision. I hope he's okay. I wish I'd get to see him again soon.

The night is long and torturous. Distant footsteps and muffled conversations remind me of my predicament. All I can hope for is the dawn of a new day and clarity amidst this storm.

When days pass peacefully, they quietly fade away, leaving no mark. They seem ordinary and forgettable. But when tough times hit unexpectedly, I genuinely appreciate those calm moments. I painfully learned this.

The long night passes, and a new day, my court day arrives. The gray of the New York County Criminal Court looms above me. Its solid concrete exterior makes me feel even smaller. The lines of police officers wear dark blue uniforms.

They patrol the entrance. It makes me feel like I'm entering a fortress, not a courthouse. My chest tightens with each step, and I can't breathe.

Inside, I'm guided to a private consultation room. With its bleak walls and dim lighting, the room does little to ease my anxiety. A young man with light yellow curly hair sits there, waiting. He stands as I enter. He offers a small smile. Given my circumstances, it feels oddly reassuring. I do not like his bright yellow tie.

"Hey there," he starts, extending his hand. "I'm Jack, your public defender."

I glance at him, disappointed. "You're so young," I blurt out unintentionally.

He chuckles softly. "I get that a lot. But trust me, I've got a fair share of courtroom battles under my belt." A light in his eyes tells me he's confident, but there's a gentle understanding there, too.

"I don't have money for bail," I don't want to beat around the bush; I'll get straight to the point. "And I swear I'm innocent."

Jack nods, scribbling down some notes. "We'll fight this. Just tell me everything, and we'll sort it out."

I give Jack a quick summary. Before we can delve more deeply, a knock interrupts us. "It's time," Jack says, helping me to my feet.

Walking through the big courthouse hallway feels so strange. It's so huge that it's a lot to take in. The shiny floors look like I could slip, and I can hear footsteps bouncing around from all directions.

But as we turn the corner to enter the courtroom, I see him, Robert. He is dressed in a crisp blue suit. It speaks of his high status and professionalism. He looks so out of place in my current world of chaos. My face burns with embarrassment, and I look down, hoping he won't recognize the girl he once shared a laugh with.

But he just walks by, his gaze never meeting mine. A part of me is relieved, yet another part is crushed. Would he think less of me now?

As we continue walking, Jack casually lifts a hand in greeting, whispering, "Hi," to Robert. It's such a simple, mundane gesture amidst the chaos of my life, but it makes me wonder: Do they know each other?

Inside the courtroom, the atmosphere is tense. The room's grandeur, with its wooden panels and high ceiling, makes me feel like an intruder in a place I don't belong. There's a low murmur of voices. Lawyers discuss cases. Families wait in fear. Defendants sit nervously.

My lawyer, Jack, and I sit at one of the tables. Opposite us sits the prosecution. A stern woman with her hair tied back reviews her notes. She occasionally glances in my direction.

"All rise," the bailiff calls out, and the room stands as the Judge enters, an older man with gray hair and glasses.

"Be seated," the Judge says, and the room obeys.

The court clerk then reads out the charges against me. "The defendant is charged with possession of illegal narcotics."

Jack rises, "Your honor, my client pleads not guilty."

The Judge nods, "Prosecution, your opening statement."

The prosecutor stands and addresses the court. "Your honor, the evidence will show that the defendant had many illegal drugs. We intend to prove that she knowingly and willingly had these drugs in her apartment."

Jack then begins our defense. "Your honor, while it's true that drugs were found in my client's apartment, she did not know of their existence. We will show that she is innocent and a victim of circumstances."

The trial proceeds. The prosecution presents their evidence. It includes the bags of drugs and the testimony of the officers who found them. They also present details of the arrest.

When Jack gets the chance, he questions the officers. He tries to find inconsistencies in their stories. "Officer, isn't it true that other people had access to the apartment?" Jack asks.

"Yes, but the drugs were found in the defendant's room," the Officer responds.

Jack continues, "Are you aware of any other individuals who might have a motive to plant those drugs?"

The Officer hesitates, "Not to my knowledge."

The Judge announces, "There is no direct evidence. We need to examine the case. So, this court will adjourn. We will reconvene in ten days for a preliminary hearing."

Jack addresses the court, "Your Honor, my client, Ms. Julia Thompson, has no prior record. She has strong ties to the community and poses no flight risk. We request that she be released on her own recognizance."

The prosecutor stands up and says, "Your Honor, Ms. Thompson has no previous convictions. But, we should consider the gravity of the current charges."

It is my turn. I speak softly but earnestly, "Judge, I assure you I will return to clear my name. I have no reason to run."

The Judge pauses, looks at the documentation, and then at me. "I will grant Ms. Thompson's request for release. I'm basing this on the facts and the nature of the crime. But, Ms. Thompson, please know that not appearing in court will lead to arrest and more penalties. Is that understood?"

"Yes, Your Honor. Thank you."

A wave of relief washes over me. Jack pats my back, "Let's go."

As we pass by the back row, a tall man stands up and joins us in the hallway.

"Well done, Jack."

Robert pats Jack's shoulder." Let's find a place to sit down."

The aroma of rich coffee wafts through the air as I face Jack and Robert in the coffee shop's intimate corner. I fidget with my hands, the weight of the situation pressing on my shoulders.

Seeing my discomfort, Jack tries to lighten the mood. "Meet Robert," he says with a grin, "We both survived Yale Law." And now, he's one of the best criminal attorneys in town."

I nod, pretending I do not know Robert. I want to keep the information I met Robert on the bench to myself.

Robert raises an eyebrow, his sharp eyes meeting mine. "Cut the introductions, Jack. We've got ten days. And if the movies have taught me anything, every second counts." His tone has a hint of humor but underlies a sense of urgency.

I take a deep breath, trying to hold back my nervousness, "So, what's the plan?"

Robert leans forward, his fingers steepled. "First, we team up. Jack'll fill me in, and I believe you. But in court, believing isn't enough. We need evidence, and we need it fast." He sips his coffee, watching me over the cup's rim.

Jack adds, "Robert's going to work with me on this, but he is expensive—"

"Well, a dinner should cover it." Robert smiles.

I look at Robert, confused. "Dinner?"

He chuckles. "Yeah, but make it somewhere fancy, okay? I've had enough coffee for one lifetime."

Their lighthearted banter helps, but the gravity of the situation pulls me back. "The person responsible is still out there. Someone who can get into my room."

Robert nods. "Coco's on our radar. We need to keep an eye on her."

I blink in surprise, taken aback. "Coco? She's my friend, Robert."

Robert's tone grows even graver. "Just be cautious. Trust your instincts." Then he looks at Jack and asks, "What about hiring a private detective?"

"I can't afford that," I say quickly, my eyes downcast.

Robert smirks. "Don't worry about it. I'll cover the cost. Consider it an early dinner payment." His humor is unexpected in a situation like this, and I can't help but smile.

Jack checks his watch. "I've got to run. Another court appearance beckons. Robert, can you represent her on the next court day?"

Robert gives him a mock salute. "Aye, aye, Captain."

As Jack leaves, Robert turns serious, saying. "Listen, you can't return to your apartment. It's not safe. I'll find you somewhere to stay."

"Thank you."

Robert puts a calming hand on mine. "Wait here. I have an appointment with my client. It may take about an hour. I will find you a hotel after the meeting."

Robert leaves in a hurry. His tie is flying in the wind.

After that, time seems to move painfully slowly. Every minute feels like an hour. I need to get my schoolbooks... and Buddy! Panic rises in my voice. The thought of Buddy alone and scared breaks my heart.

I can't wait anymore. I must see my Buddy now.

The chilly breeze brushes against my face as I make my way home. I walk and run, run and walk. I put my hands into my pocket to ensure I got my cell back. Yes, it is inside my pocket. Everything happened in the twenty-four hours like a dream, but they are all real.

When I approach my apartment, I hear muffled voices. Curious, I open the door quietly. Peeking through the slightly ajar door, I freeze.

There, in my bedroom, stands Coco, handing a small bag to a young man with a snack tattoo on his neck. Drugs.

I feel my stomach drop. Suddenly, everything becomes clear. Robert is right. It was Coco who stashed those drugs in my closet. She betrayed me. And worse, she put my future in jeopardy.

With my heart racing, I want to close the door and call the police. But, before I close the door, Buddy already finds me. He runs to me excitedly. Buddy's action alerts Coco. Her sharp eyes catch the movement, and in a split second, she's upon me, her sweet demeanor replaced by cold fury. The young man pulls me inside, closes the door behind me, and drags me into the living room. I fight back as hard as possible, but they pin me together.

"Coco, I thought you were my friend, but you—"

"But you are stupid." Coco's voice is low and icy cold.

Terror courses through me. I scream, but my voice sounds weak and distant. Just as things seem most dire, there's a ferocious growl. Buddy.

My loyal dog lunges, teeth bared, snapping at the young man and Coco. He doesn't let up, defending me with every ounce of his being. The young man, clearly outmatched, decides to bolt, leaving Coco fending for herself.

Amid the chaos, the piercing sound of sirens fills the air. The police! Someone must have heard the commotion and called them.

With Buddy keeping Coco at bay, the officers rush in, handcuffing her. She doesn't resist. Instead, she shoots me a look of pure venom.

"Are you okay? Are you hurt?" one Officer bends down and asks me.

"I'm fine, thank you." I smile at him. Now, I do not have to fear their uniform anymore.

As the police lead her away, I sink to the floor, a whirlwind of emotions crashing over me. Relief, sadness, shock. But amid all this, one feeling stands out—gratitude.

Buddy trots over, his tail wagging, licking away my tears. "Good boy," I whisper, hugging him tightly. "You are my guardian, my savior."

Then I hear my phone ring. I pick up my phone, my fingers trembling.

"Where are you?" Robert's voice is nervous.

"Robert," I manage to say, my voice strained, "Coco's been arrested. Buddy... he saved me."

Robert's response is immediate, the urgency in his voice palpable. "Stay put. I'm coming."

About thirty minutes later, the roar of a car engine signals his arrival. I open the door. The scene inside my apartment shows the recent chaos. Furniture is overturned. Items are scattered. The floor is marked by our scuffle.

He steps inside, taking in the mess with a glance. "Are you okay?"

"Thanks to Buddy," I reply, patting my loyal dog, who wags his tail.

Robert suggests a walk to help me process everything. Soon, the three of us, Robert, Buddy, and I are strolling along the familiar streets.

The cool evening air does little to calm the storm of emotions raging inside me. But walking beside Robert, the streets are lit by the city lights. I feel an unexpected romantic undertone.

We find ourselves in front of a familiar bench. It's the very one where I first stumbled upon Robert on that cold winter night, without realizing it. We both look at it, a silence settling between us.

"That was both my worst and best night," Robert says softly.

I turn to him, puzzled. "How can both those feelings come together?"

He gazes upwards, pointing towards the night sky. "See how the moon rises as the sun sets? There's beauty in both the end and the beginning. That night, on the bench, I felt lost and abandoned. But it also led me to you."

His words, spoken so sincerely, cause my heart to race. The moonlight bathes us in its soft glow, and Robert looks into my eyes. "You have a soul as captivating as the moon. It shines even in the darkest times."

Buddy barks lightly. He senses the change. He wags his tail and playfully circles us.

Robert takes a deep breath. "Your case is clear now. I won't be your lawyer. How about I be your boyfriend instead?"

For a moment, I'm speechless. A smile slowly forms on my face. "From a strange man on a bench to this? Life has a funny way of surprising us."

He laughs, and his brilliant smile lights up his face. "So, is that a yes?"

I nod, chuckling, "Yes, Robert. Yes."

Buddy happily leads. The two of us continue our walk hand in hand. We are ready to face the future together.

The True Kindness

The bell above the door jingles softly. A homeless man hesitantly steps into my small grocery shop. The winter chill seems to cling to him, his coat tattered and several sizes too big. He pauses just inside. His eyes scan the warm, cozy interior. It is bathed in the soft glow of early morning light.

"Good morning," I call out, my voice echoing slightly in the quiet store. "Can I help you find anything?"

"Morning." He takes a moment to answer, looking around at the fresh fruits and homemade stuff on the shelves. He seems really tired as if he's carrying a heavy load. Slowly, he moves closer, stopping near Mrs. Thompson's bread.

The bread costs $3.20. His hand almost reaches for the bread, then stops, and the homeless man sighs softly.

Something in my heart twitches. I see a silent battle between need and pride. Without a second thought, I step out from behind the counter and pick up the loaf of bread.

"Here," I say, offering it to him.

For a moment, he just stares at me, his expression unreadable. Then, slowly, a smile breaks through, transforming his face. It's a smile filled with gratitude, relief, and disbelief.

"Thank you," he murmurs, his voice rough like gravel. "I... I can't remember the last time someone did something nice for me."

"It's no trouble at all," I reply, feeling a warmth spreading through my chest.

He nods, clutching the bread like a precious treasure. "I wish I could pay you back somehow."

"Your smile is more than enough payment," I assure him, meaning every word. As he turns to leave, the bell jingles again, a slightly cheerier sound this time.

I watch the door closing softly behind him. A sense of rightness fills me.

In my little shop in the heart of the small town, I meet so many people, each carrying their own stories and burdens. But in moments like these, I'm reminded of what connects us all—a simple yet profound need for kindness.

The next day, Mrs. Green, who lives two blocks down, comes in. Her hands shake slightly as she counts coins for a carton of milk. "I'm just a bit short," she whispers, her cheeks tinged with embarrassment.

Before I know it, I say, "It's not worth worrying about, Mrs. Green. Consider it a gift."

Her eyes well up with tears. "Bless you, dear. I don't know what I would do without this shop."

Words of my small gestures begin to spread. It's like opening a gate. People start coming, not just for groceries, but with their stories and struggles. Each story tugs at my heartstrings, compelling me to help.

A young father with a restless toddler in his arms, his face etched with worry, talks about his layoff. I slip a bag of apples into his cart and receive a grateful hug in return.

Mr. Jenkins, an elderly man with a limp, shares his struggles with medical bills. I can't let him leave without adding a few essentials to his bag.

Each day brings new faces and new stories.

A single mother juggling two jobs, a student trying to make ends meet, a family reeling from a recent tragedy.

My shop becomes more than a place to buy food; it's a sanctuary, a haven of compassion.

But as days turn into weeks, I notice the strain on my shop. The register that once chimed steadily with sales now sings less frequently. I close up at night, my feet aching, and tally up the day's earnings, feeling a knot form in my stomach.

The shelves seem emptier daily, and I find myself dipping into my savings to restock. My heart says, "Keep going; they need you," but my head whispers warnings of a sinking ship.

The shop, once bustling and bright, now whispers of struggle. My heart aches with the weight of decisions I know I must make.

In those moments of doubt, I remember the homeless man's smile, Mrs. Green's grateful tears, and the young father's hug. They are reminders of why I started this—it's not for profit but for people, for kindness.

But the reality of my situation is too hard to ignore. I know something must change. I just need to figure out what or how.

Before I figure out what to do, the problem hits me. One morning, the bakery, where I usually get my supplies, has lost power. This means they can't bake or deliver the bread to my shop as usual, throwing off a routine we've always relied on.

"Uh, what's happening? Where's the bread I always get?" a customer asks, his voice filled with confusion as a hush falls over the room.

"Where's the bread? I can't start my day without my usual loaf," a regular customer complains loudly. His brows are furrowed in frustration.

I can feel their disappointment and frustration. They are directed towards me and it's over-whelming. These people I've served for years have always greeted me with smiles and grat-itude. But today, their expressions are foreign, their words laced with annoyance.

"I understand your frustration, and I apologize. We're doing our best to sort this out," I explain, my voice barely above a whisper.

As the morning wears on, the tension only grows. I feel helpless. I stand amid chaos, miss-ing the warmth and connection that usually fill the space.

"I come here every morning for bread," an el-derly lady snaps. "What am I supposed to do now?"

"I'm really sorry," I respond softly. "It's out of my control."

Her scowl deepens. "This used to be a reliable place."

The murmurs turn into complaints, each customer voicing their dissatisfaction. The situation escalates. Some demand more discounts. Their hopes are fueled by my past kindness.

"We know you've been giving breaks to others," one man says, his voice edged with frustration. 'Why can't you do the same for us?' The sense of entitlement in the air adds another layer of pressure.

I stand there, torn between my desire to help and the harsh reality of my dwindling profits. Each discount demand feels like another tug at my resolve. It also tugs at the shop's finances.

Amidst the chaos, the door opens, and a tall man steps in. He has a commanding presence. His gaze sweeps over the shop with an unreadable expression. He doesn't speak immediately, just observes, as if taking in every detail of the scene before him.

Then, he pulls me to the corner.

"You can't help everyone." His voice is calm but carries an authority that silences the room. "If you keep doing what you have done, you can only bring yourself down."

I bristle at his words. Who is he to judge my decisions? His tone, though measured, feels like a rebuke, a cold splash of reality.

"I'm trying to help my community," I retort, my voice more assertive now. "Isn't that important?"

He looks at me, his eyes unyielding. "Helping is good, but not at the expense of your livelihood or to the wrong people. There's a line."

His words stung. I want to argue, to defend my choices, but a part of me knows he's right. The shop is struggling, and today's events are just a symptom of a more significant problem.

"But what about the people who rely on me?" I ask, my voice tinged with desperation.

"They should find their way," he responds. "People are resilient. But if you go under, what happens to your help then?"

"Who are you? Why should I listen to you?"

"I'm Richard." His voice is firm and calm. "Just want to help you."

The room is silent now, and the customers are watching our exchange. I feel exposed and vulnerable. His words are a harsh reminder of the reality I've been trying to ignore.

"You need to think about sustainability," he continues, his voice softer now. "Kindness is a virtue, but it needs to be balanced with practicality."

He turns and leaves. His departure is as quiet as his entrance.

I'm left amidst the half-lit aisles and empty shelves, feeling a profound sense of loss. I felt a loss for my shop. It was losing vitality. I felt a loss for the community spirit I'd nurtured. And, I felt a loss for the belief that kindness alone could fix everything.

His words echo in my mind, a stern warning intermingled with truth.

I realize then that my desire to help has blinded me to the practicalities of running a business. The shop, my grandfather's legacy, is more than just a place of trade; it symbolizes my dreams and values.

As the next day dawns, I unlock the door to my shop with a heavy heart. The usual chirpiness that accompanies the start of a new day is absent.

The first customer of the day is Mrs. Henderson, a regular who often benefits from my discounts.

Today, she approaches with a basket of essentials. Her face shows the usual worry about money.

"I was hoping," she starts, her voice trailing with hope.

I take a deep breath, feeling a knot tighten in my stomach. "I'm sorry, Mrs. Henderson, I can't offer the discounts anymore."

Her expression shifts from hope to disbelief. "But you've always helped us out."

"I know, and I wish I could continue, but it's not financially possible anymore." My words feel like stones in my mouth, heavy and hard.

She leaves, her disappointment palpable, and I feel a piece of our connection fray and snap.

The day wears on, and with each denial of a discount, the atmosphere in the shop grows colder and more distant. Friendly banter once filled the air. Now, it's replaced by strained silence. The silence is broken only by the sound of transactions.

The locals, who once greeted me with smiles and stories, now pass by with barely a nod or a glare of resentment. I can feel the community's warmth fading, replaced by a chill that seeps into my bones.

One evening, I close the shop and sit in the dimming light, the shadows playing across the empty aisles.

I think of my grandfather, who started this shop with dreams of it being a community cornerstone. Now, I'm watching those dreams slip through my fingers like grains of sand.

The decision to put up the "For Sale" sign feels like admitting defeat.

I stand before the shop window, the sign in my hands trembling slightly. I place it on the window. Each letter feels like a betrayal. It's not just of my family's legacy but of the community I've tried to support.

That night, sleep eludes me. I toss and turn, the sheets tangling around my legs, each twist and turn a reminder of the day's events. The moon casts a pale glow through my window, painting the room in shades of silver and shadow.

In the dim light, the room feels larger and emptier. On the dresser is an old photo of my grandfather, taken outside the shop on its opening day. His smile, once a source of inspiration, now feels like an accusation. I can almost feel his eyes on me, heavy with disappointment. It's as if he's in the room, watching the legacy he built crumble.

I sit up, hugging my knees, the cold air nipping at my skin. The silence is oppressive, filled with the echoes of the day. I see the disappointed faces of my customers. I see the resentment in their eyes. It all plays on a relentless loop of failure in my mind.

My thoughts spiral, and guilt and regret intertwine.

The image of my grandfather in the photo morphs, his expression shifting from pride to sorrow. I imagine him asking me why I couldn't keep his dream alive, why I let the heart of the community fade away. The questions hang in the air, unanswerable.

I lie back down and close my eyes, willing sleep to come, but it's futile. My mind is a whirlwind of memories, doubts, and fears.

As the night stretches on, the room grows colder, the chill seeping into my bones. I pull the covers tighter around me, seeking comfort in their warmth. But even that feels hollow, a poor substitute for the warmth of the shop, of the community I've lost.

Finally, the first light of dawn begins to filter through the curtains. Sleep mercifully claims me.

The day I sell the shop is like saying goodbye to an old friend. The sign comes down—replaced by one that reads SOLD—and with it, a part of me.

The pain of closing the doors for the last time is indescribable. I turn the key in the lock, feeling the finality of the click.

A week later, curiosity gets the better of me, and I find myself walking past the old place. It's buzzing with workers and noise. And there's Richard, overseeing everything. My heart sinks. He's the new owner?

I approach him, my steps hesitant.

"Richard, why are you here?" I ask, trying to keep my voice steady.

"I bought the shop." He turns, a bit surprised to see me. "I'm planning to turn it around."

I fold my arms, feeling defensive. "Turn it around? It was fine before."

He steps closer, his expression softening. "I know. But sometimes, change is necessary."

I don't know what to say. My gaze lingers on the shiny new double doors Richard has installed. The old door, a silent witness to many memories, lies discarded in the front yard.

"Can I keep the old lock?" I find myself asking Richard,

"Of course," Richard replies, signaling to a worker.

The worker carefully unhinges the lock from the old door. Richard then takes a moment to gently clean the dust off the lock with a paper towel. He acts deliberately and respectfully. It's as if he understands the value of this small, mundane object to me.

He places the cleaned lock in a small box and hands it to me. As I take it, the weight of history is palpable.

Months fly by, and the old grocery shop transforms. It's part of a sleek restaurant chain, buzzing with life. It's so different, so not mine anymore.

I'm walking by one day, and Richard is leaving the new restaurant. He spots me and waves me over.

"Hey," he says, a small smile on his face. "You should come see the inside. It's changed a lot."

I hesitate, then nod. "Okay, why not?"

We walk in, and I'm struck by how different everything looks. It's modern and stylish, and I feel out of place.

"It's nice," I admit, though it's hard to say.

Richard looks at me, and there's a gentleness in his eyes. "I wanted to honor the shop's history. Keep some of its spirit."

I'm surprised by his words, and my expression must show it.

He chuckles lightly. "I'm not all business, you know. I care about this place, too."

My lifestyle changes from a shop owner to a coffee maker at a local café.

Working at the local coffee shop has become my new routine. The smell of fresh coffee and the buzz of morning customers are comforting. They provide a backdrop. It's a simple job, but it keeps my mind occupied.

One day, Richard walks in. He's become somewhat of a regular face. He's always polite and gives a nod of acknowledgment as he orders his usual black coffee. Sometimes, he's alone. But, most times he's with a friend or a business associate. They discuss things in low, earnest tones.

"You're usual, black, no sugar?" I ask as he approaches the counter.

"That's right," he answers with a small smile. "How are you settling in?"

"Getting there," I reply, pouring his coffee. "It's different but good."

He nods, sipping his coffee thoughtfully. "I've got a proposition for you," he says suddenly. "Manager at one of my other locations. It's more than just making coffee."

I'm taken aback, unsure what to make of his offer. "Why me?" I ask.

"You've got potential," he says simply. "Think about it."

And think about it: I do. Eventually, curiosity wins over hesitation. I accept Richard's offer.

The new job is a whole different world. Richard's other location is busier and more dynamic. And there, I see sides of him I hadn't noticed before.

He's everywhere checking in with staff, reviewing numbers, thinking, and planning. He's smart. That much is clear. And he works hard, harder than anyone.

But he's also strict, a stickler for rules. "Consistency is key," he tells an employee one day. "We can't afford mistakes."

Yet, he's kind to his staff, always fair. "Good job today," he says after a particularly hectic shift. "I knew you'd fit in."

His blend of firmness and fairness is something new to me. It's inspiring but also intimidating.

One afternoon, I find the courage to ask him about it. "You're so strict with how things are done, but you're not... harsh. How do you do that?"

He leans against the counter, considering his answer. "I've learned that being hard doesn't mean you can't be kind. You need rules to run a business, but you also need people to run it. And people need understanding, not just orders."

His words make me think. There's depth to him, a balance of strength and empathy I hadn't seen before.

Working alongside him, I understand how he thinks and sees the world better than I do.

And as days turn into weeks, I look at him differently. New surprises keep coming to me. Richard is not just my boss but a person I respect and even admire.

It's a strange feeling, growing slowly and subtly. But it's a newfound respect for a man I once thought I had it all figured out.

One day, I overheard him talking on the phone. "Yes, we'll continue the program," he says firmly. "It's important. These kids depend on it." My curiosity is piqued; what is he talking about?

A coworker explains, "We're in a program. It helps feed low-income middle school kids." A part of our profits goes to it."

I'm so surprised by how deeply he is involved in helping the community. It's a side of him I hadn't even considered.

One afternoon, Richard invites me to join him at a school. They're distributing meals from our program. Seeing the kids' smiles and genuine gratitude is eye-opening. This is what sustainable kindness looks like.

As we drive back, I share my thoughts. "I used to think you were just about the bottom line, but I was wrong. What you're doing here... it's remarkable."

He smiles a rare, genuine smile. "I learned the hard way that helping others isn't just about giving things away. It's about creating a system where you can keep giving without losing yourself."

"Richard, I've been thinking about what you said. My mistake was to give everything away until I had nothing left."

He nods. "It's a common mistake." He glances at me. "Smart kindness is true kindness."

His words make me pause. Smart kindness. It's a concept I hadn't considered before.

I grow up under his guidance, not just in my job skills but as a person. "Richard, I've learned a lot from you."

He looks thoughtful. "Sometimes, we learn the most valuable lessons a bit late. But the important thing is that you're learning them now."

As we return to the restaurant, the night has fully settled in, dark and brushed with a cool, windy embrace. In the parking lot, Richard notices me shivering. Without a word, he puts his jacket over my shoulders. The warmth from the jacket envelops me. It's a comforting, gentle gesture that says a lot.

His thoughtfulness in that simple act warms my heart. It goes far beyond the comfort it brings.

The day Richard invites me for dinner feels like a scene out of a movie. The setting sun paints the sky in orange and pink. I walk into the restaurant, a flutter of excitement in my chest.

He's already there, looking more relaxed than I've ever seen, away from the hustle of work. "I'm glad you could make it," he says, his smile genuine.

As we sit down, our conversation flows easily. I feel warmth growing since I started seeing the other side of him. The clink of glasses and the soft hum of the restaurant create a cozy ambiance.

Then, suddenly, Richard says something that makes my heart skip a beat. "I've liked you since the first day we met. It wasn't just your natural beauty but the heart behind it. You have something special."

His words wash over me like a warm tide. I've felt the change in our dynamic. It was a shift from boss and employee to something more. But, hearing it in words is different.

"Richard," I whisper, "I didn't think you noticed me that way. I've come to see so much in you, too. Your wisdom and care for others have changed how I see the world."

There's a pause, a moment charged with unspoken emotions, as our eyes meet. "I'm looking forward to what the future holds," I say, my words feeling like a promise.

He reaches across the table, his hand covering mine. "So am I."

As we leave the restaurant, the night air is crisp and fresh. I think about the journey I've been on. I went from the heartache of losing my grandfather's shop to finding a new path with Richard. It's been a roller coaster of emotions.

"We work well together, huh?" Richard says, snapping me out of my thoughts.

"Yeah, we do," I reply, looking up at him with a smile. He taught me what true kindness means.

Under the Same Roof

I glance around my modest living room. It's more used for old college furniture and secondhand bookshelves. Not for people like Lisa Morrison, my realtor. She sits across from me at the dining table, and her dark brown eyes can speak. Her presence is like a burst of color in my monochrome world. Her stylish outfit contrasts starkly with my well-worn jeans and faded T-shirt.

"So, it's official, then?" I ask, tapping my fingers nervously on the table. The papers before us scream finality, a contract signaling the end of my time in this home.

Lisa smiles, her eyes sparkling with professional pride and genuine warmth. "Yes, as soon as I fax this executed contract to the buyer's agent, we will legally enter into a contract. Anthony. Congratulations. Forty-five days to closing. You did great."

I nod, the reality sinking in.

Forty-five days to say goodbye to the walls that have seen my highest highs and lowest lows. "Thanks, Lisa. I... I just didn't expect it to happen so fast."

She leans forward, her expression softening. "I get it. It's not just a house. It's your home. But think of it as a step forward, a new chapter."

Her optimism is contagious, but I struggle to catch it. New does not necessarily mean good. "A forced chapter, more like. If I had a choice, I wouldn't be selling." My voice carries a hint of bitterness, a sentiment I've become too familiar with lately.

I wasn't born with this negative tone. People used to call me "Sunshine Boy."

Lisa's demeanor stays the same. Her resolve strengthens. "I know it's tough, Anthony. But you're doing what's necessary. And who knows? Maybe this is the universe nudging you towards something better."

I scoff lightly, amused by her unwavering positivity. "You really believe that?"

"I do," she says firmly, her confidence unshakable. "Sometimes the best things in life come from the unexpected. Trust me, I've been there."

There's a story behind her words, I can tell, but I don't pry. Lisa might have been born into wealth. We all speak English. Yet, even the same punctuation can hide different meanings. These meanings are shaped by our distinct worlds. Instead, I shift the conversation. "All right, so what's next? I've never... you know, done this before."

Lisa's business side kicks in. "Well, we are waiting for the inspection and the appraisal. In the meantime, keep the house presentable. And no changes, of course."

I nod, taking mental notes. "Got it. Presentable. No sledgehammering walls."

She laughs, a light, straightforward sound that momentarily lightens the room. "Exactly. Oh, and one more thing—be prepared for some back and forth with the buyers during the option period. It's normal."

"Back and forth, huh? Sounds like dating." I try to sound lighthearted, but the joke falls flat even to my own ears.

Lisa picks up on it, though. "A bit, yes. But hopefully with a happier ending."

We both know she's talking about more than just the house sale. There's an unspoken understanding. It's a shared sense of battles fought and scars earned, even if the details remain hidden.

As Lisa gathers her papers, preparing to leave, a sudden thought strikes me. "Hey, Lisa?"

She pauses, looking back. "Yes?"

"I, uh, I appreciate this. You helped me through all this." It's not easy for me to express gratitude, but with Lisa, it feels right.

She smiles, and it's like a promise of better days. "It's what I'm here for, Anthony. We'll get through this together."

She walks out the door. Her three-inch heels click confidently. I can't help but feel a flicker of hope. Maybe she's right about those unexpected turns leading to something better. After all, Lisa Morrison believes in a brighter future. She has unyielding optimism and relentless drive. Who am I to argue?

Two days after executing the contract, the buyer does the inspection.

The day of the inspection dawns clear and bright, but my nerves are anything but calm. I'm in the shower, trying to wash away the stress of the past few weeks when I hear the front door open. Panic seizes me. I'm not ready.

"Hello? Inspection service!" a voice calls out.

"Just a minute!" I yell, hastily wrapping a towel around my waist. My heart races as I rush out. But, I come to a sudden stop at the sight of the inspector in my living room. He is holding a supra key card. He's already let himself in using the key from the Supra key box. Now, he is standing there with the buyers—a middle-aged Russian couple.

"Sorry, I was under the impression we agreed on 9:00 a.m.," I stammer, striving to maintain composure.

He checks his watch nonchalantly. "It's 8:45. I prefer starting early. I must head to another inspection on the other side of the city. I hope that's not an issue."

Before I can reply, a loud meow interrupts us. My cats, startled by the stranger, dart around in panic. "Excuse me," I mutter, scrambling to gather them up. The inspector raises an eyebrow but says nothing.

Chaos ensues. I try to herd the cats into the master bedroom closet. I do this while keeping some dignity in my towel. The buyers glance. The inspector occasionally coughs in impatience. This only adds to the tension.

Finally, after ensuring the cats are secure, I quickly get dressed and head to my office to begin working. I pass through the living room. I see the inspector inspecting the oven and dishwasher. He is carefully jotting down notes on his clipboard. The buyer's wife is examining my curtains, almost as if she's already the owner. At the same time, her husband measures the dimensions of the fridge. My phone erupts in a burst of vibration on the kitchen counter

I glance at the screen. It's the call I've been waiting for about a potential contract job, my second phone interview. This call could be my lifeline, a chance to earn the desperately needed extra money. Filled with urgency, I quickly stride into my office, closing the door firmly behind me. I take a deep breath to compose myself, then sit down and press the answer button.

"Hi, Anthony Wilson speaking...."

The interview starts well, but I'm barely a few sentences in when a shrill beep cuts through the air. The inspector is testing the smoke alarms. I wince, apologizing to the interviewer, but the damage is done.

The call ends abruptly, my chances with it.

Feeling defeated, I turn on my computer and force myself to focus on my current task—I must beat the deadline.

The buyers trail the inspector throughout the inspection, peppering him with questions. Their voices and footsteps ebb and flow through the house. The front door opens and closes intermittently as they move in and out. At one point, the inspector climbs onto the roof to complete his assessment.

About three hours later, the inspection draws to a close in the kitchen. The inspector is there, addressing the main concerns of the buyers. "Everything looks good," he tells them. He says it reassuringly. They gather their things, ready to leave. "I'll send over the complete report by tomorrow."

My house falls silent again, starkly contrasting the morning's frenzy.

I'm pulled from my reverie by more meowing. The cats, poor things, are hungry. I get up to feed them, my movements slow, heavy. As I watch them eat, a pang of hunger hits me. I can't remember the last time I ate a proper meal.

Standing in the kitchen, I lean against the counter, the reality of my situation sinking in.

I'm tired of the uncertainty, financial strain, and constant need to put on a brave face.

My phone lies silent on the table. I think about the job interview, how crucial it was, how it fell apart in seconds. I'm walking on a tightrope; any slight misstep could send everything crashing down.

The cats finish their meal and wander over, rubbing against my legs, oblivious to the chaos of human life. I envy their simplicity. They can live in the moment. It doesn't bother them the complexities that keep me up at night.

As the day fades into the evening, I sit there, lost in thought. Once, the house was a source of pride and comfort. But, now it feels like a chain around my neck. It's pulling me into an ocean of debt and despair.

I should eat something and take care of myself. But motivation eludes me. Instead, I let the silence envelop me, a temporary respite from the storm of my life. Tomorrow, I'll face it all again—the uncertainty, the struggle, and the faint hope Lisa brings.

But for now, I sit alone with my thoughts. The fading light casts long shadows across the room. They mirror the darkness that seems to edge closer to my heart.

Seven days after signing the contract, Lisa returns with an update.

"Good news, Anthony," she announces, a note of relief in her voice. "The option period is over. We're now in contract pending."

"So, does this mean the deal is solid?" I ask, allowing a flicker of hope to surface.

"Unless the buyer can't get loan approval, your home should close on time." Lisa's energy fills up the space as she steps through the door.

"Ready for a little tour of your own home?" she asks, a playful glint in her eye. "We need to get ready for appraisal."

I smile despite the circumstances. "Lead the way, tour guide."

We start at the entry and then stop at my living room, where she suggests minor rearrangements. "Create more open space here. It'll make the room feel bigger," she advises, pushing the couch back against the wall.

As we move from room to room, I tell the small, unimportant stories of random objects. Lisa listens, genuinely interested, or at least does a great job pretending to be.

When we reach the small balcony, my favorite spot, I lean against the railing. "I spent countless nights out here, just staring at the stars, clearing my head," I murmur. I'm lost in the memory of quieter, happier times. At this moment, I realize how deeply I have been attached to this home.

Lisa joins me, her presence comforting. "It's a great spot. Peaceful. You've got good taste. I love your home too, Anthony."

I chuckle dryly. "Good taste, bad luck, it seems."

She doesn't offer false reassurances, just a sympathetic smile. "Sometimes life hits hard. But it's how we get back up that counts."

I glance at her, appreciating her empathy. "You sound like you've had your share of getting back up."

She nods, her gaze lingering on the horizon. "We all have our battles, Anthony. Mine just doesn't involve losing a home."

Her words hang in the air, a reminder of the reality I'm facing. The tour continues, with Lisa offering tips on maximizing appeal to the appraiser. She's professional. Yet, there's a gentleness in her approach. She understands the emotional cost of what I'm doing.

In the front yard, she points out the bushes. "They need a very nice haircut. Sets a good impression before the appraiser enters your home."

I nod, taking in her advice. "You know your stuff, Lisa."

She replies simply, "I want to make sure you get the highest appraisal value."

As the day wears on, my initial resistance to the sale begins to wane, replaced by a reluctant acceptance. Lisa is an expert. Her support, though unexpected, is welcome. It makes the process easier.

Before she leaves, I find the courage to voice a concern nagging at me. "Lisa, what if... what if the house doesn't sell in time? You know, I'm one month behind on my mortgage payment."

This moment leaves me feeling a pang of shame.

Once, I was the team leader on a significant project and was respected and secure. But then, my entire department was laid off. Now, as a contractor, my life is full of instability and uncertainty. It's far from the stability I once knew.

She stops, turning to face me. Her expression is serious but not grim. "Then we find another way. A loan modification, a short sale. There are options, Anthony. We'll find the one that suits you the best."

Her assurance is a small comfort, but a comfort, nonetheless. "Thanks, Lisa. For everything."

She smiles, and there's a promise in that smile—not of miracles, but of unwavering support. "That's what I'm here for."

I feel sorrow and gratitude as she leaves in the now-rearranged living room. Selling this house, my home is one of the hardest things I've ever had to do. But having Lisa at my side makes it seem just a little bit more bearable. And in this moment of turmoil, that means everything.

The next few days pass in a blur of anxiety and restless nights.

Monday morning. I'm sitting at my cluttered desk, surrounded by unpaid bills and overdue notices, when my phone buzzes. I feel hope and dread when Lisa's name flashes on the screen.

"Hey, Lisa," I answer, trying to keep my voice steady.

"Anthony, I have some news," she begins, and her voice instantly sets off alarms in my head. "The buyer... they've backed out. They couldn't secure the loan."

The words hit me like a physical blow. "What? But they said—"

"I know, I know," Lisa cuts in, her voice laced with frustration. "It's out of our control. The market is unpredictable."

I stand up abruptly, my chair scraping loudly against the floor. "Unpredictable? Lisa, I'm about to lose my home and credit here! We need to do something."

"We will, Anthony. I'm already looking into other potential buyers. But these things take time, and—"

"Time? I don't have time!" My voice rises, a mixture of fear and anger boiling over. "I'm on the verge of foreclosure, Lisa. Do you understand that?"

There's a pause on the line, and when Lisa speaks again, her voice is calm but firm. "I understand, Anthony. Better than you think. I'm doing everything I can. We're not giving up."

I take a deep breath, trying to rein in my emotions. "I'm sorry, Lisa. It's just... this is all I have."

"I know," she says softly. "Let's meet tomorrow. We'll go over our options. There's always a way."

After hanging up, I pace the room, my mind racing. I feel trapped, cornered by circumstances beyond my control. Every plan, every hope seems to be slipping through my fingers.

The knock on the door startles me out of my thoughts. I open it to find Lisa standing there, an unexpected sight. "Lisa? What are you doing here?"

"I couldn't wait until tomorrow," she says, stepping inside. "We need to talk, face-to-face."

We sit at the kitchen table, where we signed the contract that now feels like a distant dream.

Lisa lays out her plans. She will reach out to interested parties again. She will consider a price adjustment and increase marketing efforts.

But all I can think about is the notice on my desk, the words "Notice of Intent to Foreclose" glaring up at me. I grab it and toss it onto the table in front of her. "This is what I'm dealing with!"

Lisa picks up the notice, her expression grave. "I see. Anthony, this changes things. We need to act fast."

"Fast? We needed to act fast weeks ago!" My voice is harsh, my patience worn thin.

She meets my gaze, unflinching. "I'm on your side, Anthony. But you need to trust me. Yelling won't sell this house. We need to work together, now more than ever."

I sink back into my chair, the fight draining out of me. Lisa's right, of course. But now, all I feel is the weight of a future on the edge. It teeters on a precipice with no safety net.

Lisa sits across from me, exuding a calm, authoritative presence. Her professional demeanor, but, only serves to ignite my growing frustration. The disparity between our situations is stark and infuriating. Suppose this deal doesn't close before it is foreclosed. In that case, Lisa will lose her $6,340.46 commission. But, what's at stake for me is far more—my home, my stability, and seven years of rebuilding my credit. We're in vastly different predicaments. These thoughts swirl in my mind. My anger, just below the surface, becomes harder to contain. Finally, I can't hold it back any longer.

"Lisa, how could this happen?" I demand, my voice sharp. "You told me this was a sure deal!"

She sets her purse down, her face a mask of calm. "Anthony, I understand you're upset, but blaming me isn't going to help."

"Help? I'm about to lose everything! You drive around in your fancy car, wearing those designer clothes, and tell me to stay calm?" My words are like arrows, each one laced with bitterness.

Lisa takes a deep breath, her composure beginning to crack. "You think I don't know what it's like? To struggle? To fear losing everything?" Her voice is a low hiss, contrasting her usual upbeat tone.

I stop, taken aback. This isn't the Lisa I know.

She reaches into her bag and pulls out a crumpled piece of paper, tossing it onto the table. It's an eviction notice. My anger falters, replaced by confusion.

"What's this?"

"My reality, Anthony," she says, her voice breaking. "This is what I've been dealing with. My luxury car? It's a rental. These clothes?" She gestures at her outfit. "Black Friday sale from the outlet. I dress like this because it's part of the job—to look professional and successful. But the truth is, I work overtime every single day, and my hourly income is less than a cashier at Walmart."

I'm speechless.

The image of Lisa, the successful realtor, shatters before me.

"You see," she continues, "most realtors live like this. We are very independent and hardworking people. We're chasing a dream, living on the edge, hoping the next deal will be our big break. But more often than not, it's just another day of scraping by."

I sink into a chair, the fight draining out of me. "I had no idea, Lisa."

She still sits down opposite me, but her usual energy is gone. "I didn't want you to know. I wanted to be a good realtor."

I look at her, really look at her, and for the first time, I see the strain behind her smile, the weariness in her eyes. A wave of guilt washes over me for my earlier outburst.

"Lisa, I'm sorry," I whisper. "I was so caught up in my own problems that I didn't even consider what you might be going through."

She gives a small, sad smile. "It's okay. We're all just trying to make it through, one way or another."

In that moment, something shifts between us.

The façade of the successful realtor and the struggling homeowner fades. It leaves just two equally vulnerable, equally scared people facing an uncertain future. But in that shared vulnerability, there's a glimmer of hope. It's a sense that maybe, just maybe, we're not alone.

Learning about Lisa's struggles shifts everything. We have a new feeling like we truly get each other. We're sitting in my living room, bathed in the gentle morning light, quietly figuring out what to do next.

"Have you heard of the Dodd-Frank Act?" Lisa asks. "It has a 120-day rule that might buy us some more time."

I look at her, a flicker of hope igniting in my chest. "What is it?"

"It gives homeowners facing foreclosure extra time to explore options," she explains. "It could give us the breathing room to figure things out."

The relief that washes over me is palpable. "That could work, Lisa. It could really work." In 120 days, I should find a second contractor position and can work on two jobs.

"Maybe we should remove the listing from the Multiple Listing Service," Lisa suggests. Her voice is hesitant. We should try to do a loan modification. "Just temporarily until we figure things out."

I nod, feeling a weight lift off my shoulders. "Yeah, let's do that."

Lisa quickly opens her laptop and starts removing the listing from the MLS. As she works, a comforting quiet surrounds me. For the first time in weeks, there's a glimmer of hope that I can keep my home.

This newfound calm feels worlds away from the tense exchanges we've had recently. It's like Lisa and I are teammates, braving the same challenging storm together.

After finalizing the paperwork, Lisa gets ready to leave. She looks exhausted, the strain of her troubles evident in her eyes. On impulse, I say,

"You know, I have a guest room. If you need a place to stay...."

She stops, surprise flickering across her face. "Are you sure? I don't want to impose."

"It's not an imposition," I assure her. "You're in a tough spot, and so am I. Maybe we can help each other out."

"I can't pay rent right now. "But, I might get a $2,590 commission check in about two weeks," Lisa says. Her smile is cautious yet hopeful. "If the buyer closes.""

I quickly dismiss her concern. "Don't worry about it." Right now, money isn't my main concern. What's more important is helping her. "You don't need to pay me rent until you're back on your feet."

Lisa pauses as if weighing my words. Then, with a nod, she accepts. "Okay. Thank you, Anthony. This really means a lot to me." I see her gratitude. It reinforces my decision to support her. This is a challenging time.

Lisa moves in that very day. Having her around is a new experience for me, but deep down, I know it's the right choice. I just have to remind myself of the little changes. For example, making sure I'm always dressed and not wandering around barefoot. It's a small price to pay for helping a friend in need.

The good thing is that most of the day, Lisa will work outside somewhere, and it is hard for us to see each other. I'm still home alone.

Over the next few days, our dynamic shifts. The house, once a reminder of my failures, starts to feel like a home again. Eventually, we fall into a routine. We share meals and talk about everything and nothing.

One evening, we sit in the kitchen with mugs of tea. It's a rare, relaxing moment in our busy lives. Lisa looks up from her laptop. "My buyer client's loan is finally approved. I will close on time. I will receive the $2,590 commission check on time."

Her determination is infectious. "And I've been applying for more contract work. Sent out a dozen applications today," I tell her, feeling a spark of hope.

"That's not all. I've got more good news," she announces with excitement in her eyes. "I just got a referral. I'll be assisting an overseas client in buying a luxury home. They're paying in cash, so they can close quickly."

That day, we talk late into the night, making plans and discussing strategies. We do not need to go through loan modification anymore. It's a partnership born of necessity, but there's more to it than that. A connection is forming, a bond forged in the fires of adversity.

My home starts to have laughter.

At home, Lisa is a different person. She's in old jeans and a simple shirt, and this other side of her is striking. It reveals a more authentic Lisa—naturally beautiful, approachable, and warm. Seeing her like this, I realize she's not just a driven professional. She's a kind, relatable person with a good heart.

Even my cats have taken a liking to Lisa, perhaps even more than to me. Most nights, they sleep on her bed like they've chosen her as their new favorite. It's a small, amusing sign of how comfortably she's fit into our home.

One afternoon, while going through some old boxes, I find a photo album from my college days. Lisa joins me, and we flip through it, laughing at the memories. It's a moment of lightness amid our struggles.

"Look at you, with hair down to your shoulders," she teases, pointing at a photo.

I grin, a little embarrassed. "It was a phase. I thought I was a rock star."

"You kind of look like one," she says, her smile genuine.

Lisa brings life into the house and my world as the days pass. Her resilience and ability to smile even when things look bleak inspire me.

And then, one quiet evening, as we share a homemade dinner, I realize something has shifted inside me. My feelings for Lisa are growing. They are becoming deeper than gratitude or friendship.

But I keep these thoughts to myself. I'm unsure if she feels the same. I'm unsure if it's suitable to feel this way given our circumstances. For now, I'm happy with the company. I like the shared struggles and the flicker of hope. I hope things might turn around for both of us.

As we clear the table and discuss our plans for the next day, I feel a sense of contentment. Yes, we're still in a tough spot, but not alone. And there's a comfort that I hadn't realized I'd been missing.

Soon, an unexpected storm changes our life.

It's about the middle of the night when the first rumble of thunder rolls in, distant but ominous. Lisa and I are in the living room, her with a stack of paperwork, me with a laptop, balancing on my knees. We both pause, glancing towards the window as the wind picks up.

"Sounds like we're in for a storm," I comment, trying to keep my tone light. Thunderstorms have only bothered me a little.

Lisa looks genuinely worried. "I hate storms," she admits, her voice tinged with apprehension. "They always make me nervous."

I'm about to reassure her. But, then the city's tornado alarm blares into the night. It's a piercing wail that sends a chill down my spine. The look on Lisa's face shifts from worry to fear.

"Anthony, can you... would you mind staying with me tonight? Just until the storm passes?" Her voice is small, almost childlike in her fear.

"Of course, Lisa," I reply without hesitation, touched by her vulnerability. I gather my laptop and follow her to her room, settling on the floor beside her bed with a pillow and a blanket.

The storm outside gets worse. Lightning lights the room. It is followed by the deep growl of thunder.

I'm tired. Usually, I can fall asleep as soon as my eyes close. But, with Lisa nearby, I can't rest.

Lisa is in bed, curled under the covers, her phone in hand. Despite her fear, she's still working, talking, and texting with an overseas buyer.

I lie there, listening to the storm, to Lisa's hushed, professional conversations. She's juggling the explanation of the transactions and soothing client concerns. She does this all while glancing anxiously at the window with every thunderclap. Her dedication, even in the face of her own fears, impresses me deeply.

As the night wears on, the storm shows no sign of letting up. Lisa's voice becomes a comforting background. It is a testament to her strength and commitment. I find myself drifting in and out of sleep, caught between fatigue and the desire to be there for her.

At one point, she lets out a small yelp during a thunderous clap of thunder. I sit up, alert. "You, okay?"

She looks over, a sheepish smile on her face. "Yeah, just... hate thunder. Thanks for staying here."

I smile back, lying back down. "No problem. Happy to be here."

We continue like this for hours. The storm rages outside. Lisa works tirelessly. I am half-awake, half-asleep, but wholly admiring the woman she is.

Sometime during the night, the storm finally begins to wane. The lightning becomes less frequent, the thunder a distant grumble. Lisa's conversations wind down, and a sense of calm is settling in the room.

In the quiet aftermath, Lisa speaks up, her voice soft. "Anthony, thank you. I know it's silly, fearing storms at my age, but—"

"It's not silly," I interrupt gently. "Everyone's afraid of something. Besides, it gave me a chance to see how hard you work. You're incredible, Lisa."

There's a pause, and then she whispers, "You really think so?"

"I do," I assure her, sincerity in my voice. "You're one of the strongest people I know."

We fall silent, the storm outside now is just a memory. In the darkness of Lisa's room, with the faint sound of her breathing, I feel a connection to Lisa that goes beyond words. It's a bond formed through shared experiences. We see each other at our most vulnerable.

As dawn breaks, the first light of morning filters through the curtains. Lisa is asleep now, breathing deeply and even. I watch her for a moment, admiring her peacefulness, her resilience.

Getting up quietly, I head back to my room, my mind and heart full. Last night wasn't about romance or closeness. It was about understanding, about seeing the person behind the façade.

As I lie in my bed, I realize that my feelings for Lisa have deepened in a way I hadn't anticipated. It's not just admiration or gratitude now. It's something deeper and essential.

A few hours later, I start my new day in the morning. The world outside seems fresh and renewed, the storm's fury replaced by a serene calm. I'm in the kitchen, making coffee, when Lisa shuffles in, her hair tousled, eyes still heavy with sleep.

"Good morning," I greet her, handing her a mug. "Sleep okay after all that?"

She takes a sip, nodding. "Yeah, eventually. Thanks to you. I don't know what I would've done without you last night."

Her gratitude is evident, but there's something else in her eyes—a recognition of the shift between us. "It was no problem. I was glad to be there."

We sip our coffee in comfortable silence. The night's events linger unspoken between us. The morning light gives the kitchen a warm glow. It reflects the subtle change in our relationship.

After breakfast, Lisa gets a call. Her face lights up as she listens. "That's great news!" Lisa exclaims. Hanging up, she turns to me, excitement dancing in her eyes. "That was my overseas client. We reached a contract pending!"

"That's amazing, Lisa! Congratulations!" I can't help but share in her excitement. Her hard work is finally paying off.

She beams a radiant smile that fills the room. "This could be a game-changer for me. The commission... it's more than I've ever made."

I grin, genuinely happy for her. "Looks like the storm brought some good luck after all."

"Yeah, it did," she agrees, then hesitates, her expression turning thoughtful. "Anthony, about last night...."

I am tense, unsure of what she's going to say. "Yeah?"

She takes a deep breath. "I felt something, being there with you. It wasn't just about the storm or the fear. It was... more."

My heart skips a beat. "I felt it too, Lisa."

There's a vulnerability in her eyes, a mirror of my feelings. "I'm not sure what this means, for us, for the house, for everything... but I don't want to ignore it."

I nod, understanding her uncertainty. "Let's just see where it goes, no pressure. We're in this together, right?"

"Right," she says, smiling, the tension passing, leaving a sense of possibility.

The sun sets, painting the sky in orange and pink. Lisa and I sit on the balcony. It's the same place where I used to find solace alone. Now, it's a place of connection, shared dreams and hopes.

"We've got a lot ahead of us," I say, looking out at the city skyline.

"We do," Lisa agrees. "But whatever happens, I'm glad you're here with me."

Her words echo my own thoughts. The future is uncertain, and the challenges ahead are daunting. But, for the first time in a while, I feel hopeful. I believe that, no matter what comes, we'll face it together.

The night falls, wrapping the world in a blanket of stars. There, on that balcony, with Lisa by my side, I realize something. Sometimes, the deepest connections are made unexpectedly. The storm may have passed. But, its impact lingers. It marked the start of something new and beautiful.

A few days later, the golden afternoon light filters through the curtains. Lisa walks through the door, her face bright with an excitement I haven't seen before. In her hands, she holds an envelope that promises more than just paper.

"Anthony, you won't believe it," she exclaims, barely able to contain her joy. "The overseas buyer closed and funded." She hands the envelope to me, "Open it."

I open the envelope and see a $25,000 check inside.

"Congratulations, Lisa."

"Congratulations to us. Anthony, now you can bring your home loan back on track."

I stand up. "That's very generous of you, but I can't accept it."

She looks at me, her eyes shining. "Do not treat it as money. Treat it as a life-turning point. It can help get your life back."

Her offer is generous. Her willingness to share her success with me fills me with an emotion beyond gratitude. "Lisa, I can't let you do that."

"Why not?" she asks, stepping closer. "We're under the same roof, aren't we?"

Her words echo in my heart, resonating with the truth I've realized over these past weeks. "We are," I say, my voice steady despite my emotions swirling. "And that's why I need to tell you something."

Lisa waits, her expression open and expectant.

"I love you, Lisa," I confess, the words flowing freely, unburdened by doubt or fear. "Not just for this," I gesture at the check, "but for everything. For being the light in my darkest times, for believing in me when I couldn't. I love you for who you are, and I want you to be part of my life, not just as a roommate, but as... well, as more."

Lisa's eyes glisten with unshed tears, a soft smile playing on her lips. "Anthony, I've felt it too. These weeks together, they've shown me what true partnership is. I love you too."

The confession hangs in the air, a beautiful truth that wraps around us, drawing us closer. I take Lisa's hand, feeling the rightness of the moment.

"Then stay with me, Lisa. Not just for now but for always. Be my roommate forever."

Her smile turns playful. "Share your guest room?"

I shake my head, my heart pounding with nervousness and hope. "No. My bed."

The laughter that bubbles up between us is light and joyful. Lisa steps into my embrace, her arms winding around my neck. "Yes, Anthony. I'd love to share the same roof with you."

In Lisa's embrace, I realize my house has become a happy home again. Under the same roof, it is now filled with love, hope, and the promise of a shared future.

My Tough Boss

Paul, the owner of the shoe company, stands at the front of the meeting room. His deep blue eyes focus on me. "Sara, you are the top salesperson this month. Can you share...?" His voice is firm, but I sense an undertone of genuine curiosity.

"Just lucky," I reply, keeping it short. I want to avoid drawing attention to myself. Paul, the owner of the shoe company where I work, is about forty and known for his gruff demeanor. He's divorced and has been single for over a decade. People say no woman wants to get close because of his stern nature. I agree; his stony face and harsh tone don't make him approachable.

Every Monday morning, we have our routine marketing meetings. Paul always asks me to share my sales strategies, but I prefer to keep my answers brief. I need to stay low-key to secure my job. I'm a single mom to a four-year-old boy named Jim, and I have a home loan that's always on my mind.

As a contractor, I don't enjoy the same benefits as full-time employees. No retirement plans, no medical insurance. It's a constant struggle, but I manage because I must.

During one of these meetings, Paul pushes a bit more. "Sara, your numbers are impressive. There must be more to it than just luck."

I hesitate but decide to give a bit more this time. "Well, I focus on understanding the customers. It's about connecting with them, not just selling shoes."

Paul nods, seemingly impressed. "That's a good approach," he admits.

The rest of the meeting blurs and Paul approaches me as we file out. "Sara, can we talk for a minute?"

I'm taken aback but nod. We move to a quieter corner. "I've been watching your performance. You're more than just lucky," Paul says, his voice softer than usual.

"I appreciate that," I respond, unsure where this is going.

"I know being a contractor isn't easy. I was thinking of offering you a full-time position. But you have to work here at least for the next four years," he says, looking directly into my eyes.

I'm stunned.

A full-time job would mean stability and bene-fits. It would change everything for Jim and me.

But I can't accept it.

"I... I can't promise you to work here for the next four years. I'm planning to complete my MBA program. But, thank you, Paul."

He smiles. It's a rare sight that transforms his usually stern face. "Think about it. Let me know."

As I leave the office that day, my mind races. For the first time, I see Paul as a demanding boss and a man who might care about his employees. There may be more to him than meets the eye.

But soon, there is one thing that changes my mind.

I'm in the breakroom, fixing myself a cup of coffee, when I overhear a conversation from the hallway. It's Todd, sounding unusually tense, and Paul, our owner, with his usual firm tone.

"Paul, I really need that bonus in advance. It's for my new house; I need it to pay my closing costs," Todd pleads, his voice echoing slightly in the narrow corridor.

"The company policy is clear, Todd. I can't make exceptions," Paul responds, his voice as rigid as his posture.

"But this is a unique situation. My family is depending on this. Without the bonus, we'll lose the house," Todd explains, his voice growing more desperate.

"Anything that can be lost was never truly yours."

"Please, Paul."

There's a brief silence, and I imagine Paul's stony face, unyielding. "I'm sorry, Todd. My hands are tied," he finally says.

I clutch my coffee cup, feeling the tension in the air. I stay quietly in the breakroom, feeling like I'm doing something wrong.

The conversation ends, and I hear their footsteps fading away. Todd sounds defeated. Paul even seems disturbed. His usually steady steps are slightly uneven.

Two weeks later, the lunch breakroom buzzes with the usual chatter. I sit at a corner table and eat my meal quietly.

Todd joins us in the middle of my lunch, looking more haggard than usual. I glance at his face and notice dark circles under his eyes, and his usually neat hair is disheveled. He may have had trouble with his house. "Todd, are you okay?" a coworker asks.

"I lost the house," he blurts out, his voice heavy with defeat. My guess is confirmed. Todd runs a hand through his hair, looking around at our sympathetic faces. "I couldn't get the advance. I lost everything. That includes the option, inspection, and loan fees. It was more than fourteen hundred dollars."

There's a collective sigh from the group. The fluorescent lights hum above us, casting a stark light on Todd's crestfallen face.

"And now, my wife and I... we can't stop arguing about it," Todd continues, his voice breaking a bit. "It's like everything's falling apart."

I feel a pang of sympathy for him.

"It's a beautiful house. I got it for a steal. All I needed was a bit of leniency from Paul. Can you believe I had to beg? But that stubborn man just flatly refused."

I take a cautious sip of my coffee, feeling the bitterness on my tongue. Todd's frustration is palpable.

I glance over Todd's shoulder and see a tall man standing just behind him—it is Paul. Our grumpy owner's expression is like chiseled stone, cold and unyielding.

For a split second, I tense up, half expecting Paul to lash out physically. My heart races, the sound almost echoing in my ears.

The other coworkers see Paul, too. They are all surprised.

There's a thick, uncomfortable silence filled with unspoken words and strained emotions.

Like a looming shadow, Paul's presence adds an intense weight to the atmosphere. The break-room is usually a place for small talk and re-laxation. But now it feels like a battleground of silent confrontations.

Our eyes meet momentarily, and I see a hint of remorse in Paul's gaze.

Paul does not confront Todd. Instead, he turns and walks away quietly. He leaves a trail of mixed feelings as he goes.

The room falls silent, all of us processing this unexpected side of our owner.

This incident changes something in how I see Paul. Behind his tough exterior, there might be a depth of feeling I hadn't considered before.

After lunch, I head back to my desk. There's a picture of my son, Jim, smiling at me. Even though he's been sick and we've been in and out of the hospital, I've kept my spot as the top seller at work. Life at the shoe company goes on like normal.

But then, everything changes. My phone rings. It's Jim's doctor. My hands start to shake as I answer. I step away from the busy sales floor to a quiet spot to talk.

"Sara, I'm afraid the tests confirm that Jim has Acute Lymphoblastic Leukemia." Dr. Davis's voice is gentle, but each word hits me like a physical blow.

I struggle to process his words, my mind reeling. "How... how bad is it? What should we do now?"

"We've outlined a treatment plan. It's aggressive but necessary," Dr. Davis explains. The call ends with a promise of an emailed treatment plan and cost estimation.

When the email arrives, I open it with a sense of dread. The numbers stare back at me, cold and unyielding—$30,000. Even with the hospital's generous discount for upfront payment, $15,000 might as well be a million.

I don't have that money!

Desperate, I start looking for a second job. My options are limited; it has to be something I can do after my regular work hours. That's when I find an ad for a nightclub looking for staff. It's not a job that suits me, but I don't have the luxury of choice.

The first night at the nightclub is a blur of neon lights, loud music, and the clink of glasses. I force a smile as I serve customers. The sound of their laughter and chatter is a stark contrast to the turmoil inside me. Each smile feels like a betrayal to my little Jim. He lies in his brown twin-size bed, fighting for his life and being cared for by his babysitter.

I imagine Jim's little face, wondering why Mommy isn't there to tuck him in. The guilt is overwhelming. I should be with him, reading bedtime stories, not here, smiling at strangers.

I bring drinks to my customers with a smile, but suddenly, I can't hold back my tears. They start to fall.

The customers look surprised and worried. One old man asks gently, "Are you okay?"

I quickly wipe my tears and keep smiling. "I'm fine, just allergies." But deep down, I want to cry out loud.

Thoughts of Jim overwhelm me. The fear that he might not make it gnaws at my heart. Am I squandering the precious moments we have left? Yet, the harsh reality is that I need to earn money for his treatment. Torn between my heart and our needs, I make a tough decision, betting on Jim's recovery.

Every morning, the sun rises, casting a warm glow through the windows of the shoe company. But, for me, it's just another day of juggling two exhausting worlds.

The routine is grueling. After a night of forced smiles and serving drinks, I get only four hours of sleep. Then, I have to face the day job again. My eyes are often rimmed with dark circles, a telltale sign of my nightly endeavors.

At work, my colleagues make lighthearted jokes, unaware of my struggles.

"Sara, who's the lucky guy? You've got those telltale dark circles of someone in love," one of them teases during a lunch break. The group erupts in laughter.

I muster a weak smile, my heart aching.

If only they knew the truth—these are not the marks of a new romance but of a mother's desperation.

My sales performance is slipping. The numbers that used to soar now barely take off.

Each Monday, the team gathers for our regular meeting. Paul goes through the sales figures, his brow furrowing when he gets to mine.

"Sara, this isn't like you. What's going on?" he asks, his tone a mix of concern and disappointment.

I swallow hard, feeling the weight of his gaze. "Just a rough patch, Paul. I'll get back on track," I reply, hoping my voice sounds more convincing than I feel.

After the meeting, I retreat to my desk, my mind racing. I can't let my performance at work slide; I need this job.

But it's hard to focus when every moment is consumed with worry for Jim and the exhaustion from the nightclub.

Once, the company's sales floor was a place of confidence and success. Now, it feels like a battlefield. I muster the enthusiasm I once had for every sale and customer interaction. But I keep making mistakes.

As the day wears on, the office's usual buzz of activity feels like a distant hum. My colleagues chat and laugh, oblivious to the turmoil churning inside me.

I glance at the clock, dreading the evening when I'll have to put on my other mask—that of a cheerful nightclub worker.

Leaving work, the setting sun casts long shadows on the streets. The drive to the nightclub feels like a transition between worlds. As I step inside, the dim lighting and pulsating music surround me. They are a stark contrast to the bright, orderly world of the shoe company.

On this night, I weave through the nightclub crowd with a fake smile. The pulsating music and the vibrant lights of the club contrast with my inner turmoil. I'm so lost in my thoughts that I barely notice the hand gently resting on my shoulder.

"Sara, is this you?" A familiar, deep, steady voice breaks through the noise.

I turn and am shocked about what I see.

It's Paul, but his tone carries a hint of surprise, different from the usual firmness I'm accustomed to at work.

He stands amidst the club's chaos, looking out of place with his friends.

His stern expression softened, and he seems less rigid in this dim but lively atmosphere. Yet, his eyes are still sharp, quickly scanning my face for answers.

"Sara, why do you work in a place like this?" Paul's voice is filled with surprise and a hint of concern. I force a smile, trying to maintain my composure. "Is this for your MBA program?" Paul looks at me, his expression unreadable.

I reply nervously, "Well, it's just a temporary job. Excuse me, I have to serve the other customers." I quickly move away, my heart pounding.

Secrets are getting out. The next day at the hospital, while the doctor and I are discussing Jim's health, I unexpectedly see Todd and his wife. They're there for her routine pregnancy check-up. Running into them here feels odd.

"I heard about Jim," Todd tells me quietly, his voice filled with concern. His wife gently puts her hand on my shoulder, offering silent support. "If you need anything, just let us know."

I thank them, touched by their offer, but I prefer to handle things independently. But, Todd has a reputation for being unable to keep things to himself. Soon enough, everyone at work knows about Jim's condition. It's uncomfortable, feeling so exposed.

Then, a few days later, I get an unexpected call from the hospital. They tell me that someone anonymously paid all Jim's medical bills.

I'm shocked and can't find the words to respond. Who could have done this?

The answer becomes clear when I see Paul at work. His eyes have a knowing look, a softness I've never seen before.

I confront him during a quiet moment.

"Paul, did you pay Jim's medical bills?" My voice is a mix of gratitude and confusion.

He doesn't deny it. "You're a valuable part of the team, Sara. I just wanted to help."

I'm overwhelmed by emotions. "Thank you," I whisper, "but why do it secretly?"

Paul shrugs, a rare glimpse of vulnerability in his eyes. "I didn't want to embarrass you. I know you're a proud person."

His kindness breaks through the wall I've built around myself. I realize that under his stern exterior, he's compassionate.

This revelation shifts something between us.

The lines of our relationship blur, and I start to see Paul not just as my boss but as someone who genuinely cares—a friend I can trust.

The days turn into weeks, and slowly, miraculously, Jim begins to recover. His improvement brings light into my life, which had been dimmed by worry and exhaustion. During this time, Paul becomes closer to me.

One afternoon, Paul visits the hospital. He brings a small, thoughtful gift for Jim whose eyes light up at the sight of the toy car. It's a gesture that warms my heart.

As Jim plays with his new toy, Paul and I talk. It's a simple conversation, but it feels different and more personal. The roles of boss and employee fade away.

I start sending small payments to Paul to repay the medical bills he covered.

I walk into his office. "Here, Paul," I say, extending the envelope toward him. My hand is steady, but there's a flutter in my heart. It's more than just money inside; it's a piece of my thanks. "I can only pay this much each time."

He looks at the envelope and then meets my eyes. There's understanding in his gaze, a silent recognition of what this gesture means. "You don't have to do this," he begins, his voice low.

"I know," I interrupt, pushing the envelope closer. "But I need to."

Paul's eyes soften, and he nods slowly, accepting the envelope. His fingers brush against mine. They send a message louder than words. He respects my decision.

My payback schedule is set for every two weeks. Each time, I manage to pay $250. Paul always nods in understanding. He accepts the amount, never questioning or refusing it.

One morning, before the Monday meeting, I overhear Todd talking to another coworker. "Can you believe Paul is taking money from Sara for her kid's bills? Seems a bit heartless, doesn't it?" Todd's voice is loud enough for a few others to hear.

"How do you know?" one of my coworkers asks, curiosity lacing her voice.

"I saw the check on Sara's desk," Todd replies with a hint of triumph in his tone. "The memo says: Thank you for paying Jim's medical bill. Think about it; $250 is a big number for us, but not for Paul. He's rich."

I feel a flush of embarrassment. My privacy is now out in the open, subject to office gossip.

At this uncomfortable moment, Paul walks into the room, his timing almost too perfect. He overhears Todd's last remark and pauses, his expression calm but firm.

"Todd, I accept those payments. I value Sara's independence and respect her pride," Paul says. His voice is steady and clear. He looks directly at Todd, then at me, his eyes conveying a message of understanding and support.

His defense takes me aback, a warm feeling spreading through me.

The room falls silent, and Todd looks embarrassed, mumbling an apology.

Paul's intervention shifts the mood of the room. As we move into the meeting, I steal glances at Paul, seeing him in a new light.

After the meeting, I approach Paul, "Thank you," I whisper.

Paul looks at me, a hint of surprise in his expression. "For what?" he asks, his tone light yet sincere.

"For standing up for me, for understanding," I reply, feeling a wave of appreciation. "I'm going to call and quit the nightclub job."

"When?"

"Now." I want to be the top salesperson again.

He gives a slight, humble shrug. "Sara, you're doing everything you can for your son. That's something to be admired," he says earnestly. Then, a playful glint appears in his eyes. "I guess we understand each other, don't we?"

His words, lighthearted yet filled with a deeper meaning, bring a small smile to my face. It's a rare moment of connection. It's a recognition of the mutual respect and understanding that's grown between us.

As the weeks pass, the bond between Paul and me strengthens. He occasionally asks about Jim, genuinely interested in his recovery. They were once filled with formalities. But now, the small interactions at work carry warmth and mutual respect.

One day, Paul invites me for a coffee after work. It's a casual invitation but a significant step in our evolving relationship.

We find a quiet café away from the hustle of the city. I am sitting across from him, outside the office. He seems more approachable and human.

"I've been meaning to ask how Jim is doing," Paul starts, stirring his coffee. His tone is gentle, a far cry from the stern boss in the boardroom.

I smile, feeling a sense of ease. "Jim is getting better every day. It's a slow process, but we're getting there. Thanks."

"He's a good boy, as strong as his mom." Paul nods.

The conversation flows effortlessly. I ask Paul one question that has lingered in my mind for a long time.

"Paul, can I ask you something?" I begin hesitantly. "Why did you refuse Todd's request for his bonus in advance?"

Paul looks at me, his eyes reflecting a depth of experience. "It wasn't an easy decision, Sara," he starts, his voice calm and measured. But if Todd couldn't pay the closing costs, he'd likely struggle with the mortgage. He'd also struggle with property tax, home insurance, and the other costs of owning a home."

I listen, realizing there's more to his decision than I had thought.

"He would have risked losing everything. His credit, his home. It leads to more trouble. Often, it brings financial strain," Paul continues. His gaze is distant as if recalling a painful memory. "Do you know?" Paul asks, a hint of seriousness in his tone. "More than 60% of homeowners will divorce after their home is foreclosed on."

Hearing this statistic for the first time, I'm taken aback. It's a stark, unsettling number that puts Paul's decision in a new light.

"It happened to me," he adds softly. "The financial stress... it was a factor in my divorce. It's a painful experience I wouldn't wish on anyone, especially not my employees."

His words strike a chord in me.

The man I once saw as unyielding and brutal reveals a vulnerable and considerate side. Paul refused to advance the bonus. His reason wasn't just strict rule adherence. It was a deep fear of the potential consequences.

I look at him, seeing the layers of his personality unfold.

Paul isn't just the stern owner or the kind benefactor. He's had loss and hardship. He uses his past to guide his decisions to help others, even if it's not clear at first.

He is a man with a golden heart.

Leaving the café that day, I feel Paul is becoming someone important in my life, someone I might even fall in love with.

Over time, my feelings for Paul grow stronger. They become profound and undeniable. I'm in love with him. It's a realization that fills me with a warmth I haven't felt in a long time.

Paul must feel the same way and invites me out more often. Sometimes, I take Jim with me, especially at the park.

One Sunday afternoon, the sun is high and bright. We find our spot in the park under the cool shade of an old oak tree. The breeze is gentle, rustling the leaves overhead. Paul sets down a picnic basket, and I spread out a blanket while Jim pulls a soccer ball from his bag excitedly.

"Bet you can't get past me, Jim!" Paul challenges with a grin, setting the ball at his feet.

"You're on, Paul!" Jim replies, his eyes alight with excitement. Jim makes a dash for the ball, and Paul pretends to stumble, letting Jim score a goal.

"Goal!" Jim shouts, throwing his arms up in triumph. Paul ruffles his hair playfully, and they both laugh.

I watch them, leaning back on my elbows, feeling a sense of contentment wash over me.

"Your turn, Sara!" Paul calls out, beckoning me to join in.

I stand up, laughing as I take my place opposite Jim. "Okay, but I warn you, I'm pretty good!"

As we kick the ball around, laughter and playful shouts fill the air. Jim's giggles are infectious. Even Paul, usually so composed, is letting loose. His laughter joins ours.

At one point, Jim kicks the ball a little too hard and rolls off under a nearby bush. "I'll get it!" he declares, running after it.

As he retrieves the ball, Paul and I share a quiet moment. "He's a great kid, Sara," Paul says, watching Jim with a fond expression.

"He really is. And he loves spending time with you," I reply, my heart full.

Jim returns, ball in hand, and we continue our game until we're all out of breath and laughing. We settle down on the blanket. Paul opens the picnic basket. It reveals sandwiches and snacks.

As we eat, Jim tells us stories about new friends he meets in the hospital. His eyes sparkle with enthusiasm. Paul listens attentively, laughing at the right moments and adding to his stories.

It feels natural and comfortable—like we've been doing this for years.

Lying back on the blanket, watching the clouds drift by, I feel a deep sense of peace. Paul and Jim are chatting beside me, their voices blending with the sounds of the park around us. It's a simple moment, but it holds so much meaning.

I realize that this is what I've been longing for—a sense of belonging, of being part of a family. Paul and Jim, with their easy camaraderie and shared laughter, have brought that dream to life.

I see it now. I stand in the shade of the old oak tree. I see the future I've always wanted. It's one filled with love, support, and an unbreakable bond.

As the year wanes, the festive spirit of Christmas begins to fill the air. The city is adorned with lights, and the scent of pine and holiday spices lingers in our home.

It's a white Christmas, the snow painting the world outside in a blanket of pristine white.

On Christmas morning, we unwrap gifts and hear Jim's excited squeals. Amidst this, Paul hands me a small, exquisitely wrapped box.

My hands tremble as I open it. Inside, I find a beautiful ring. It sparkles under the lights of our Christmas tree.

I look up at Paul, my eyes brimming with tears of happiness. He takes my hand gently. "Sara, you've brought me so much joy and strength. I want to be there for you and Jim, always. Will you marry me?"

The question hangs in the air, a moment suspended in time. My heart beats wildly, overwhelmed by the love and sincerity in his eyes.

"Yes, Paul. Yes, I will marry you," I reply, my voice filled with emotion.

Sensing the moment's significance, Jim runs over and hugs us both. "Are we a family now?" he asks, his eyes wide with hope.

"Yes, Jim. We're a family," Paul answers, his voice warm and full of promise.

I watch Paul and Jim make a snowman later that day. Their laughter mixes with the soft sounds of the winter afternoon. I feel love and a sense of wholeness I hadn't known I was missing.

That evening, we're cozied up by the fireplace, the gentle glow reflecting off the ring on my finger. I snuggle closer to Paul, enveloped in the comfort of his embrace. Glancing over, I see Jim sleeping soundly on the couch, adding to the serene atmosphere.

Together on this magical Christmas. It feels like we're starting a heartwarming journey. It's beautiful and we're doing it as a family.

Shines in the Darkness

The park is alive under the sun, light playing hide and seek through the leaves. I'm here with my camera, snapping shots of everyday magic. A mom is cooing over her baby in a stroller, and a girl is laughing as she and her golden retriever race the wind.

I'm trying to capture a giggling kid chasing pigeons when suddenly—Bam! I'm knocked off-balance, and my camera slips from my hands. "Oh no!" I gasp, reaching out too late.

"Hey, watch it!" a deep voice grumbles.

I spin around, ready to give a piece of my mind, but then I see him. He's like a thundercloud on a sunny day. He's tall and rough around the edges. He has a slightly intimidating frown. But there's something in his eyes, a softness that doesn't match his stern look.

"Uh, sorry about that," he says, sounding like he's not used to apologizing. His eyes flicker to my camera. "Is it okay?"

Before I can bend down, he's already scooped it up. He's gentle with it, which surprises me. "Looks all right, I think."

My heart's still racing, and not just from the scare. He's an attractive man who's all clouds and shadows. He stands awkwardly, then offers, "I'm Ethan," with an unexpectedly warm hand.

"Lily," I respond, feeling a strange mix of calm and excitement.

He glances at some skateboarders, a hint of regret crossing his face. "Got distracted," he says, almost like it's hard to admit.

I smile, finding the whole situation amusing. "Happens to all of us. I was after the perfect shot, anyway."

He gives a small, almost shy smile. "You a photographer?"

"Trying to be," I say, feeling more like myself. "I love capturing the little happy moments."

He looks at me like he's trying to figure out a puzzle. "That's... cool," he finally says, and it seems complicated to admit something's nice.

The wind picks up, swirling leaves around us. Ethan's hair gets all messed up, and he suddenly looks less intimidating and more... human.

"Can I make it up to you?" he asks, slightly uncomfortable. "Coffee at a place I know, just around the corner?"

This catches me off guard. Grumpy, mysterious Ethan wants to grab coffee? My curiosity wins. "Sure," I say, "but you'll have to tell me what's so interesting about those skateboarders."

He laughs, a sound that seems new to him. "Okay, you've got a deal."

Walking to the café, I feel this random bump-into might be the start of something unexpected. Ethan has a stormy exterior. I am always chasing sunshine. We seem like we're from different worlds. But maybe, just maybe, we'll find some common ground.

We reach the café, a quaint little place with a cozy vibe. The bell jingles as we enter, drawing a few curious glances. Ethan leads the way to a corner table, away from the bustling crowd. It's quieter here, more intimate.

As we sit, I notice how out of place Ethan seems in this cheerful café. Yet there's an undeniable intrigue about him.

"So, Ethan," I start, sipping my coffee, "what brings you to the park on a day like this? You don't strike me as the type who enjoys basking in the sun."

He shrugs, a guarded look in his eyes. "Just passing through, I guess. The park seemed like a good place to clear my head."

His answers are brief, but I'm still determining. There's more to him than this rough exterior, and I'm committed to finding it out. "Clear your head? Sounds serious. Everything okay?"

Ethan hesitates, then sighs. "Life's complicated, but I'm fine."

I nod, understanding more than he realizes. "I get that. Photography is my escape."

He looks at me then, really looks, and for a moment, the gruffness in his eyes softens. "That must be nice," he says, almost wistfully.

"Ethan, what do you make for a living?"

"I'm my own boss."

The conversation shifts to lighter topics. Ethan's responses are always brief, but warmth creeps into his words. It's like the sun slowly breaking through the clouds; I want to see more of it.

I talk about my photography, how I started, and what inspires me. Ethan listens. His expression is thoughtful. He occasionally asks surprising questions.

"You really love what you do, huh?" he says, a hint of a smile tugging at his lips.

"Absolutely," I beam. "There's nothing like capturing a moment, knowing it's yours to keep forever."

We continue talking, and the atmosphere around us shifts as we do. The café's warmth seems to seep into Ethan, melting away some of his iciness. He's still guarded, but there's a curiosity in his eyes, a spark that wasn't there before.

Ethan leans back as we finish our coffees, regarding me with a newfound interest. "You know, Lily, you're not what I expected."

"And what did you expect?" I'm amused.

He shrugs, his half-smile still playing on his lips. "I don't know. But not someone who could make me forget my troubles, even for a little while."

I laugh, feeling a surge of accomplishment. Beneath that grumpy façade, there's a natural person, and I've just caught a glimpse of him.

We leave the café together, and I realize this spark of interest isn't one-sided. Ethan, with his mysterious aura and grumpy demeanor, has piqued my curiosity. And something tells me this isn't the last time we'll share coffee.

A week later, just as I suspected, I meet Ethan again at the same café.

He's already there when I arrive, a book in his hand, looking every bit the brooding intellectual. As I approach, his eyes lift from the pages. There's a flicker of something in his gaze—amusement, perhaps. It's as if he's shifting from a private world into the present.

"Seems we both favor this spot," I say as I sit down.

Ethan closes the book, his expression a blend of amusement and challenge. "I suppose that's true for both of us," he replies.

We exchange small talk. But, Ethan quickly steers the conversation to something more substantial. We discuss art and the city's untold stories. His insights are sharp and thought-provoking, pulling me into deeper contemplation.

Out of the blue, Ethan asks, "Have you ever used your photography to narrate a story? Really capture the essence of this city?"

I'm intrigued. "What exactly are you suggesting?"

He leans forward, the gruffness fading into intensity. "This city is a labyrinth of untold stories, hidden gems. We could use your photography to reveal them, show the world what lies beneath."

The idea excites me, but I wonder about his sudden interest. "That sounds fascinating. But why me? And why now?"

Ethan hesitates, then says, "It's personal. People ignore aspects of this city, stories lost in the hustle. I want to bring them to light. And you... your photography has a way of capturing the soul of a moment. It's honest, unfiltered. That's what we need."

His words strike a chord with me. He sees my purpose, not just my work.

"So, what's the plan?" I ask, my curiosity now thoroughly piqued.

"We explore, document, and narrate," he explains. "We show the hidden heart of the city, the parts that are forgotten or ignored. Maybe in doing so, we can understand it better, and ourselves too."

His proposal is more than an adventure. It's a journey into the city's heart and, maybe, into each other's worlds. I sense Ethan's genuine passion for this project despite his guarded nature.

As we leave the café, a plan is taking shape for our venture, and I feel excitement. Ethan is intellectually deep and mysterious. He has presented a challenge that I eagerly accept.

Walking home, my mind races with possibilities. This project isn't just about photos. It's a quest to uncover truths about the city and the enigmatic man who proposed it. It's a chance for discovery, connection, and something deeper. It's more profound than I first realized.

Our project starts with a promise and a camera. Ethan and I roam the city's less-known streets. We capture everything from abandoned buildings to hidden murals. His knowledge of the city's nooks and crannies surprises me. He's seen a side of the city that's remained invisible to most.

"Ethan, how do you know about these places?" I ask, snapping a photo of an old, ivy-covered wall.

He shrugs, a shadow crossing his face. "I've been around," he replies curtly, his tone closing off further inquiry.

His evasiveness sparks my curiosity. Each location we visit is personally significant for him, a story he's unwilling to share. His grumpiness becomes more pronounced, especially when I probe too deeply.

"Ethan, there's something about these places, isn't there? Something personal?" I venture, trying to tread lightly.

He stiffens, his camera hanging idly by his side. "Can we just focus on the project, Lily? Not everything needs to be a heart-to-heart."

His sharpness stings, but I don't let it deter me. There's more to Ethan than this defensive front.

One day, while exploring an old art hub in a forgotten part of town, we encounter someone from Ethan's past. Perhaps a former classmate greets him with a familiarity that Ethan doesn't share.

"Lily, meet Alex, an old... acquaintance," Ethan says, introducing us, his voice strained.

Alex's eyes are full of unspoken stories. "Ethan was a legend back in the day, weren't you?" he says, a knowing look in his eye.

Ethan's discomfort is palpable. "That was a long time ago," he says dismissively.

After Alex leaves, the air between us feels heavier. "Ethan, who were you 'back in the day'?" my voice is gentle but persistent.

He looks away, the lines of his face hardening. "Someone you don't want to know," he answers, his words clipped.

I reach out, touching his arm. "Maybe I can help you carry some of that past."

He pulls away slightly, anger and vulnerability in his eyes. "I don't need help, Lily. Especially not with the past."

I step back, giving him space. His gruffness hides a pain I'm only beginning to understand. Despite his walls, I see glimpses of the person beneath. He is thoughtful, complex, and fighting inside battles.

Our project continues, but now there's a tension that wasn't there before. Each photo we take and each story we uncover feels like it's bringing us closer to something hidden in Ethan.

We sit in the café, reviewing our photos. Ethan's gaze lingers on a particular image. It shows a lone figure in a vast, empty street. "This one... it's good." His voice is softer.

I look at him, seeing the layers slowly peeling away. "You're good, Ethan. You just hide it well."

He meets my gaze, and for a moment, the grumpiness fades, replaced by something akin to gratitude.

I look into his deep blue eyes. I warn myself: I must uncover the city's secrets and unravel Ethan's mystery.

The city's hidden corners become our canvas, the lens capturing its untold stories. But with each camera click, Ethan grows more introspective. His usual grumpiness is tinged with something deeper, more reflective.

On a brisk evening, we walk through the cobblestone alleys of the old city district. I decide to confront the elephant that's been following us. "Ethan, you've shown me so much of the city but nothing about yourself. Why the secrecy?"

He stops, his back to me, his shoulders tense. "It's not easy, Lily. The past... it's complicated."

I step closer, my voice soft but firm. "I'm not asking for everything. Just a glimpse, Ethan. Just enough to understand."

He turns slowly, the streetlight casting shadows across his face. "You know those graffiti walls we photographed? I used to be a part of that world. Art was my escape, my voice. But it led me down some dark paths."

His admission hits me like a wave. The man I've been spending my days with is mysterious and grumpy. Suddenly, he becomes more human, more real.

That's why this project is like revisiting ghosts. Ethan continues in a mere whisper.

I reach out, taking his hand. "And now? What does art mean to you now?"

He looks down at our entwined hands. "A second chance," he says, "to beat down the ghosts, make things right, to find peace."

The revelation brings us closer, the air between us charged with a new understanding. We resume our walk, the silence comfortable, filled with unspoken acceptance.

In the following days, our project takes on a new depth. Each photograph tells a story, not just of the city, but of Ethan—the pain, the redemption, the hope.

Ethan's phone buzzes as we sit in the café, poring over our latest shots. He glances at the screen, his face paling. "I have to go, Lily. It's my brother, he's... he's in trouble."

The urgency in his voice is unmistakable. "Do you need help?" I ask, concern lacing my words.

He shakes his head, a storm brewing in his eyes. "No. I need to handle it alone."

He leaves in a hurry, and I feel I'm foreboding. Ethan's past is catching up with him. I fear what it might mean for us and our future. We're just starting to build it.

Days pass without a word from Ethan. The city feels different without him—less vibrant, more somber. I revisit our photography spots, each one echoing with his absence.

Ethan returns after several tense days. We meet on a weathered brick street, the backdrop accentuating his tired appearance. Dark circles under his eyes and his black coat against the gray wall paint a stark picture. He seems weary yet resolute.

As we sit on a worn bench, Ethan begins to un-ravel the story of the past few days. "My brother got involved with some bad people," he starts, his voice heavy. "Debts, threats... it was messy. I thought I had left that world behind, but I couldn't let him deal with it alone."

He explains how he had to dive back into the shadows of his past, confronting figures he once knew all too well. "It was like walking back into a nightmare I thought I'd woken up from," he admits. "Every step I took to help my brother felt like the darkness I fought so hard to escape was trying to pull me back."

Ethan recounts late-night meetings in dim al-leys and tense negotiations. He struggled to keep his brother safe without getting trapped again in the life he left. "I had to be tough and play the part, but every moment was a battle against who I used to be and who I am now."

He looks away, his gaze distant. "In the end, I managed to get him out, settled things without... without going back to who I was. But it was too close, Lily. It reminded me of the darkness I carry inside, the part of me I'm trying to change."

As Ethan shares his story, I see his layers of conflict. He battles his past and present, his darkness and his light. It's a peek into the depths of his struggles. It's a reminder of the strength needed to leave a troubled past and strive for something better.

Sitting there with him, I see how much Ethan has fought to become the person he is. I also see how much he still fights each day. His story isn't just about the past few days. It's about his whole journey, the darkness he's leaving behind, and the light he's reaching for. I hope to help him find and hold on to that light.

I wrap my arm around his and lean on his broad shoulder, proud of his bravery.

Ethan's hand inches towards mine, hesitating momentarily before finally grasping it. His hand is large and warm, providing a comforting touch.

"We've got one last place to photograph," he says, a spark returning to his eyes. "It's where my journey began, and I want you to see it."

The place is an old art studio hidden in a forgotten city. It's here that Ethan first found his love for art, and it's here that he wants to conclude our project.

As we set up for the final shot, Ethan turns to me. "Lily, you've shown me there's more to life than dwelling on past mistakes. You've given me a reason to look forward."

I smile, realizing how far we've come. From strangers to partners, from conflict to understanding.

"Our project may be ending," I smile, "but I feel like this is just the beginning for us."

Ethan nods, a genuine smile breaking through. "Yeah, the beginning of something real."

We capture the studio in our lens, the light, the shadows, the echoes of a past that's shaped us both.

With all its stories, the city has become a part of us. In turn, we became a part of each other's stories. They are tales of resilience, redemption, and new love.

The days following our visit to Ethan's old art studio are filled with tense anticipation. I can sense there's more Ethan hasn't shared, secrets that loom over us like dark clouds. Despite my apprehension, I know it's time to face what's been unsaid.

We meet at our now-familiar café. The ambiance starkly contrasts the gravity of our meeting. Ethan seems restless, a storm brewing beneath his usual gruff exterior.

I take a deep breath. "Ethan, we need to discuss what's been happening with you. I can feel there's something you're not telling me."

He avoids my gaze, his hands fidgeting with the coffee cup. "Lily, it's not that simple. There are things about my past... things I'm not proud of."

I reach across the table, offering a reassuring touch. "I'm not asking you to bare your soul, Ethan. Just let me in, even if it's just a little."

Ethan's gaze shifts, focusing on something far away in his mind. "My dad is a general contractor. He died when I was eight," he begins, his voice laden with old pain. "After that, my mom worked tirelessly to care for us, her three boys. She'd been saving up to fix our leaking roof, but... I took that money. I used it to buy drugs, and I almost got my best friend killed because of it. That chaos and the sheer terror of that night shook me awake. I left home, couldn't bear to face what I'd done."

He pauses, collecting himself. "I started doing all sorts of jobs, anything to earn and send money back home. I kept at it, got myself into college, and studied architecture. Now, I have my own company."

His story is a narrative of regret and redemption. It paints a picture of a man who walked through darkness to find the light. "But that night, my mistake, it's a weight I carry always. It drives me to do better, to be someone my dad would've been proud of, someone who fixes things, not breaks them."

I listen, my heart aching for the pain he's endured. I understand him more.

"Ethan, thank you for trusting me with this," I say gently. "Your past doesn't define you. What matters is who you are now and want to be."

He nods, a weight visibly lifting from his shoulders. "I want to be someone better, Lily. For you, for myself."

Ethan's barriers crumble. They reveal the real man. He is complex and flawed, but inherently good.

As we leave the café, the setting sun casts a warm glow over the city. It feels symbolic, like the closing of one chapter and the opening of another.

Something changes between Ethan and me. This happens in the days after our revealing conversation. The air is lighter, and our interactions are more open. He's no longer just a grumpy enigma; he's Ethan, with all his complexities and newfound openness.

We decide to revisit some of the spots we've photographed, but this time it's different. We're not just collaborators; we're partners in a sense that goes beyond our project.

One evening, the city lights twinkle like stars in the night sky. Ethan takes me to a secluded part of the riverbank. It's away from the usual hustle of the city, a hidden gem bathed in the golden glow of the setting sun.

"I used to come here to think," Ethan shares, his voice softer than I've ever heard. "It's where I found peace in my turbulent times."

The tranquility of the place wraps around us. The river gently laps the shore. Leaves rustle in the breeze. Both feel like nature's melody, playing just for us.

Ethan turns to me, his eyes holding mine. "Lily, these past weeks with you... they've changed me. You've shown me a light I thought I'd lost."

His words send a warm rush through me. I step closer, the proximity sending my heart into a flutter. "Ethan, you've shown me so much too. You've opened my eyes to the beauty in the shadows, the stories hidden in plain sight."

He reaches out, brushing a strand of hair from my face. The touch is tentative yet filled with emotion. "I was lost in my own darkness, but you... you were like a beacon, guiding me back."

Our gazes lock, the world around us fading into a blur.

Slowly, as if drawn by an unseen force, we lean in. Our lips meet in a gentle but deep kiss. It's a merging of two souls. They've found understanding and comfort in each other. The kiss deepens, speaking words we don't need to say.

As we pull away, breathless, Ethan smiles, a genuine, heartfelt smile. "Lily, you've turned my world upside down in the best possible way."

I laugh, the sound mingling with the night air. "I could say the same, Ethan."

We sit by the river, talking, laughing, and sharing dreams of the future.

As the night deepens, we make plans, not just for our photography but for us.

The next day, the afternoon light filters through the café windows. Ethan and I are in our usual spot, surrounded by our latest photographs. He pauses at one image. His eyes trace the scene with deep thought. It's a candid shot of him, lost in thought against an old brick wall in a narrow, forgotten alley.

"You captured something in my memory," Ethan murmurs. His finger delicately traces his silhouette in the photo. "I used to paint on this wall when I was a teenager."

His admission piques my curiosity. "What did you paint?" I ask gently, sensing the depth of the memory.

Ethan's eyes hold a distant, almost pained glimmer. "Bread, food... when I was hungry." His voice is a soft echo of a past filled with longing.

I reach across the table, covering his hand with mine. "Ethan, you were painting your hope. You were seeking light in the darkness."

He looks up, our eyes locking in a moment of shared understanding. In his gaze, there's a vulnerability rarely shown, a window into the soul of the man I've come to love.

"It's strange," he continues, the words flowing like a whispered confession. "Back then, those paintings were my escape, my way of filling the void. But now, looking at this photo, I see something different. It's like you've captured not just me but a piece of my past, transforming it into something... hopeful."

My heart swells with a mix of compassion and admiration. "That's the power of art, Ethan. It transforms, heals, and reveals. You painted to express your hunger, your need. And now, through your lens, you show the world its hidden beauty, its potential."

Ethan's expression softens, the corners of his mouth curving into a tender smile. "I never saw it that way. But with you, Lily, I'm starting to see things differently. You bring out the colors in my life."

Our conversation drifts to dreams of the future. The possibilities stretch beyond our cameras. Ethan, with a newfound determination in his voice, shares his vision.

"I've been thinking about an art gallery," he says, a flicker of excitement in his eyes. "A place where stories like mine, like ours, can be told. Maybe we can inspire change. We can bring a new view to the city's planners. We can help them see our community's beauty and needs."

I feel a surge of excitement. "That's more than an art gallery, Ethan. It's a mission, a way to connect our art with the world, to make a difference."

As the café dims, signaling the day's end, I realize that with Ethan, I've found not just a partner in art but a soulmate.

The grand opening of our exhibition surpasses all my dreams. The gallery rooms buzz with energy, filled with guests from all walks of life. Among them, the head of the city zoning department and the Mayor himself stand out. Our photographs line the walls, each frame a story, a call to action, a slice of life.

As Ethan and I mingle, I feel a tap on my shoulder. Turning around, I come face-to-face with City Department of Commerce representatives. Their expressions are a mix of curiosity and admiration.

"We're very impressed with your work," one of them says. He extends an official-looking envelope. "We'd like you both to attend our next meeting. There's much to discuss about the role your art can play in our city's future."

Ethan and I exchange a glance, our excitement barely contained. "We'd be honored," I reply, the significance of their invitation sinking in. This is our chance to really make a difference.

The Mayor, a charismatic man with a keen eye, approaches us next. "Ethan, Lily, your exhibition is the talk of the town. It's incredible how you've captured the city's spirit."

Ethan, usually reserved, responds with a warmth that surprises me. "Thank you, Mayor. We wanted to show the city as we see it—not just the beauty but also the challenges and potential future."

"And you've done it splendidly," the Mayor says, his gaze sweeping over the photographs.

As we chat, a renowned architect known for her innovative city designs joins us. Her eyes are alight with enthusiasm. "Your work is a vital reminder of the people and stories behind our urban landscapes," she says. "It's artists like you who inspire my designs."

The Mayor nods in agreement. "Would you two be up for a photo? It would be a great way to commemorate this evening."

"Of course!" Ethan and I say almost in unison.

The cameras flash, capturing the moment—us, the Mayor, and the architect, all smiling. This photo is more than just a memory. It's a testament to our journey and our art. It reaches beyond the gallery walls into the city's heart.

As the night goes on, the conversations continue. The laughter and clinking of glasses create a symphony. It is a symphony of celebration.

Ethan squeezes my hand, a silent acknowledgment of our journey together. From the riverbank to this gallery, our shared vision has brought us closer. It has brought our city to life through our lens.

Two weeks later, the exhibition ended. The city zoning department bought several of our photos for their future plans.

As the evening winds down, Ethan and I escape to our sanctuary by the riverbank, the place where it all began. The city skyline, illuminated against the night, is a backdrop to our personal tale.

"The exhibition was a success," I say, my voice a blend of pride and contentment. "But it feels like it's more than just about the photos, doesn't it?"

Ethan nods. "It's about making change through our lens."

Ethan pulls out a photo—just him and me, captured in a candid moment of laughter and love.

"Can I frame this one?" he asks, holding the photo like a precious gem.

"You picked this from the group photos?" I inquire, a smile playing on my lips.

"Yep," he replies, his eyes locked on mine.

"Nice." My heart flutters with an emotion I can't quite name.

"If you like it, I can hang it on the wall," he suggests, a hint of nervousness in his voice.

"Which wall?" I ask, feigning confusion.

"The one we'll share for life if you agree." His words hang in the air, a proposal wrapped in simplicity and sincerity.

For a moment, I'm speechless, overwhelmed by the depth of his sentiment. Then, with a joy that bubbles up, I answer, "Yes, Ethan. I'd love that."

We stand hand in hand. The water mirrors our first kiss. It reflects the love that has grown between us.

Night arrives. I see Ethan's eyes shining in the darkness, and I know how beautiful they are.

Sunlit Secrets in the Café

The scent of fresh coffee wraps around me like a familiar hug, signaling that I'm in my cozy hideaway. This little café, nestled in the heart of Chico, California, offers me an escape from everyday life.

This café is my daily haven. It's where my thoughts spill into my novels.

There's a unique charm here. The way sunlight filters in feels right. So do the well-used tables and the gentle jazz backdrop. My days usually have a simple rhythm: work, write, rewind, but not today.

I am scribbling away. I barely notice when a tall man with dark hair gets a coffee and chooses the seat opposite me. Only when I glance up and meet those intense blue eyes do I pause. He seems oddly familiar. It's like a forgotten song that I still know all the words to. The café's hum fades as our gazes remain locked.

"Sorry to intrude. Everywhere else was taken," the tall man says, breaking the silence. His tone is cautious, even hesitant.

"No worries," I reply with a friendly smile, eager to cut through the tension. "I'm Lila."

"Adrian," he responds, his voice striking a chord of familiarity in me.

I strike up a conversation. "I come here often, but I've never seen you before."

Adrian stirs his coffee slowly and deliberately. "I'm new in town," he admits, taking a tentative sip.

Intrigued, I lean forward, curiosity evident in my tone. "Oh? Where did you come from?"

For a moment, he looks trapped, as if caught off guard by my question. The cheerful ambiance of the café feels miles away as tension wraps around our table.

He sets down his cup, avoiding my gaze. "Different places," he finally says, his voice low and guarded.

Feeling the atmosphere shift, I can't help but press further. "Why? Did you move here for work? Family?"

Adrian hesitates, his fingers tapping a nervous rhythm on the table. "Just... needed a change of scenery," he mumbles. The weight of his gaze is palpable when he finally meets my eyes again. "Some memories are better left buried."

His cryptic response leaves me with more questions.

Just as I'm about to delve deeper, Adrian glances out the window. He abruptly stands, looking slightly anxious. "I have to go."

As he hurries away, a small envelope slips from his pocket.

"Adrian!" I shout, but he is quickly lost in the crowd.

I know I shouldn't do it, but my curiosity increases, and I open the envelope. Inside, there's a photo of Alex and my best friend,

Jane, their smiles wide and genuine. The date stamped on it from two years ago. The shot sends a chill down my spine. Alex and Jane passed away only a few days after they took this photo.

A whirlwind of emotions engulfs me. It follows a flood of questions that fills my mind.

Who is this Adrian?

How did he get this photo?

Why can't I remember this man who clearly knows me so well?

And what brought him back into my life today?

The photograph feels heavy in my hands, its implications sinking deep into my psyche.

Sleep eludes me that night. Whenever I close my eyes, the photograph and my encounter with Adrian replay in my mind.

Why doesn't any of this make sense?

Why does my heart feel this strange ache when I think of Adrian, the strange man?

Is he an extraordinary man?

Morning finds me resolute. I can't let this enigma remain unsolved. The writer in me, always inquisitive, constantly yearning for answers, takes over. I need to find Adrian.

I start with the café. Maybe the regulars or the staff have seen Adrian before. If not, I'll check the nearby places, ask around, and look for clues.

It feels like I'm stepping into one of my own stories, but the stakes are real this time, and I'm the protagonist.

As I head out, I'm determined. I vow to find every hidden secret and memory. Whatever it takes, I'll find the missing pieces of this puzzle and put them back together.

The next few days are a blur of relentless searching. But it all leads to dead ends.

One evening, I felt tired and frustrated. I find solace in my old writings about Jane, my lost friend. I've continuously poured my heart into words, seeking clarity in the face of confusion. Maybe, somewhere in these pages, I'd find a hint, a memory, or even the comfort of familiarity.

As I leaf through my journals, a particular entry from two years ago catches my eye. It's titled "The Enigma Death." I begin to read. With every line, my heartbeat quickens. These words are still haunting me. "After a party night, on their way home, they both disappeared. Two weeks later, Jane's body was found in Horseshoe Lake, surrounded by hundreds of acres of dead trees."

The description of "Alex" is uncanny. It mirrors Adrian in detail. His blue eyes are mesmerizing. There's an almost touchable air of mystery around him.

I sit back, stunned. Alex and Adrian - the parallels are undeniable.

Are they brothers?

No matter what, Adrian must have some relationship with Alex. The more I think about it, the more my head spins.

With this newfound clue, my resolve to find Adrian intensifies. I need answers, not just for his mysteries. I also want to understand the eerie link between our encounters. The pieces are beginning to form a picture, but the image is still hazy.

Determined, I decide to retrace my steps from two years ago. I will revisit the Horseshoe Lake, where I lost my best friend.

The following day, armed with my journal and the photograph, I set out.

Horseshoe Lake looks much the same as it always did. The landscape around Horseshoe Lake exudes an unsettling atmosphere. It has hundreds of skeletal trees stretching upwards. Their barren branches claw at the sky.

Once proud and robust, these trees now stand lifeless, like Jane. I remember the shapes they cast on the ground. This was especially at dusk and dawn. It created an unsettling dance of shadows. I had been here many times two years ago, hoping to find out who killed my best friend.

The air is thick with a tangible silence. It's broken only by the rustling of leaves underfoot. This sound makes the feeling of desolation stronger. The lake is surrounded by these ghostly sentinels. It reflects a somber gray, adding to the chilling atmosphere.

I remember the countless times I sat by its edge. I jotted down snippets of conversations with Jane, fleeting emotions between us. I was missing my best friend, and I can never forget about her.

But today, it feels different, like the lake holds a secret it's been waiting to share with me. I need to find out what is behind Jane's death.

I walk along the familiar path. Gravel crunches under my feet. Birds chirp in the distance, creating a comforting soundscape. I'm so lost in my thoughts. I almost don't notice the elderly woman on a bench. She fixes her gaze on the water. She looks up as I approach, a hint of recognition in her eyes.

"You're back," she says, her voice soft, like the rustling of old parchment.

I'm taken aback. "Have we met?"

She nods, her eyes distant. "It's been two years. You used to come here a lot. Always with that notebook." She gestures to the one in my hands.

I look at her tiny body, but I cannot recognize her, and I'm not expecting to meet anyone here either.

"I live nearby. This is a quiet place. Other than you, I've only met a few people."

"Have you seen a young man? Dark hair, intense blue eyes?"

"Sure, I did. He always looked like he carried the weight of the world. But he never spoke much."

My heart skips a beat. This man could be Adrian. "What's his name?"

She nods again. "I don't know, dear. He never told me."

We sit silently for a few minutes, the weight of memories filling the air.

"Do you know where he might be now?" I finally ask.

She shakes her head. "No, dear. But I remember the last time I saw him here, just a few days ago. He looked broken. He'd stay for hours, staring at the lake, as if seeking answers."

A chill runs down my spine. I realized that Adrian and I were sharing something very close. Our paths almost crossed.

"Thank you," I whisper, my voice choked with emotion.

She smiles kindly, her wrinkled hand briefly touching mine. "My dear, life has a curious way of weaving its tapestry. When the moment is just right, it brings souls together. If destiny wills it, you'll find your paths again entwined."

Feeling elated and overwhelmed, I leave the lake, my determination renewed. I must find Adrian and find out what's the cause of Jane's death.

A week later, I find Adrian in the café. Across the room, in a dimly lit corner, Adrian sits engrossed in a book. My heart races as our eyes meet, that same unspoken connection pulling at us.

Taking a deep breath to steady myself, I approach him.

He looks up, a mix of surprise and something else—perhaps regret—playing across his features.

"Adrian, or should I say Alex?" I challenge gently, holding up the photograph of Alex with Jane.

For a moment, he looks like a deer caught in headlights. He visibly swallows, his gaze shifting between the photograph and my eyes. With a resigned sigh, he gestures for me to sit opposite him.

"Adrian's my real name," he admits, voice wavering with emotion. "Alex... was my twin brother. After his death, after what happened to him and Jane, I had to vanish."

The mention of Jane makes my heart clench. "You knew Jane?" I ask, although deep down, I already know the answer.

He nods, pain evident in his eyes. "More than just knew her, Lila. I know you too, through her. Actually, I've been looking for you."

He pauses, struggling to find his words. When he speaks again, his voice is thick with emotion. "It wasn't... I was the real target. They wanted to kill me and mistakenly put Jane and my brother Alex in peril."

My hand reaches out instinctively, covering his. The warmth of our touch bridges the chasm of lost years between us. We've got a deep bond. It may come from the shared tragedy of losing loved ones to the same terrible act. It feels like we have known each other for a lifetime.

The days that follow our reunion are a whirl-wind of emotions. Adrian and I've gravitated towards each other, the pull too powerful to resist. Our talks last for hours. We move from cafés to long walks along the city streets. Some-times, we sit by Horseshoe Lake, where so many memories linger.

The pain of losing Jane and Alex is a shared wound, raw and fresh; in its healing, we find so-lace in each other's company. We spend nights sharing stories. We laugh at shared memories and comfort each other in grief.

Yet, with each passing day, a new kind of dan-ger casts a shadow over our budding romance. Letters with no return address start appearing at my apartment. They contain veiled threats.

One reads, "Stay away from him if you know what's good for you." Another, "He's caused enough pain. Don't be his next victim."

Adrian's face goes pale when I show him the notes. "They're from my past," he admits, regrets clear in his eyes. When I was undercover, I made enemies—dangerous ones. They think I betrayed them."

"Adrian, how do we find the person who took Alex and Jane away from us?"

"Lila, I'm already deep into this. I've gotten closer, closer than I've ever been. But I need you to promise me something."

"What is it?"

"Stay away from this. Lila, it's dangerous, and I can't bear the thought of anything happening to you."

"Can I help in any way? "

Adrian smiles and hugs me gently. "The best way you can help is by keeping yourself safe. I've ventured into some dark places and don't want you anywhere near them."

It is a long and warm hug.

Despite the looming threat, our love refuses to be overshadowed. If anything, the danger only strengthens our bond. We become each other's haven. We find strength in our shared resolve to face the menace head-on.

With each challenge, shared fear, and every moment of vulnerability, our love deepens. It becomes a beacon. It guides us through the darkest times. It promises that we'll face it side by side. No matter what the future holds.

One afternoon, we are back at Horseshoe Lake, a place holding special significance for both of us. The water's calm surface reflects the sunlight's glow, casting a golden light around us.

Adrian, always observant, scans the area, his sharp eyes missing nothing. "We shouldn't discuss Jane's case at the café," he murmurs, a hint of reproach in his voice. "It's public. We could've been watched."

I chuckle, trying to lighten the mood. "You underestimate my sense of adventure! I'm a suspense novel writer. Besides, the café's my turf!"

He looks at me, his intense eyes softening. "Lila, this isn't one of your stories. The danger's real."

I face him, and my determination is evident. "Adrian, I'm not some damsel in distress. I've faced challenges before, and I'll face them now. With you."

He sighs, pulling me close, his warmth enveloping me. "You're fearless, you know that? But these people are worse than animals. They play dirty."

"I'm not scared," I reply, my voice firm. "We've got something they can never understand or break: love."

A smile tugs at the corner of his lips. "Always the optimist, aren't you?"

I grin. "Someone has to balance out your broodiness."

He chuckles, the sound echoing in the stillness of the night. "Together, then?"

"Together," I affirm, sealing our pact with a kiss.

As evening arrives, we leave.

After leaving Horseshoe Lake, we stop by the café. The café is cozy. This contrasts starkly with the chilly evening outside. After dinner, as Adrian and I get ready to leave, I can't shake off a nagging feeling of unease.

I glance around, trying to spot anything out of place, but everything seems normal. People are chatting. The barista is behind the counter. Soft jazz plays in the background.

We walk out. The street's dim glow quickly replaces the café's warm light. The usual bustling city sounds are oddly muffled, giving the night an eerie stillness.

We start walking, our footsteps echoing on the pavement. I feel like we're being watched many times. I catch fleeting shadows in my side vision.

Adrian tugs me into an alley, pressing us both against the wall. His eyes scan the street, his body tense. "We're being followed," he murmurs.

Before I can respond, a dark figure steps into view at the alley's entrance. "Thought you could run from your past, Adrian?" The voice is low, chillingly so.

It's Vincent, the murderer," Adrian whispers to my ear and uses his body to cover mine.

Vincent takes a step closer, a menacing grin on his face. "Did you think changing cities would save you?"

From behind us, two more figures emerge, effectively trapping us.

The darkness around us was thick and suffocating. It was the kind that feels almost touchable, pressing into us from all sides. My breath catches in my throat. Every passing second makes the sinking feeling in my gut worse. We might not make it out alive. Adrian tightens his grip on my hand. We are both paralyzed by Vincent's looming threat in the shadows.

Then, just as despair threatens to consume us, the distant wail of sirens cuts through the night. Growing louder and closer, they become our beacon of hope. Suddenly, powerful headlights slice through the gloom, revealing a fleet of police cars.

An officer, gun drawn, shouts, "Freeze!"

Vincent, caught momentarily off guard by their sudden appearance, stumbles back. His face, now visible under the police lights, contorts with rage and disbelief.

Adrian steps forward with newfound confidence, points, and yells, "That's him! He's the one!"

"There are two more," I roar, pointing at the pair sprinting away. A team of officers is already in pursuit.

Vincent, realizing the odds are now against him, spits out with venom, "You'll regret this, Adrian!"

Several officers close in on Vincent without missing a beat, swiftly handcuffing him. His threat is neutralized, and the air around us feels lighter and safer. The night's terror is finally over.

A familiar voice calls out, "Thank you, Officer." The old lady from the lake stands at the alley's entrance, behind her, the lights of police cars flash.

Now, the trio are all handcuffed even as they protest.

The old woman approaches us, her eyes sharp but concerned. "I saw him by the lake earlier," she says, nodding towards Vincent. I felt bad, so I followed him into the city. I'm glad I did."

Relief washes over Adrian as he nods, gratitude clear in his eyes. "Thank you. You saved us."

The old lady smiles, "I'm a retired cop," gently patting Andrian's arm. "Just keep an eye out, both of you. And take care of each other."

As the police cars drive away, the night's events weigh heavily on us. We stand there momentarily, the reality of what could have been sinking in.

But then Adrian turns to me, his eyes filled with relief and love. "Lila," he whispers, pulling me close, "It's over. We're free."

And as we embrace, I tell Adrian, "It's not over yet. We need to fight with them in the courtroom."

The court day is finally arriving. The courtroom is quiet and tense. It is broken only by the occasional whisper or rustle. Behind a high wooden desk, the judge sits at the center, gazing sternly over his glasses at the room below.

On one side of the room, Vincent, looking disheveled and defiant, sits flanked by his lawyers. The evidence against him is vast. But, his demeanor suggests he still has a shred of hope.

Opposite him, Adrian is seated, his face pale but determined. Beside him, I clasp his hand, offering silent support. The memories of Jane and Alex weigh heavily on our hearts, and today, we hope for justice.

The prosecutor rises, her voice clear and confident. Your Honor, the evidence clearly shows that Vincent was involved. He was involved in the tragic deaths of Jane Moore and Alex Turner. They were innocent bystanders caught up in his dangerous games. They were brutally taken from us, leaving a void that can never be filled."

As she recounts the night of their deaths, the room's atmosphere grows heavier. The details are harrowing, and many in the gallery wipe away tears.

Vincent's lawyer attempts a defense, suggest-ing a lack of motive and questionable evidence. But the case against him is strong. Security footage, witnesses, and damning evidence link him to the crime scene.

Vincent's eyes dart around, avoiding Adrian's gaze. Guilt, fear, or both make him fidget in his seat.

As the trial progresses, the weight of the ev-idence becomes undeniable. Witnesses come forward, and pieces of the puzzle fall into place. The atmosphere in the courtroom grows thick with anticipation.

Finally, after what feels like an eternity, the jury returns.

The foreperson stands. Her voice does not waver. We find the defendant, Vincent Lopez, guilty. He's guilty of the first-degree murders of Jane Moore and Alex Turner.

A collective sigh sweeps through the court-room. Vincent's face pales, the weight of his actions finally sinking in. The judge sentences him. His voice is solemn. "You've committed terrible crimes. They caused immense pain to families and loved ones. For that, I sentence you to life in prison without parole."

As the gavel falls, Adrian and I embrace, tears flowing freely. The journey to justice has been long and painful. But today, we find peace. We know that Jane and Alex's souls can finally rest.

After the criminal guys were arrested, we often go back to that same quaint café. We've penned our memories of Jane and Alex and how I met Adrian. It's our true story.

The process of writing together is almost magical. Our words weave together. They draw from our shared experiences and turn into captivating stories. The manuscript comes from our work. It won't just be a bestseller. It will be a testament to our journey of love and resilience.

While the café is always abuzz with people, it turns into our own little world. It's where we first met. It's where our love story began. It's where we vowed to face the future hand in hand. Every corner and table has a memory etched into it. They hold whispered secrets, soft kisses, and dreams of tomorrow.

Adrian asks me, "What's the book's name?"

"Sunlit Secrets in the Café," I reply.

Whispers of Fire

On the first step into this little coastal town, my heart is about to burst out of my chest. The sun sparkles on the water, and seagulls dance in the sky. There's an old lighthouse in the distance. The kids are playing on the beach. There are colorful houses with white picket fences. I'm here for an art residency program. I can't wait to dip my brush into the colors of this town.

I drag my art supplies along as I enter a cozy-looking café that promises warmth and a delicious coffee aroma. The bell above the door jingles, announcing my arrival. A man stands behind the counter. He isn't smiling, and shadows cover his eyes. But, something is captivating about him. Maybe it's the way he moves with purpose or the intensity in his gaze. He's not your typical sunny barista.

"Hello," I greet, my natural enthusiasm pouring out. "This place looks amazing! Can I get a latte, please?"

He nods, his voice deep and gruff as he says, "One latte coming up."

I study him a bit more. "You know, there's something about this town, this café, that feels so... unique. Is there a story behind it?"

He glances away, irritation flickering in his eyes. "Was a firefighter, not a historian."

I blink in surprise. "A firefighter? You must be very brave!"

A hint of sadness crosses his face, and he shrugs. "Just did what I had to do."

We share a few seconds of silence. His demeanor contrasts mine, but oddly, it feels... comforting. Genuine.

"My name's Ella, by the way," I say, trying to inject warmth into the conversation. "I'm here for an art residency."

He pours the latte into a mug and places it before me. "Max," he introduces me simply.

"Nice to meet you, Max," I say with a grin. "I'll visit often, not just for the coffee."

Max gives me a small, almost imperceptible smile. It doesn't reach his eyes, but it's there. "We'll see."

Our exchange is brief and odd. But, I leave the café with a strange feeling. This isn't the last important talk I'll have with Max.

Over the next few days, I make it a ritual to visit the café. I am drawn to the place for a quick coffee break or a leisurely lunch. And maybe, just a little bit, to the enigmatic Max.

One morning, I sit at a window table, sketch-book in hand, lost in the sea's wave patterns. I overhear snippets of a conversation from a nearby table.

"Can't believe Max even shows his face around here after what happened."

"Poor Max... but he should've known better."

Curiosity gets the better of me, and I turn slightly to catch more. They're talking about the fire. The one where Max lost someone close.

I feel a pang in my chest, a mix of sadness and sympathy. Later, when I approach the counter to order, I can't hold it anymore. "I overheard your story about losing your friend. I'm sorry for whatever happened, Max."

His gaze hardens, and tension is in the air. "Some things are better left unsaid," he replies, his voice colder than I've ever heard.

Flustered, I stutter, "I-I didn't mean to intrude. Just... if you ever want to talk—"

"I don't." His interruption is sharp. He hands me my coffee, and the message is clear: this is the end of the conversation.

Walking back to my table, my cheeks burn with embarrassment. What was I thinking, prying into Max's past?

The next day, when I hesitantly step into the café, Max doesn't acknowledge me. He's avoiding my gaze. The once comforting place now feels heavy with unspoken words.

I've ruined any chance of getting to know him better. Every artist needs inspiration, and Max, with his layers and depth, would be mine. But perhaps some stories are too painful to share, even with a sunshine-filled girl like me.

As the days pass, the town's whispers become hard to ignore. Snippets of Max's story reach my ears at local shops, by the beach, and even at the residency where I paint.

"It was a terrible fire at the old Thompson mansion," Mrs. Peters, the local baker, tells her friend. I pick out pastries. "Such a shame. Max tried to save them, but...."

"But he failed," her friend replies. He lowers his voice and casts a sorrowful glance. He probably realizes I was eavesdropping.

Each tidbit adds to the haunting puzzle of Max's past, and I'm torn. I yearn to know the whole story. I want to understand the layers of pain and regret that seem to shadow Max's every step. Yet, another part wants to give him space, to let the past remain buried if that's what he needs.

One afternoon, as I paint by the sea, Clara approaches me, a fellow resident artist who's lived in the town for years. I knew her before I came here.

"Clara, can you tell me what happened at the old Thompson Mansion?"

Noticing my distraction, she asks, "Yes, but why?"

Nodding hesitantly, I admit, "I wonder about Max and the fire. Everyone hints, but no one says what happened."

Clara sighs, looking out at the waves. "It was a dark time for this town. The Thompsons were beloved, and their mansion was the town's landmark. It caught fire unexpectedly. Max was the first responder. He saved the children but couldn't reach the parents in time. The weight of that loss, the guilt—it changed him. Thompson and Max were best friends. His younger sister was Max's girlfriend. She left Max after the fire."

A heavy silence settles between them. Now I can feel Max's pain. It makes my earlier curiosity seem almost invasive.

"I wish I hadn't pried now," I confess, guilt-ridden. "I pushed Max, and now there's this wall between us."

Clara places a comforting hand on my shoulder. "It's not just you. He's built walls around himself, keeping everyone out, maybe even himself."

I ache for Max. His pain is so deep. His gruff exterior hides such profound wounds. I'll respect his boundaries, no matter how much my heart wishes to reach out to him.

The coastal town unveils its charm with each day, but the natural allure for me is the little café by the shore. It isn't just the delicious brew or the pastries—it's Max.

Our chats start with hellos. They grow into longer talks about the weather, the town, and my art. We find a rhythm and a comfort that wasn't there before.

One morning, as I sip my coffee, I notice an elderly lady struggling with groceries outside. Before I can offer to help, Max is there, carrying her bags and listening intently as she talks. The sight tugs at my heart. Behind his gruff exterior, small gestures reveal a tenderness. They show a gentle soul that perhaps only a few get to see.

When I sit with my canvas in the evenings, it's not just the ocean or the lighthouse that I paint anymore. Subtle elements of Max begin to weave into my art. The silhouette of a strong man stands against a fiery backdrop. The warm glow of a café at twilight. The gentle steam from a coffee mug mirrors the mist from the sea. He becomes my muse, filling my canvases with emotion and depth.

A few days later, I'm lost in painting a scene of the café with a lone figure at the counter. I sense a presence. Looking up, I find Max watching, his gaze locked onto the canvas.

"You've captured it," he murmurs, voice thick with emotion. "The essence of this place, of... me."

Our eyes meet. There's an intensity, a silent nod to the bond growing between us. It's as if, through my art, I've seen parts of him he rarely shows.

He steps closer, his fingers lightly grazing the wet paint. "You make it look... beautiful," he whispers, and I can't tell if he's talking about the painting or the world around us. But in that moment, with the golden hue of sunset enveloping the café, everything truly is.

Just like that, our once distinct worlds start blending. They create a mix of emotions we had not expected.

One overcast evening, the café is tranquil. I'm sketching by the window when Max approaches, two cups of hot chocolate in hand. He sets one in front of me and takes a seat opposite. His eyes have a heaviness, a vulnerability I haven't seen before.

"You've been... kind," he starts hesitantly, looking out at the rain-speckled sea. "You see things, Ella. Things others don't. And I think you've seen parts of me I've tried to hide."

I wait, pencil pausing, sensing the significance of the moment.

He took a deep breath, his gaze distant, lost in memories. "You know, Ella," he began, his voice low and filled with pain, "That night... it haunts me. Not just because of the loss, but because of the choices I had to make."

I remained silent, giving him the space to continue.

When I arrived, the flames were everywhere. The heat was intense, and the smoke was choking," Max describes, his voice quivering. "I'd managed to get the kids out, but I knew Thompson and his wife were still inside. The house... was beginning to collapse. Every instinct told me that I might not make it out if I went back in. But there was this voice in my head, this relentless voice screaming at me to be brave, to try."

He paused, taking a shaky breath. "I stood there for what felt like hours, battling with myself. I wanted to go in, be the hero, and save them. But the reality was brutal. The risk was too great. And the worst part? Living with that decision."

I reach out, holding his hand, trying to offer some comfort. "Max, bravery isn't just about taking risks. It's also about living with our choices, no matter how painful. You did your best, given the circumstances."

He looked at me, tears glistening in his eyes. "Thank you, Ella. For understanding, for listening."

The night grows dark. But, in that moment, amid the pain and shared confidences, a strong, unbreakable bond forms. It's profound.

The days that follow are lighter. Max's guarded demeanor begins to thaw, and our interactions have a new ease. Yet, curiosity keeps gnawing at me. The story behind the fire, the gossip, the whispers—it doesn't add up.

Late one evening, as I wander around the older section of town, I stumble upon a dilapidated building. Its charred remains evoke a strong sense of familiarity, recalling tragic tales. I feel my artist's instinct kick in. I start sketching the mansion's haunting silhouette. I aim to capture its somber beauty.

A rustling behind me makes me turn. An old man with a hunched back and weathered face observes me with keen eyes. "Sketching the old Thompson place?" he inquires.

I nod. "It has a story, doesn't it?"

The old man sighs, looking at the mansion. "Yes, one of pain and mystery. They say it was arson, you know? But the culprit was never found."

My heart skips a beat. "Arson?"

He nods. "Some say it was a vengeful act by a man. Others believe it was just a tragedy. But no one really knows."

A chill runs down my spine. This changes everything. Was Max's guilt misplaced? Was someone else responsible for the pain he'd been carrying all these years?

"Who was the man."

"He was from out of town. I only met him once when I was pumping gas downtown."

Driven by a newfound urgency, I turn to the old man. "Can you remember what he looked like?"

He squints, trying to recall, "He was an older fella with a particularly long nose and had a snake tattoo on his neck."

With a sudden idea, I pull out my sketchbook. My hands move swiftly, drawing a rough sketch based on the old man's description. Holding it up, I ask, "Is this close?"

The old man studies the drawing, pointing to the nose. "His nose was even longer."

I make the adjustments, elongating the nose further. "How about this one?"

He nods, his eyes widening in recognition. "Yes, that's him. That's the man I saw."

Holding the sketch, I feel a mix of dread and determination. I now have a face to the mystery and am more resolved than ever to uncover the truth.

"Thank you," I whisper, still processing this revelation.

He nods and shuffles away. He leaves me with a sketchbook full of shadows and more questions.

That night, I lie awake, debating whether to share this discovery with Max. Would it offer him solace or further torment him? The weight of this secret presses down on me.

But as dawn breaks, I make up my mind. Even if it means unraveling more of the past's dark tapestry, Max deserves to know.

The next day, I take the sketch and a printed old article about the fire I found online. I go to the café. The bell jingles softly, announcing my presence. Max looks up, his face brightening momentarily before he notices my serious demeanor.

"Max," I start, my voice trembling, "I found something you should see." I place the article on the counter. I watch his face. He scans the headline: "Thompson Mansion Fire: Tragic Accident or Deliberate Act?"

His eyes widen, and his fingers clutch the paper tightly. "Where did you find this?" he asks, his voice barely above a whisper.

"Internet," I reply, showing him the sketch of the mansion. "And there's more. An old man told me rumors of arson that it might not have been an accident. The suspect looks like this man."

His face pales. "Ella, I've been receiving messages lately, letters left at the café, in my mailbox. Cryptic ones that hint at the fire, making it sound like someone is watching, taunting."

I gasp, "You think it's the arsonist?"

Max nods slowly. "It's possible. Someone who knows what happened that night and is playing a dangerous game."

"If the blackmailer is the person who set the fire, he must be extremely stupid," It's hard to believe someone could be so foolish.

"Or lawless, extremely malicious, deriving joy from others' suffering and believing he can never be caught," Max replies, handing me a cup of coffee.

We decide to go to the police. The officer on duty is a stern woman named Officer Davis. We give her all the strange letters, notes, and drawings I made about the suspect. Officer Davis listens intently, her face grave. "We had suspicions back then but never enough evidence to pinpoint someone. Max, these messages you've been receiving could be the lead we've been waiting for."

"But," she adds cautiously, "you both need to be careful. If it really is the arsonist, and they feel cornered, they might act unpredictably."

As we step out of the police station, the weight of our discovery looms over us. Still, there's also a determination. It's a silent promise. We'll face whatever comes next together.

Max's face is a mix of hope and apprehension. He squeezes my hand. Gratitude is evident in his eyes. "Thank you, Ella. For not looking away, for helping me confront this."

With the threat of the arsonist lurking in the shadows, the quaint coastal town takes on a new hue. Each rustle, each unfamiliar face, brings a jolt of apprehension. But amid this tension, something unexpected blossoms—Max and I grow inseparable.

Our evenings are filled with hushed conversations at the café. There, he shares more about his firefighting days. He talks about the camaraderie, the risks, the lives saved, and, sadly, the lives lost. Each tale brings with it a rollercoaster of emotions, drawing us closer. We lean on each other, finding solace in shared silences and whispered confidences.

One breezy evening, as we walk along the beach, Max turns to me, his eyes reflecting the golden hues of the setting sun. "You've brought light into a very dark corner of my life, Ella. I can't thank you enough."

I smile, squeezing his hand, feeling the warmth of our intertwined fingers. "We're in this together."

My art residency ends with an exhibition. It will show all the pieces I've made here. I was inspired by Max's stories and the firefighters' resilience. They led me to theme my display as a tribute to these brave souls. Canvases filled with roaring fires and silhouetted heroes dominate the room. But the centerpiece? It is a poignant depiction of Max. He is staring at the remnants of a burnt building. Pain and determination are etched on his face.

The day of the exhibition is buzzing with activity. The town comes together. People's eyes show admiration as they move from one painting to another. But I watch Max standing before his portrait. Tears stream down his face. I know the tribute has touched him the most.

"I never imagined I'd see myself this way," he murmurs. He pulls me into a tight hug.

As the townsfolk applaud and appreciate, the atmosphere is bittersweet. The looming threat casts a shadow, but for now, we bask in the glow of art, admiration, and our deepening bond.

The night is in full swing, the gallery alive with chatter and admiration. But amidst the sea of familiar faces, one stands out. It is a man, his eyes concealed behind glasses, and he has a very long nose.

A knot forms in my stomach.

Max's face turns ashen as he spots the man. "It's him," he murmurs, barely audible.

The atmosphere suddenly thickens. Why is he here?

 "Is there something you want?" Max confronts him, voice steady. My heart racing, but resolved to stand by Max's side.

The man chuckles, the sound hollow and chilling. "Just wanted to see the famous exhibition, especially the 'hero' everyone's talking about."

Before Max can respond, Officer Davis spots Bill Williams through the crowd. Her steps are measured and silent, her eyes locked onto her target.

"Bill Williams," Officer Davis announces, her voice clear and commanding, cutting through the chatter like a knife. The room falls silent abruptly. Bill turns, his face a mask of feigned confusion.

"You are under arrest," she continues, her tone steady and resolute.

"For what?" Bill's voice wavers slightly, a hint of panic underlying his question.

"For arson, resulting in the death of two individuals, and drug trafficking," Davis states, stepping closer. The gallery attendees gasp, and whispers begin to swirl around them.

Bill's eyes dart around, seeking an escape, but Davis is unyielding. "You have the right to remain silent. Anything you say can and will be used against you in court. You have the right to an attorney. If you cannot afford one, one will be appointed for you."

As she speaks, she deftly pulls out handcuffs and moves to secure Bill's wrists. His initial shock gives way to a scowl, but he offers no resistance, his options dwindling.

"You think you've got the right guy?" Bill sneers, trying to salvage some defiance.

"I don't think, I know," Davis replies, her gaze never leaving his. "We have evidence of your crimes, Bill. This is the end of the line for you."

With Bill handcuffed, Davis nods to a nearby officer who steps forward to assist. Together, they lead Bill out of the gallery, the eyes of the town upon him. Max watches from a distance, a complex look of relief and sorrow on his face, his ordeal with Bill finally ending.

As Bill is escorted out, murmurs fill the gallery. The shock of the arrest disrupts the evening but leaves a sense of justice in its wake.

Max, looking overwhelmed, turns to me, his eyes filled with gratitude. "You stood by me, Ella. Even when things got dangerous."

I smile, taking his hand. "Always."

The evening, which could have taken a dark turn, becomes a celebration. A celebration of art, bravery, a town's unity, and two people discovering strength in each other.

As the last guest leaves, Max pulls me close amidst the paintings that tell our story. "This town, these people, and especially you, have given me something priceless. They gave me closure."

I rest my head on his chest, listening to the steady beat of his heart. "And you've given me a story, a muse, and a bond I'll cherish forever."

In the heart of the gallery, we are surrounded by canvases showing courage and love. Our two souls were once hurt by the past. But, we now find comfort and hope in the promise of a shared future.

In the days following the climactic events at the exhibition, the coastal town is abuzz with talk.

But amidst the chatter, a serene calm settles between Max and me.

One evening, as the sun casts a golden hue across the sea, Max and I sit at our favorite spot on the beach. He turns to me, eyes reflecting the vast horizon, "Ella, I've been through storms, both literal and of the heart. But having you by my side, supporting and believing in me, anchored me. Thank you."

I smile, squeezing his hand, "Life has a funny way of bringing people together, doesn't it? I came here looking for inspiration and found so much more."

There's a gentle pause, our gazes locked, voices unspoken, but hearts communicating. "I care about you, Ella," Max admits, his voice filled with warmth.

"And I love you, Max," I whisper back, leaning into his embrace.

The days that follow are magical. My exhibition, already the talk of the town for its art and drama, has become a resounding success. People from neighboring towns visit. They come drawn by the tales of bravery, love, and resilience shown on canvas.

But more than the acclaim, the transformation in Max stands out. He begins to smile more, the weight of his past slowly lifting. The café was once just a shop for him. Now, it hosts community events. This further intertwines his life with the townsfolk.

And as for us? Our bond deepens. We become an inseparable duo—the brave firefighter and the sunshine artist.

The days fly by, and before I know it, my art residency draws to a close. I have to choose whether to return to the bustling city, to the life I once knew. Or, I can embrace the new world I've found here in this coastal haven.

As I pack my paints and canvases, memories of the past weeks flood my mind. I think of the first brush strokes. The café owner was mysterious. A mystery unraveled, revealing a surprising love story. The decision becomes clear.

It is the last day of my residency. The morning sun casts golden patterns on the cobbled streets. I stand in front of the café. Max emerges, a hopeful smile playing on his lips.

"I've decided to stay," I tell him, my voice filled with conviction.

His face lights up, the joy unmistakable. "I was hoping you would."

We stand there, hand in hand, not as the artist and the café owner, but as two souls ready to start a new chapter together. The café's sign creaks in the breeze. It symbolizes new beginnings. As the sun rises, our shared story unfolds.

My Off-Limits Protector Next Door

EVA STONE

Contents

I Will Marry You

"What's your name?" the ten-year-old girl in my arms asks, her voice barely above a whisper against the crackling backdrop of the burning house.

"Alex Jones," I reply, trying to mask my concern calmly as I navigate the smoky chaos.

"I'm Julia," she says, her tiny fingers clutching my jacket. "I will marry you when I grow up, Mr. Jones." Her innocent and sincere words momentarily distract me from the roaring inferno.

As the paramedics take her from my arms, her declaration lingers in my mind. It's the first time anyone has said something like that to me. At twenty, I'm more familiar with the heat of fires than the warmth of such words.

However, it's just a kid's way of saying thanks.

In the weeks following the fire, Julia regularly visits the station. She always comes bearing gifts—small tokens of gratitude. The latest is a Christmas candy jar brimming with festive treats, which she proudly shares with my crew.

"Merry Christmas, everyone!" She beams, excitement filling the station more than the bright lights and decorations adorning the walls.

The guys, a tough bunch, softened by her presence, gather around to partake in the sweets. I lean against my fire truck, watching the scene unfold with a smile I can't entirely suppress.

"And this," Julia announces, turning towards me with a smaller, carefully wrapped package, "is for you, Alex."

She hands me a homemade cupcake, the icing a bit uneven but made with undeniable care. "I made it myself," she adds, her eyes seeking approval.

"Thank you, Julia," I say, genuinely touched. "It looks great."

My crew doesn't miss a beat. "Looks like Alex has got himself a little sweetheart!" they tease. Laughter echoes around the station, but I shake my head, chuckling.

"She's just a little friend, guys," I protest, but it's a feeble attempt.

Julia, unfazed by the teasing, stands with quiet confidence. "I wanted to thank Alex for saving me," she states, and I'm struck by her resilience, her spirit.

The station, usually resonant with the sound of alarms and the rumble of engines, is filled with a different energy during her visits. Her curiosity about our work and her endless questions about firefighting bring a lightness to our routine.

I reflect as the afternoon fades and Julia's mom arrives to pick her up. I've always seen myself as just an ordinary guy, easily overlooked. But through Julia's eyes, I'm reminded that sometimes, being ordinary can still mean being someone's hero.

I watch their car disappear down the street, the cupcake in my hand a simple, sweet reminder of the unexpected bonds that life can bring.

Three years have passed since I first met Julia in the burning fire.

Today marks my twenty-third birthday, which starts just like any other day at the fire station—filled with the usual drills and the background hum of radios. But there's an undercurrent of excitement among the crew; I can tell they've been planning something.

The surprise comes at midmorning. Julia bursts through the doors, her face bright with a smile that could light up the gloomiest day. She carries a clumsily wrapped gift, her steps hurried, eager.

"Happy Birthday, Alex!" she exclaims, presenting the gift with a flourish. I grin at her enthusiasm.

"Thanks, Julia. You don't have to," I add, but I'm genuinely pleased.

She's grown so much since I carried her out of the fire that night. She's almost a teenager now.

But today, there's another figure trailing behind her, hesitantly pushing open the station door. Luby, my girlfriend of six months, steps in, her eyes scanning the room before landing on me.

"Hey, Birthday Boy," Luby says, a hint of a smile on her lips. She's holding a store-bought cake. I know her attempt at a gesture doesn't come quickly to her.

Luby works in sales at Dillard's. She's lovely and usually stands out in a crowd, sparkling with charisma. But today, around my buddies, she seems shy, a side of her I rarely see.

The room's warmth dissipates as Julia's bright smile falters, her gaze flickering between me and Luby. There's a trace of something in her eyes—confusion, maybe, or a tinge of disappointment that didn't belong on a young girl's face.

"Who's she?" Julia's question cuts through the muffled sounds of the station, her voice climbing a notch, unsteady.

"This is Luby, my girlfriend," I introduce, aiming for a casual tone to ease the sudden tension.

Luby extends a polite smile, a practiced curve of her lips that doesn't quite reach her eyes.

Julia's response is a simple, elongated, "Oh," laden with unspoken words, the kind that hover and thicken the air. I catch a flicker of something—a shadow, a thought, a feeling—crossing her face before she masks it with a semblance of neutrality.

The birthday celebration continues, but we're all actors in a poorly rehearsed play. Julia's vibrant energy, usually so infectious, is subdued. She picks at her cupcake, glances towards Luby, and is loaded with a complexity that seems beyond her years.

At one point, I find myself standing beside her, trying to bridge the widening gap with small talk. "You know, Julia, having more people in our lives just means there's more love to go around," I say, hoping to lighten her mood.

She looks up at me, her eyes searching mine for an answer to a question she hasn't asked. "Does it? Sometimes it seems like it just divides it up, makes it... less," she says, her words striking a chord deep inside me.

When it's time for her to leave, I say, "See you, Julia."

Julia's eyes carefully avoid mine as if she fears what they might reveal. "I don't want to say 'see you,' Alex."

I watch her go. A part of me wants to call her back, but I think she is too young to understand my explanation. She's just a little girl.

Since then, Julia has never shown up at the fire station.

Christmas rolls around, and instead of Julia's usual visit, I find a card in the mail, signed simply, "From Julia." It's a small gesture, but it speaks volumes of the distance growing between us.

Life, as it does, keeps moving. My relationship with Luby deepens. We become a couple, a step that feels both exciting and daunting.

Luby is different from anyone I've ever known—independent, strong-willed, with a social circle that spans the entire city.

Our home has become a hub of activity, with friends and acquaintances coming and going. Luby is always at the center, vibrant and lively.

I adapt to this new life, the quiet firefighter in a world of loud personalities.

Yet, in quiet moments, when the noise fades, and I'm alone with my thoughts, I miss my quiet world.

As the years pass, those Christmas cards become the only constants from Julia. Eventually, she faded from my busy life.

***

Now, at thirty, my life looks different.

I've been married to Luby for six years, and we have two kids: Kim is two years old, and Jim is about five. They are the center of my world. But honestly, it's not the happy picture everyone sees from the outside.

Luby, with her vibrant personality and never-ending social energy, is the star of our neighborhood. She's the one who knows everyone's business, from who's expecting a baby to the latest gossip about someone's rocky marriage.

At dinner, she's always animated, sharing stories and news. At the same time, I find myself just listening, often feeling like a spectator in my own life.

"Did you hear about the Thompsons? They're finally getting a pool," she'd say, her eyes sparkling with excitement. I'd just nod, my mind drifting away from the gossip. Instead, I'm thinking about Kim needing a new shoe or Jim's latest painting, still stuck on the fridge, full of vibrant colors and childlike imagination.

"Alex, are you even listening?" Luby's voice snaps me back to the present.

"Sorry, just tired from work," I mumble, forcing a smile. But the truth is, it's more than just physical exhaustion. It's this growing sense of disconnection from Luby, from the life we've built together.

"I see." Luby hands me a bowl of soup. "Hey, Alex, are you attending the Hendersons' party next Saturday?" Luby's voice is tinged with excitement, as she flips through a magazine filled with party themes. Her eyes don't leave the glossy pages, but I know she's expecting a positive response.

I pause, then say, "I... might have a shift, Luby," my voice trailing off, unsure.

The thought of another social event, another night of forced smiles and small talk, weighs heavily on me.

She looks up, her expression shifting to mild frustration, a crease forming between her brows. "Alex. You are just a captain, but you are busier than the mayor. You know when you're here, you're not 'here'?" Her words, though spoken softly, hit hard. They're a reminder of the gap that's been growing between us.

"I know, I'm sorry. But I'm not a party fan," I reply, a familiar sense of guilt settling in my chest.

In less than ten minutes since I came to the dining table, I have already apologized more than ten times.

I watch her reaction closely.

Luby sighs, a slight frown creasing her forehead as she returns to the magazine. In that brief exchange, a moment of potential connection flickers and then fades, slipping away as quickly as it appeared. The gap between us widens a little more.

Later, as I sit on the couch, the TV sounds are just dull background noise, and I reflect on my days. With its relentless demands and unexpected emergencies, the job used to feel fulfilling. Coming home was the relief, the comfort.

But now, home feels like stepping into a foreign land where I'm constantly trying to find my footing.

Luby is there, but we live parallel lives under the same roof. Her world revolves around social events and maintaining appearances. At the same time, mine is about life-and-death decisions and the chaos of emergencies.

I glance over at Luby, who's now animatedly talking on the phone, likely planning another event. I stand up, needing to escape to find some cool night air.

Before I walk out, I hear a little voice.

"Can you put us to bed tonight, Daddy?" Kim's small voice is full of hope as she tugs at my sleeve one evening.

"Of course, sweetheart," I reply, grateful for the chance to escape the noise and be with my kids.

But as I sit there, reading bedtime stories in their dimly lit room, I can't shake off the feeling of being out of place everywhere else. I love my family and want to be a good husband and father. But with each passing day, I feel like I'm losing a part of myself, a part that Luby and I used to share.

***

I'm jolted awake by Luby's laughter, ringing loud and clear through the house. She's on the phone, her voice bubbling with excitement. I glance at the clock—it's earlier than I'd hoped to be up on my day off. Rubbing my eyes, I try to cling to the remnants of sleep, but it's futile.

She sees me stirring and immediately switches gears. "Alex, let's go shopping today." Her tone is cheerful, leaving no room for argument.

I groan inwardly. Shopping with Luby is an all-day affair, especially when she's hunting for something specific—like the perfect dress for the Hendersons' party. And I know it means the kids and I will spend hours trailing after her in the store.

By midday, we're deep in the throes of her shopping spree. The kids are restless and hungry; I'm tired and overwhelmed by the endless parade of dresses Luby keeps trying on. She flits from one mirror to another, her energy undiminished.

"What do you think of this one, Alex?" she asks, twirling in front of the mirrors.

I offer a halfhearted thumbs-up, my attention divided between her and keeping an eye on Kim and Jim, who are getting more fidgety by the minute.

"This is your payback for not coming to the party," Luby jokes, but her voice has an edge that makes me wince.

I want to find Kim a new pair of shoes—she's been needing them for weeks—but Luby's preoccupied with dress after dress. I glance at Kim, her small face looking up at me with boredom and hope.

"Soon, sweetheart," I whisper to her, but I'm unsure when.

By the end of the day, we've spent nearly $450. The party dress costs $360, and the rest goes to dining out. But seeing Luby's glowing face, her happiness is evident in every smile and laugh.

It's clear that the expense is justified to her, even though she already has more than enough clothes hanging in the closet. Each new addition brings her joy, contrasting my more practical view of necessities. As I watch her admire her latest purchase, I can't help but tally the cost, both monetary and in terms of the time and energy spent, wondering if it's all worth it.

Sitting next to Luby at the restaurant, I feel disconnected, wondering how our perspectives on something as simple as clothing can vastly differ.

Soon, my birthday arrives. Luby confronts me before I head off to work, her voice strained with frustration. "I've invited everyone, Alex. Can't you skip just this once?" she pleads.

I nod first and then shake my head, a heavy feeling settling in my chest. "I wish I could, but you know I can't guarantee it," I reply, the weight of my duty as a firefighter making it impossible to acquiesce.

As the sun sets, casting long shadows over the city, my phone buzzes insistently in my pocket. I'm just minutes away from home to attend my birthday party, but the moment I see the caller ID—it's the fire chief—I know that any plans I have are about to change.

"Jones," I answer, my voice automatically shifting to a tone of readiness.

"Captain, there's a fire, residential, on Fifth Street. It's near a factory. We need all hands," comes my chief's brisk, urgent reply.

My heart sinks, but duty overrides personal disappointment. "On my way," I respond, already turning the car around.

As I approach the scene, the sky is painted with ominous plumes of smoke. The fire has engulfed a two-story house, flames licking hungrily at the walls, threatening to spread to neighboring homes. The street is chaotic, filled with the noise of sirens and the shouts of my fellow firefighters.

As captain, I quickly put on my turnout gear and take charge of my teams.

"Listen up," I say, my voice steady and clear, "we need to sweep the building and ensure everyone's out. Reports suggest someone might be trapped on the second floor!"

My team nods in unison, their faces set with determination. We've trained for this, and we move as a cohesive unit under my leadership. The heat from the burning building is almost a physical barrier, but we push through it, our focus unwavering.

As we enter the building, the smoke is like a thick fog, reducing visibility to nearly zero. I lead the way upstairs, the heat intensifying with each step. The structure groans ominously under our boots, a stark reminder of the risks inherent in every step.

"Fire department, call out if you can hear me!" I yell, my voice echoing through the smoky haze.

Then, a faint sound—a cough. My trained ears pick it up immediately. I signal my team and head towards the source, a small room clouded with smoke. There, under a window, is a young woman and a little girl, their eyes wide with fear.

I reach them quickly, my presence offering her some comfort. "I've got you," I assure them, my voice calm and confident even through the mask. Gently, I lift the girl into my arms, her weight light but her grip tight, a silent testament to her fear.

I look at the young lady, urgency apparent in my eyes. "Follow me, quickly," I instruct, guiding her towards the stairs. As we start descending, two other firefighters, part of my team, join us. They move in swiftly, one leading the way and the other following behind us, ensuring we have support on both sides as we navigate through the smoke and potential hazards. Together, we work as a unit, focused on getting them to safety as efficiently as possible.

"Team, we're coming out. Prepare for extraction," I communicate through my radio, leading the way back through the treacherous, smoky passageways with the victim in my arms.

Every second is crucial; the building could collapse at any moment. But it's more than just a job for me; it's a commitment, a vow to protect and save lives, no matter the danger. As we emerge into the night, the cool air hitting us like a wave, I know that this is what being a captain is all about—leading from the front, saving lives, and bringing my team back safely.

Back outside, the cool night air is a stark contrast to the inferno inside. Paramedics take the woman and the girl. Now, they are safe.

My phone buzzes again with a message from Luby. I know it will be filled with disappointment and frustration.

When I return home, exhausted and longing for rest, the aftermath of the missed party hits me in full force. The house is quiet; Kim and Jim are already in their beds. But Luby's anger is loud and clear. Her disappointment manifests in a heated argument, louder and more intense than any we've had before.

"You missed your own birthday party, Alex!" Luby's voice is sharp, a cutting edge that slices through my exhaustion. "Do you know how embarrassing it was to explain to everyone why you weren't there?"

I lean against the wall, feeling the tension in my shoulders tighten. "There was a fire, Luby. Someone's life was in danger. I couldn't just leave—" I begin, my voice weary yet firm.

"But there's always a fire, isn't there? Always some emergency!" Her hands are on her hips, her stance rigid with frustration. "What about the emergency here, at home? What about us?"

Luby steps closer, her voice tinged with frustration and disappointment. "Do you know how many hours I spent cooking in the kitchen for your birthday meal?"

I run a hand through my hair, struggling to find words to bridge the chasm between our worlds. "I'm a firefighter, Luby. This is what I signed up for. Saving lives—it's not just a job, it's a calling."

"A calling?" Luby scoffs, her voice rising. "What about your calling as a husband, as a father? Do those mean anything to you?"

The accusation stings more than the heat of any fire I've faced. "Of course they do," I shoot back, my frustration bubbling up. "But I can't control when emergencies happen. I wish I could be in two places simultaneously, but I can't!"

Luby's expression hardens, her eyes glinting with unshed tears of anger and hurt. "Sometimes I wonder if you even want to be with us."

That hits a nerve, and I'm at a loss for words for a moment. The gap in understanding between us feels more comprehensive than ever. I'm torn between my duty and my love for my family, and it's a balance I'm constantly struggling to maintain.

"I always want to be here," I say quietly, the fight draining out of me. "But I also can't turn my back on people who need me—"

I stop midsentence as I notice Jim and Kim standing in the hallway. Their faces are etched with fear and confusion, clearly scared by the intensity of our exchange. This moment brings a stark realization of how our conflicts resonate beyond just the two of us, touching the innocent lives we are responsible for.

The room falls into a heavy silence, our words hanging like smoke. At that moment, it's clear that the fire I fight at work isn't the only blaze I'm struggling to contain. The fire at home, burning through my marriage, is proving to be just as challenging, if not more so. And right now, I'm not sure how to extinguish it.

In the end, I lay on the couch, alone in the dim light of the living room. Though sharing the same roof, Luby and I are worlds apart, sleeping with different dreams and growing frustrations.

Lying there, I can't shake off the guilt that clings to me, heavier with each passing day. I love my family, but the rift between Luby and me seems to widen with every missed party and every unshared moment. I'm caught in a constant battle between my duties as a firefighter and a husband, feeling like I'm failing at both.

As the night stretches on, I'm left with my thoughts, the house's silence amplifying the sense of disconnection that's become my constant companion. The joy of family life I once longed for now feels like a distant dream, slipping further away with each passing day.

The air in our home carries a weight, thick with unspoken words and the echoes of recent arguments. It feels as if the walls themselves have absorbed the tension, the sadness.

We're on the path to divorce.

***

This evening, we sit across from each other at the kitchen table, feeling like we're facing strangers.

"Alex, I need more than this," Luby says, breaking the silence, her voice firm yet tinged with unmistakable weariness. "I've spent six years waiting for you to change—they were the best years of my life. I can't do it anymore."

I look at her, the woman I once thought I'd spend my entire life with, now a stranger in her home. "Luby, isn't there a way we can make this work?" My voice is a plea, a last grasp at a slipping thread.

She looks down, then up again, her eyes sad. "No, Alex. We are done," Luby says, her voice devoid of the warmth it once held. "I need to find out who I am, find a better man, and live a better life."

Her words are sharp, cutting through any remaining hope of reconciliation. They echo in the room, a stark testament to the end of what we once had.

"What about Kim and Jim?" I worry about our kids. They are so young.

"I love them, I really do. But I'm just so lost, Alex. I need space to make my life better. The kids will be okay with you." Luby's voice is firm, but her eyes tell a different story. There's pain there.

"They're both so young," I say, thinking about how much they need their mother.

"Being young is better. Kids won't remember much or hurt as much as I do." Luby lifts her chin, trying to sound confident.

Her words are like a punch in the gut. She's so distant, even talking about our own kids. That's when I know for sure—I need to be the one who's there for Kim and Jim. They deserve a fully present parent who cares about their every little need.

Over the next few days, Luby packs up her things. The kids are confused, not really understanding what's happening. I try to explain, but it's hard. They just look at me, not really getting it.

So now, I'm a single dad, navigating a world that feels familiar and alien. Each morning is a battle, a juggling act of preparing breakfast, packing lunchboxes, and double-checking that Kim and Jim have everything they need for preschool and kindergarten.

The house, once filled with Luby's laughter and endless chatter, now echoes with the sounds of children's shows and the occasional bickering of siblings. The chair where Luby used to sit at dinner is now just an empty space. Her side of the bed is cold and untouched.

I try to fill these gaps with extra love for Kim and Jim—more hugs, longer bedtime stories, and forced smiles. But their little eyes often wander to that empty chair, filled with questions they can't put into words.

One night, I walk down the hallway to check on Kim and Jim. I gently push Kim's bedroom door open and see her curled up on her little bed. In the soft glow of her nightlight, I notice her small arms clutching something tightly to her chest. I move closer, treading softly to avoid waking her, and realize that she's holding on to one of Luby's old sleeping shirts.

The sight is both tender and heart-wrenching.

I stand there for a moment, watching her. These quiet, unguarded moments reveal the depth of the kids' feelings and the silent struggle they face in understanding the changes in our family. I feel a mix of emotions—sadness for their loss, anger at Luby for leaving this void, and a fierce determination to be all that my children need.

Quietly, I walk over and gently adjust the blanket around Kim, careful not to disturb her. Leaning down, I whisper a soft "I love you," hoping my presence can offer comfort, even as she sleeps.

I step back and take another look at Kim. She's still holding her mom's shirt. In the quiet light of her room, I promise myself again, not just to be there for her and Jim but to help them feel better, to help them understand and get through this tough time. It's a big job, but I'm ready to do it. They mean everything to me, and I'll do whatever I can to make them feel okay again.

The days leading up to Luby's visits are the toughest. Kim and Jim mark off the days on the calendar, their excitement growing.

"Daddy, only two more days until Mommy comes!" Kim exclaims one morning, her eyes bright with joy.

"Yeah, I can't wait to show her my new drawing," Jim adds, his voice filled with a rare enthusiasm.

I smile at their happiness, though some of me dreads Luby's commitment unpredictability. Then, my phone buzzes. It's a text from Luby: I am on vacation with my boyfriend, so I won't make it for the visit.

I look up at Kim and Jim, their expectant faces making this even more complex. "Kids, I just got a message from Mommy," I start, my voice gentle.

"She's not coming, is she?" Kim asks.

"No, honey, not this time. Mom's... away," I say, trying to keep my voice steady.

Jim's face falls instantly, his disappointment a tangible thing. "But she promised," he murmurs.

Kim turns away, tears in her eyes.

I kneel to their level, feeling a surge of protectiveness. "I know, and I'm sorry. But how about we do something special instead? Just the three of us?" I suggest trying to salvage their spirits.

"Can we make pancakes for dinner?" Kim asks a slight quiver in her voice.

"And watch a movie?" Jim adds, still not looking up.

"Absolutely," I reply, wrapping them both in a hug. "We'll make it a fun night, I promise."

I have a happy day with Kim and Jim. As I tuck them in at bedtime, their little arms cling to me a bit tighter. "We love you, Daddy," they murmur, and my heart aches with love and pain.

I stare at the ceiling in bed, feeling glad the kids ended their day happily. Tomorrow will be another challenging day.

The following day is Sunday. Amidst the usual morning chaos, there's a knock at the door. I open it to find a young girl in her early twenties holding a pie. She has a friendly, familiar smile, but I can't place her.

"Hi, I'm Jane Willow, your new neighbor," she extends a pie towards me. "I thought I'd introduce myself."

I take the pie from her, noticing it's freshly baked and still warm in my hands, a bit surprised by this unexpected kindness. "Thanks, that's really kind of you. I'm Alex," I reply, stepping aside to let her in.

As she enters, her eyes briefly scan the living room—toys scattered, breakfast dishes on the table, a clear sign of our rushed life.

"You've got your hands full here," she remarks with a sympathetic smile.

"Yeah, it's been a bit hectic since… well, since I started doing this solo," I admit, feeling self-conscious about the mess.

Jane nods understandingly. "I work at Jim's elementary school. I see you dropping him off sometimes."

As I pour milk for Kim, I turn to Jane with curiosity. "What do you teach?" I ask.

Jim, overhearing our conversation, pipes up with a smile. "Ms. Willow is our art teacher," he says proudly.

Jane hesitates momentarily, then offers, "If it helps, I could take Jim to school. I'm heading that way anyway. It might make your mornings a little easier?"

I'm taken aback by her kindness. "That would be... actually, that would be a huge help. Thank you."

We chat a little more—Jane is easy to talk to, and something about her is reassuringly familiar. As she leaves, I feel a weight lifted off my shoulders.

A few weeks pass, and Jane's help with Jim has become a routine that I'm incredibly grateful for.

But the unpredictability of my job as a fire-fighter still looms large. One afternoon, I get an emergency call just as I'm supposed to pick up Kim from kindergarten. I rush to the scene, the stress of being late to pick up Kim gnawing at me.

By the time I'm done and rush to the YMCA to pick up Jim, I'm met with disapproving looks and a penalty for late pickup.

The next day, Jane notices my distress. "Rough day?" she asks gently.

I nod, explaining the situation. Jane listens. Her expression is thoughtful. "How about I pick up Jim and Kim whenever you need me? I can bring them home and care for them until you arrive. It's no trouble."

I'm overwhelmed by her offer. "I... I don't know what to say. That would be amazing."

I stand at the front door as Jane leaves, reflecting on her kindness. It brings a warmth to my heart, a feeling that's been rare in these challenging times.

As time passes, Jane becomes more than just the lady next door who helps out. She's kind and easygoing with the kids—it's like she becomes a part of our everyday life. Gradually, I look forward to seeing her, to hearing her knock on the door. Her simple and warm smile makes everything feel a bit lighter for me.

One evening, duty calls me away unexpectedly, and I can't pick up Kim and Jim. Without a second thought, I dial Jane's number. "Jane, I'm sorry to ask, but could you—?"

"Don't worry, Alex. I'll pick them up," she answers without hesitation, her voice a soothing balm to my frayed nerves.

When I return home that night, the house is tidy and calm, unlike the usual mess. Jane's sitting by Kim and Jim's beds, reading them a story. Her voice is soft and sweet, filling the room with quiet peace. It's like looking at a cozy picture, everything calm and gentle.

In the kitchen, there's dinner ready on the table. It's nothing fancy, but Jane put her heart into making it.

Jane looks up as I enter, and in the soft lamp-light, her face holds a serene beauty that catches me off guard. She dresses simply, contrasting Luby's preference for makeup and high fashion. Her simplicity is elegant, a genuine quality that resonates deeply with me.

"Thanks, Jane. I don't know what I'd do without your help," I say with sincere gratitude.

"It's nothing, really. I enjoy it," Jane replies with a smile that reaches her eyes.

After the kids sleep, we sit at the dining table, discussing Jim's latest painting. Jane's eyes light up as she discusses his talent.

"Jim has a real gift," she says earnestly. "His use of color, his expression—it's remarkable for his age. He has a great imagination."

I watch her enthusiasm for Jim's hobby and her belief in him. My feelings for Jane begin to shift in these small, genuine moments. What starts as gratitude slowly blossoms into something more profound that surprises and scares me. I wasn't searching for love, yet it has found me in the most unexpected ways.

As Jane prepares to leave, I am reluctant to see her go.

There's a connection between us, subtle yet undeniable. It's a far cry from my tumultuous and passionate relationship with Luby. With Jane, it's like a quiet melody, soothing and reasoning.

That night, lying in bed, I couldn't stop thinking about Jane—how kind she is, how simply and beautifully she carries herself, and the quiet comfort she's brought into our lives. She's so different from Luby, with all the ups and downs we had. Being around Jane is soothing; she's gently healing all the hurt without even meaning to.

I start realizing that what I feel for her has changed, and grown into something bigger than I ever thought it would. It's scary but also exciting. After all the tough times, love has returned to me.

But this time, it's different with Jane. It's quiet, not showy, but deep and genuine.

My feelings for Jane deepen as time passes, but I hold back, wary of scaring her away. She's young, full of life and beauty, and in my eyes, she deserves someone far better than me. So, I tread carefully, keeping my growing affection under wraps.

Jane, perceptive as always, seems to sense the shift in my emotions. But she remains the same—a steadfast, caring friend, never over-stepping boundaries.

It's a delicate dance we're in, both aware of an undercurrent of something more, yet neither of us dare take the first step.

Then, one quiet evening, after the kids have drifted off to sleep, Jane turns to me with a seriousness I've not seen before. She hands me a folder with a mysterious smile.

Curious, I open it to find an old newspaper clip-ping—a picture of a firefighter holding a little girl. It's me, a decade ago, and Julia is the girl I saved from a fire.

Why does Jane show me this old newspaper?

"Alex, I need to tell you something," Jane starts, her voice barely above a whisper. "My first name is Julia. Jane is my middle name. I'm that girl you saved."

The revelation hits me like a wave. Julia—the little girl who promised to marry me, who visited the station, who drifted away... and now here she is, in front of me, as Jane.

She continues, her eyes locked on mine. "I've always seen you as my hero, the man who saved my life. I've admired you, cared for you, for as long as I can remember."

I sit there, stunned, trying to process the enormity of what she's saying. "You... you've been here all this time? Watching over me? Over us?"

Jane nods, her expression a mix of vulnerability and hope. "Alex, I need to ensure that I can bring happiness to you. And I needed to know if your kids could accept me."

The room feels like it's spinning, my mind racing to piece together all the moments and interactions with Jane—no, Julia.

The care, the connection, the unexplained familiarity—it all makes sense now.

I look at her, really look at her, seeing not just the neighbor, not just the woman who's become a friend, but Julia, the girl who grew up holding on to a memory, a promise.

"Julia," I call her name.

Her name feels both new and familiar on my lips. "I... I don't know what to say. You've been right here, and I...."

Words fail me, but the emotions don't. I reach out, pulling Julia into a hug, feeling the pieces of a puzzle I didn't even know were missing falling into place.

We hold each other, and in that embrace, I feel a sense of completeness and rightness I haven't felt in years.

It is the embrace of our souls.

Life is indeed a beautiful mystery, unpredictable and full of surprises.

As Julia and I sit close that night, everything feels right. It's like all the puzzle pieces of our lives have finally fit together.

When we tell Jim and Kim about us the next day, I'm a bit nervous. But Julia squeezes my hand, giving me courage.

"Kids," I say, "you know Jane, right? Jane's first name is Julia. We really like each other and will be together like a couple."

Kim's eyes light up. "Does this mean Julia will be here more?" she asks, hope in her voice.

"Yes, it does," Julia answers with a smile. "If that's okay with you."

Jim looks at us, then nods. "That's cool," he says, and I can tell he means it.

I look at Jim and Kim, their faces open and trusting, and take a deep breath. "Do you guys want Julia to be like your mom?" I ask gently.

Their smiles come quick and bright. "Yes," they both say, almost in unison.

Their simple, heartfelt response fills the room with a warmth that touches my heart. It's a moment full of love and hope, a sign that we're moving together into a new, happy chapter of our lives.

The room feels warm and happy. Later, watching Julia with the kids, I see how easily she fits into our family. It's like she was always meant to be here with us.

In bed, I recall little Julia's cute voice, "I will marry you when I grow up, Mr. Jones." I smile from the bottom of my heart before I fall asleep.

My Kiddie, Parrot, and Firefighter

My Kiddie, Parrot, and the Firefighter

I push open the door of Pet Mart, balancing my ten-month-old baby boy, Jamie, on my hip. He's my little bundle of joy, the sunshine in my otherwise routine life as a single mom and teacher. I'm here for cat food.

As we step in, Jamie's giggles blend with a wave of laughter echoing from the back of the store.

Curious, I maneuver through the aisles, a familiar voice rising above the rest. It's Eric, my next-door neighbor. He's a firefighter known around our small town for his bravery, pranks, and boundless humor.

There he stands, a crowd gathered around him, a parrot perched on his shoulder.

"Come on, Shakespeare, say 'hippopotomonstrosesquipedaliophobia,'" Eric coaxes, his eyes twinkling with mischief.

The word, meant to be funny because it's about fearing long words, confuses the parrot. It just squawks instead of repeating it, making everyone laugh again. I know parrots are clever, but the word Eric picked is too hard—even my middle school students would struggle to say it.

Jamie claps his hands, clearly entertained.

I can't help but smile. Eric's antics have a way of lighting up any room.

A red-haired young salesperson approaches me, assisting with placing a bag of cat food into my shopping cart. However, her somber expression casts a shadow over her helpful gesture.

"The poor parrot has been here too long. If no one buys it by today, we have to put it down," the salesperson says quietly, a frown on her face.

I look at the parrot, then at Jamie. I'm busy enough with my boy and a black cat, but I cannot watch the parrot die.

"I'll buy it," I say decisively.

The salesperson looks surprised, then relieved. "Really? Oh, thank you!"

The salesperson happily leads me to the parrot. "This bird is sold."

Eric overhears and turns to me, a broad grin on his face. "Look at you, Lucy, always the hero. First teaching our future generations, now saving parrots from my torture."

I roll my eyes, though I'm fighting back a smile. "Someone's got to counteract the trouble you cause."

Eric's chuckle ripples through the air, and he steps closer, his playful manner easing into a gentler tone. "Let me help you with the adoption. It's the least I can do for our new feathered friend."

Eric fills the air with jokes and easygoing chatter as we approach the counter. He's a natural entertainer—not just with Jamie, whose giggles echo in response to Eric's funny faces, but also with everyone around us. The customers nearby can't help but smile at his antics, and even the cashier looks amused, a break from her day's routine. Eric's presence is like a beam of sunlight, warming everyone it touches.

"All right, Shakespeare, welcome to Team Lucy," Eric announces, handing me the paperwork with a flourish. The parrot squawks, almost as if it understands and approves, sending another wave of laughter through the store.

"Thanks for the help, Eric," I say with genuine gratitude.

"Anytime, Lucy. And remember, if Shakespeare here gets cheeky, I'm just a shout away for a parrot pep talk," he replies with a wink.

I can't help but smile, shaking my head in amusement. "We'll be fine but thank you."

As we leave Pet Mart, the moment's warmth stays with us. Eric's grin never fades, and I am happy with my new pet. It's a simple yet comforting end to an unexpected adventure.

After the day at the pet store, I often run into Eric. Fate enjoys playing matchmaker with neighbors. His house, a kaleidoscope of colors and quirky garden gnomes, stands out next to my more subdued abode. Seeing him has become as regular as the morning paper.

On Saturday morning, while I'm lost in petunias and pansies, Jamie is in his baby car, happily gnawing on a teething toy. Eric jogs past, his smile bright enough to compete with the morning sun.

"Morning, Lucy! Is Shakespeare causing a ruckus yet?" he calls out.

I laugh, shaking my head. "That bird's a bigger drama queen than any of my middle school students!"

He pauses, resting his hands on the fence, his grin unwavering. "Need a hand? I've become quite an expert in bird psychology... and kiddie entertainment."

"No, thanks. We're somehow surviving the Shakespearean drama," I reply, touched by his offer, even if it's just neighborly politeness.

At that moment, Captain, my supposedly intelligent cat, decides to enact his great escape. He nudges the front door open with the finesse of a cat burglar and darts off, clearly mistaking himself for a feline James Bond. His target: the unsuspecting goldfish in Eric's pond. He zigzags along the fence line, then, with Olympic-level agility, leaps over into Eric's yard.

"Eric, quick! Captain's playing secret agent in your backyard!" I yell, a mix of amusement and alarm in my voice.

Eric springs into action, his jog turning into a sprint. Balancing Jamie on my hip, I follow him, curious and slightly anxious.

In Eric's backyard, we're greeted by the sight of Captain, now a proud conqueror, scaling an ancient oak tree. He ascends with the grace of a seasoned climber, reaching dizzying heights until he's just a rebellious dot against the sky.

I assume Captain will come down when bored, but a sudden, pitiful meow suggests otherwise. My heart sinks. He's stuck.

Eric glances at me, the corners of his eyes crinkling with amusement. "Captain wants to test the local firefighter's cat-rescuing skills."

He sheds his jacket, revealing a T-shirt titled "Local Hero at Work." In a few smooth motions, he's up the tree, moving confidently, making it look like a walk in the park. Reaching Captain, he gently coaxes my adventurous cat into his arms and begins the descent. He's back on solid ground in no time, looking every bit the hero from a Saturday morning cartoon.

"Your cat's quite the escapologist," Eric comments, setting Captain down. Now realizing his adventure wasn't as thrilling as anticipated, the cat scurries towards home, dignity slightly ruffled.

Eric's laughter is light and infectious. "Well, the fish had a narrow escape. I think they'll enjoy a vacation indoors for a bit."

"Thank you, Eric. I owe you big time," I say, relief washing over me.

His eyes twinkle with a familiar mischief. "Owe me? I'm a simple man. I accept payments in coffee. How about tomorrow?"

I hesitate, and then a smile breaks across my face. "Coffee it is." After all, how could I say no to my cat's dashing rescuer?

I have to call my babysitter to take care of Jamie tomorrow.

Having coffee with Eric is like accidentally walking onto a sitcom set filled with laughter. We're nestled in a corner of the local coffee shop.

Eric leans back, his chair creaking slightly under his weight. He continues his story loudly.

"So, there I was, right? Knee-deep in floodwater and this tiny pug is just yapping away on the roof of a car," he begins, his hands animating each word.

Initially engrossed in their own worlds, the surrounding patrons start glancing over, drawn by the magnetic pull of his storytelling. Laughter bubbles from his lips, infectious and hearty, and soon, it's not just our table but the whole room echoing with mirth.

"But you should've seen the owner's face, Lucy! Like I'd handed her a bar of gold instead of a sopping wet, disgruntled pug." He chuckles, eyes twinkling with the joy of sharing.

I offer a small, somewhat restrained smile, sipping my coffee. While Eric's tales are hilarious, the increasing attention from others makes me shrink inward. The spotlight, even by association, feels glaring on my introverted soul.

I enjoy Eric's company—his easy charm, his vivid recounting of everyday heroics. But I feel a mismatch. I crave stability, a specific educational parity, and a secure life.

"Hey, you've gone quiet on me," Eric observes, his smile softening into a look of concern. "Everything okay?"

I nod, forcing my smile to widen with just a touch. "Yeah, just... overwhelmed by the crowd, I guess."

He leans in, lowering his voice. "I sometimes forget how loud I can get. Sorry about that, Lucy. I don't mean to make you uncomfortable."

"It's not just that," I murmur, fidgeting with the handle of my cup.

Eric's expression shifts to one of understanding, tinged with a hint of disappointment. "I get it," he says, nodding slowly. "You need someone who's more your speed. Guess I'm a bit too much of a free spirit, huh?"

A bittersweet smile crosses my lips. "Maybe just a bit."

The following weekend, my kitchen turns into a scene straight out of a sitcom. Water cascades from the dishwasher, turning my cozy nook of yellow walls and potted plants into a miniature lake. The wooden cabinet under the sink, soaked through, looks like it's decided to take an impromptu swim.

I'm frantically throwing towels onto the ever-expanding puddles when a knock at the door startles me. Swinging it open, I find Eric, an armful of misdelivered mail in his grasp.

"Looks like the mailman's playing puzzles with house numbers again," he says with a grin, which quickly falls away as he steps into the aquatic chaos of my kitchen. "Whoa, do you need a plumber or an ark?"

His light tone is a stark contrast to the flood's severity. "At this point, I'd take either," I reply, my voice laced with stress.

Eric doesn't miss a beat. He dives under the sink to turn off the water valve, then darts out and returns, toolbox in tow, wading into the water with an almost comical determination.

While he battles the rebellious plumbing, I retreat to check on Jamie, who's blissfully ignorant of the chaos. Eric's muffled instructions to Shakespeare, my unusually quiet parrot, drift from the kitchen.

Curiosity piqued, I tiptoe back, only to discover Eric, now ankle-deep in water, animatedly chatting with Shakespeare. "Repeat after me, 'Eric is the best plumber,'" he instructs, a mischievous sparkle in his eye.

I can't help but laugh, the absurdity of the situation is cutting through my stress. "Really, Eric? A parrot plumber's apprentice?"

He shoots me a grin, his hands still busy with the pipes. "Hey, everyone needs a sidekick. Shakespeare's got potential."

The crisis eventually subsides, and my kitchen returns to its usual dry state. In relief and gratitude, I hand Eric a box of candy. "For your heroic plumbing skills... and the unique entertainment."

He winks, accepting the treat. "Anytime. I'm all about saving the day—or causing harmless chaos."

It's only the next day, returning from work, that I'm greeted by Shakespeare's new phrase: "Eric is the best match." The bird's imitation of Eric's voice is uncanny.

Shaking my head, I scribble a note to Eric and leave it at his door, a playful jab at his latest antic: "Parrot brainwashing is not neighborly."

Despite everything, how Eric seamlessly blends into my life is starting to make an impression on me. His humor and readiness to help, without a moment's hesitation, are hard to ignore.

Our coffee date fades into memory, and life resumes its comfortable rhythm, with Eric weaving himself into the fabric of my days. His jokes and easygoing nature become a familiar presence. Yet, I find myself at a crossroads when he suggests moving beyond casual meetups.

I'm cautious, torn between the warmth of gratitude and the pulse of something more profound. In my quieter moments, I envision a future husband who is not just kind but also brings the stability of education and a steady career. With his laughter and lightness, Eric offers solace but not the security I crave.

One bright afternoon, while I'm absorbed in the dance of gardening, Eric's voice drifts over the fence. "Hey, Lucy, how about dinner tonight?"

The question catches me mid-prune. I look up, meeting his hopeful eyes. "Eric, you're wonderful, but I don't see us like that. I'm sorry."

His smile doesn't falter, but there's a fleeting shadow in his eyes that he quickly masks. "No worries, Lucy. Worth a shot, right?"

This scene becomes a recurring motif: Eric, undaunted, finds creative ways to ask me out—a bouquet of flowers one day, a handcrafted invitation another. Each refusal I offer is tinged with a blend of affection and guilt.

In the meantime, my thoughts increasingly linger on Daniel, a CPA I met at a recent teacher's conference. His lecture on tax strategies was insightful and delivered with a charming blend of intelligence and wit. He seemed to embody the qualities I yearned for—knowledgeable, kind, and grounded.

Yet, dating as a single mom is a puzzle, with pieces like childcare always needing to be placed, and sometimes the babysitter is unavailable at short notice.

One evening, while contemplating this, an idea forms. A gesture of gratitude towards Eric: a homemade cake for his continuous understanding and support.

Holding the cake, I knock on Eric's door. He greets me, his face lighting up at the sight of the dessert... and perhaps a little at seeing me.

"Is this a peace offering?" he teases, accepting the cake.

"In a way," I laugh. "Actually, I have a favor to ask."

His eyebrows arch in interest. "Oh? What is it?"

"I have a date this weekend. Could you... maybe babysit Jamie?"

The surprise in Eric's eyes is evident but swiftly replaced by a warm smile. "Of course, I'd love to. Jamie and I are going to have a great time."

The date with Daniel is a mix of nerves and excitement. Returning home, I find Jamie asleep, a contented smile on his face. Looking happy and tired, Eric shares stories of their evening's adventures. His enthusiasm and the warmth in his voice bring me unexpected joy.

"Thanks, Eric. I really appreciate this," I say, feeling deeply grateful.

"Anytime, Lucy. Jamie's a great kid, and you're an amazing mom," he responds, his sincerity resonating with me.

As I close the door behind me, a wave of gratitude and something else—a flicker of doubt—washes over me. Unbeknownst to me, this evening has set in motion a chain of events that will challenge my perceptions, mainly as Daniel's first visit draws near.

On Sunday afternoon, when I meet Daniel at the park, Daniel unexpectedly requests to visit my home. He wants to meet Jamie and see where we live, a sudden but understandable request from someone as methodical as him.

As Daniel and I walk into my living room, the familiar warmth of home greets us—soft couches, Jamie's scattered toys, and the walls adorned with family memories. Eric is also sitting cross-legged on the floor, deeply engaged in a block-building mission with Jamie.

"Hey, Lucy! And this must be Daniel," Eric says, his voice blending warmth and welcome.

Daniel politely nods, his gaze taking in the scene with a calculative air. "Nice to meet you. Your name?"

"Eric. My name is Eric."

Jamie, spotting Eric, abandons his blocks and toddles over with a bright smile. "Dad!" he exclaims, reaching up to him.

The word hangs in the air like a misplaced note, and I see Daniel's brows furrow in confusion. "Dad? Why is he calling Eric that?"

I rush to clarify, feeling the tension rise. "Oh, Eric's just a good friend from next door. Jamie adores him."

Daniel's eyes don't stray from Eric, his voice laced with professional skepticism. "Is that so?"

Before I can further smooth the ruffled feathers, Shakespeare, ever the opportunist, chimes in from his perch. "Eric is a good match!" he squawks, repeating his newfound favorite phrase.

I laugh nervously, trying to lighten the mood. "This parrot, I swear, becomes a chatterbox whenever we have visitors."

But the damage is done. Daniel's expression shifts from mild curiosity to something more intricate, more calculating. "A neighbor and a parrot are both quite... involved in your family life, it seems."

Struggling to keep my tone light, I respond, "It's really not what it looks like, Daniel."

Eric rises to his feet, his face etched with concern. "Honestly, Daniel, it's just fun with Jamie and the bird. Nothing serious."

Daniel's eyes linger on Eric, then shift to me, his voice laced with a hint of disapproval. "Lucy, our relationship should be built on transparency. This is... unexpected."

Stammering, I attempt to dispel his doubts. "Daniel, please, you're misunderstanding the situation."

Daniel's posture stiffens, his expression morphing from curiosity to suspicion. "I see. "

My attempts to smooth things over are desperate. "Daniel, it's not what it seems. Eric has been a great help, but that's all there is to it."

Eric stands, dusting off his hands. "She's right, Daniel. I just enjoy hanging out with Jamie. No hidden agendas."

Daniel's response is measured, his CPA-like precision surfacing. "A neighbor teaching your child to call him Dad, and a parrot echoing sentiments of compatibility. You must admit, it's peculiar."

I feel my face flush with frustration. "It's just a misunderstanding, nothing more."

Daniel regards me with a look that weighs and measures my words. "I value honesty, Lucy. This feels less than straightforward."

Sensing the gravity of the situation, Eric takes a step towards Daniel. His usual playfulness is replaced by a seriousness rarely seen. "Look, Daniel, I didn't mean to cause any confusion. I care about them, sure, but just as friends and neighbors."

Daniel's gaze shifts between Eric and me, weighing his words.

I'm stammering now, trying to find the right words. "Daniel, please understand it's not what you're thinking."

Daniel looks at me, his expression one of calculated decision. "I appreciate honesty above all, Lucy. This situation seems muddled."

With a curt nod, he makes his way to the door, his steps deliberate. "I thought we had a transparent understanding. I may have been mistaken."

His departure leaves a void filled only by the echo of the closing door. Shocked, I sink into the nearest chair, my mind racing.

Eric kneels beside me, his voice soft. "Lucy, I'm so sorry. I didn't mean for any of this to happen."

I look up at him, his genuine concern contrasting Daniel's calculated withdrawal. "It's not your fault, Eric. It's just... complicated."

As Eric nods understandingly, I can't help but wonder about the striking differences between the two men. One is so quick to bring joy and ease into our lives, and the other is so quick to judge and depart at the first sign of complexity.

Eric, also surprised, sits down next to me, his characteristic cheerfulness subdued by the gravity of the situation.

"Lucy, I was just trying to add a bit of humor to Jamie's day. I never imagined it would lead to this," Eric says, his voice laden with sincere regret.

In the aftermath of Daniel's departure, I find myself deep in thought, Eric's presence a comforting constant beside me.

The contrast between Eric's playful, caring nature and Daniel's rigid, unforgiving demeanor becomes strikingly clear.

"Lucy, I know I can be a bit much sometimes," Eric begins, his voice soft and earnest. "But I care about you and Jamie, genuinely. I just want to bring a little happiness to your lives."

I look at him, seeing the truth in his eyes. "Eric, you've always been there, making us laugh, helping out. You've been more of a partner than I realized."

He nods a gentle kindness in his gaze. "Life's too short not to spread a little joy, Lucy. Especially to those who deserve it most."

As the evening unfolds, Eric helps put Jamie to bed, his gentle way with my son further warming my heart. We then sit down to share dinner. Our conversation flows more deeply than ever before.

As the night draws closer, Eric moves towards the doorway, signaling it's time for him to head home. He pauses and turns to me, his expression warm and filled with sincere reassurance. "Actually, I've grown really fond of Jamie. I truly hope, one day, he might come to call me 'Dad.'"

Watching him leave, a sense of clarity washes over me. With its unexpected events, this chaotic evening has shed light on what truly matters in a relationship.

The support, the care, the laughter Eric brings into our lives. A man's kind nature is more valuable than book-smart in real life.

What I've been looking for has been here, with Eric, all along.

The following weekend, after my heart-to-heart with Eric, my phone buzzed with an unexpected call. It's Daniel. My heart skips a beat, a mix of surprise and unease settling in. I take a deep breath and answer, bracing myself for the conversation.

"Lucy, I've been thinking," Daniel says, voice-controlled as always. "I believe we might have acted hastily. I'd like to meet and discuss things."

His words hang in the air, a proposition I wasn't prepared for. But at this moment, with new-found clarity and the warmth of my feelings for Eric still fresh, my decision is evident.

"Daniel, I appreciate your call, but I don't think there's anything left to discuss," I reply, my voice firm yet polite.

There's a pause, and I can almost picture Daniel's brows knitting together in confusion. "Are you sure? I think we could work things out, reconsider—"

I cut him off gently but resolutely. "I'm sure, Daniel. My decision is final. I'm moving forward, and we both should do the same."

There's a brief silence, a sign that my words have registered. "Well, if that's your decision, then I wish you the best, Lucy," he says, his voice revealing a hint of disappointment.

"Thank you, Daniel. I wish you the best too."

As I end the call, I feel relief. Standing by my decision and choosing my own path feels empowering. I glance over at Jamie, playing with his toys. I've made the right choice for us all. Eric will be a good father.

Later that day, I stand outside Eric's door with Jamie, my palms sweaty and my heart racing. This is it, the moment of truth. I knock, and he answers, his face lighting up as he sees me.

"Lucy, everything okay?" he asks, concern flickering in his eyes.

I take a deep breath, finding the courage to speak my truth. "Eric, I need to tell you something. It's important."

He steps aside, inviting me in. We sit on his couch, the room bathed in the warm afternoon light, creating an intimate atmosphere.

"I've ended things with Daniel," I begin, my voice trembling slightly. "And it's made me realize something important. I... I have feelings for you, Eric. But I'm scared. Scared of rushing into something, of getting it wrong."

Eric reaches out, his hand covering mine, a tender gesture sending shivers down my spine. "Lucy, I've cared about you for a long time. But

I'll go at whatever pace you're comfortable with. There's no rush. I just want to be with you, to make you and Jamie happy."

His words, so simple but sincere and full of warmth, make my heart swell. The uncertainty holding me back melts away, replaced by a growing hope and excitement.

"Eric, you've brought so much joy and laughter into our lives. I want to see where this goes with you," my voice soft but filled with emotion.

He smiles. It's a smile that reaches his eyes, radiating pure joy.

"Lucy, that's all I've ever wanted. "

Eric walks me back to my house, gently cradling Jamie in his arms. His manner is tender and protective, like a father carrying his child.

In the soft glow of the evening, Eric and I sit together on my backyard porch, the air filled with the sweet scent of blooming jasmine. The setting sun paints the sky in shades of orange and pink, creating a romantic backdrop to our quiet conversation.

"Lucy, I know we've both been through a lot," Eric starts, his hand finding mine, his touch sending a warm thrill through me. "But I want to do this right, take it slow, make sure it's built on a strong foundation."

I nod, my heart swelling with emotion. "I want that too, Eric. To build something real and lasting together."

We sit there, hand in hand, watching the stars begin to twinkle in the evening sky. The warmth between us is palpable, a promise of things to come.

I lean closer to Eric and feel he is my rock. Our lips meet in a tender kiss, a perfect seal to our shared hopes and dreams.

The security offered by a man's golden heart, warm and invaluable, far surpasses the cold comfort of mere book smarts.

Harmonies and Heartbeats

I'm engrossed in practicing my singing, hitting some challenging high notes, when I suddenly hear an off pitch wailing outside. It sounds like… is that a dog trying to mimic my singing?

Annoyed, I stomp to the window, preparing to give the owner a piece of my mind. But as I pull it open, the sight before me causes my annoyance to give way to giggles. My new neighbor, a handsome guy, is lounging on his patio swing chair, and next to him is a massive dog, head thrown back, belting out his version of my song.

"Um, excuse me?" I call out, trying to stifle my laughter. "Your dog seems to think he's the next big thing in opera?"

The neighbor looks up, startled, and then breaks into a sheepish grin. "Oh! I'm so sorry. That's Thunder. He gets a little carried away when he hears music. Thinks he's a canine Pavarotti or something."

"I can see that," I reply with a smirk. "I mean, I've had fans before, but this is a first."

He chuckles, "Well, it looks like you've got yourself a new duet partner. By the way, I'm Rober. The charming new addition to this community."

Laughing, I reply, "Lana. The already charming resident. Welcome to the madhouse!"

"Pleasure to meet you, Lana. And apologies again for Thunder's... um... performance."

"Tell Thunder he might need a few more lessons before his big debut," I tease.

Rober chuckles, patting Thunder's head. "Hear that, buddy? You've got work to do."

We share a friendly wave, and I return to practice, silently hoping for more interruptions from my amusing new neighbors.

Before I close my window, Whiskers, my Russian Blue cat, jumps to the windowsill and touches me with his head. His green eyes tell me it's time for him to play outside.

Sunlight filters through the curtains as I start my vocal warm-ups. The notes flow smoothly, and the rhythm is right on point. My primary performance is just around the corner, and every practice counts. As I hit a high note, I'm rudely interrupted by a series of deep, booming barks.

Not again.

Thunder. That big, adorable, incredibly noisy furball. Why did he pick my singing time to showcase his vocal range? I try to continue, hoping he'll stop, but the barks grow louder and more insistent, matching my pitch and rhythm.

Enough is enough. Marching to the window, I fling it open, ready to confront the canine opera singer. But instead, I lock eyes with Rober, lounging on his patio swing chair, seemingly enjoying the ruckus.

"Really?" I start, my tone sharp, trying to hide my obvious annoyance. "Is this a daily duet now?"

Rober smirks, looking unfazed. "Ah, Lana! Thunder here seems to think you guys could form the next hit duo. You know, bring a bit of canine charm to the music world."

"This is hardly the time for jokes, Rober," I retort, hands on my hips. "I have an important performance in a few days. I can't afford these... disruptions."

He raises an eyebrow, a playful glint in his eyes. "Ah, c'mon, it's just a bit of fun. Besides, it's good to have a backup singer, right?"

"I need silence, not a barking 'backup'!" I exclaim, my patience thinning. "You need to control your dog. And for the record, a good owner would teach his dog manners."

Rober's smirk fades, replaced with a touch of defiance. "Hey now, Thunder's just being himself. Can't fault him for having a bit of musical flair. Maybe you should try embracing it."

I'm flabbergasted. "Are you serious right now? Your dog is disturbing the peace, and you're defending him?"

He chuckles. "Well, when you put it that way.... But Lana, he's still getting used to the place. Give him some time."

I take a deep breath, reminding myself to stay calm. "Rober, I'm all for animals being themselves. But not at the cost of my practice. Not when it jeopardizes my performance."

He leans back, looking thoughtful. "All right, point taken. But you've got to admit, his barks have a rhythm."

I sigh, trying hard not to smile. "You're impossible, you know that?"

He grins. "Been told that before. We'll work on the barking. No promises on the singing, though."

We share a brief moment of understanding before I close the window, hoping for a more peaceful practice session next time.

The evening sun casts a golden hue, enveloping the neighborhood in a serene warmth. I enjoy a quiet moment on my patio when an unexpected commotion shatters the peace. It's Whiskers' alarmed meow, unmistakable and urgent. I spring up, my heart pounding, to find my beloved cat being chased by Thunder, who looks like he's having the time of his life.

To escape the massive dog, Whiskers climbs up a tree, her eyes wide with fear, her tail bushy, and her body pressed close to the branch. I can hear her terrified meows echoing in the stillness of the evening. Thunder sits below, wagging his tail, seemingly pleased with the chaos he's caused.

Adrenaline courses through my veins, and I'm livid. Without a second thought, I storm towards Rober's house, not caring that I'm still in my pajamas, and bang on his door.

A few moments later, Rober, looking bewildered, opens up. Before he can utter a greeting, I point accusingly toward the tree. "Your dog has scared Whiskers half to death!"

Rober looks in the direction I'm pointing, taking in the scene. He seems to stifle a laugh but quickly turns it into a cough. "Ah, it seems Thunder is making friends," he quips, his tone light, but I'm not in the mood for humor.

"Making friends? Your dog is terrorizing my cat! Whiskers is terrified!"

Rober raises an eyebrow, then sighs, his humorous facade dropping. "I'm sorry, Lana. I genuinely am. Thunder has a playful spirit; he didn't mean any harm."

"Playful spirit? My cat is up a tree, terrified because of your dog! You need to control him."

Rober looks apologetic. "I'll get Thunder inside and help get Whiskers down. I promise I'll work on keeping him in check."

We head outside together. Rober calls Thunder, who obediently follows him inside. Once sure that the threat is gone, I coax Whiskers down. Her petite frame trembles in my arms, her heart racing.

Rober stands beside me, a sheepish look on his face. "I'm really sorry, Lana. This won't happen again."

I give him a sharp look, but my anger is slowly dissipating. "It better not. Whiskers doesn't need this kind of excitement in her life."

He chuckles, "Neither does Thunder, it seems. Let's call it a truce?"

I sigh, nodding, "Truce. But keep Thunder away from Whiskers."

He salutes. "Will do, ma'am."

"Rober, do you know how to train your dog? There's a training school only a few miles away—"

"I don't think it is necessary," Rober interrupts me and rejects my suggestion directly.

I look at his handsome face and impressive muscular body, wondering what kind of father he could be if he had a kid.

"Imagine something about me?" Rober senses my thought.

"Yes. I want to know how badly you will spoil your kid if you luckily have one."

"Wow." He laughs. "Do you want to know how badly I will spoil the beautiful girl who will help me to produce the kid?"

His electric-blue eyes are shining and charming. I unexpectedly feel my heart skip a beat. I turn around and carry my cat home.

I have never had this feeling before. From that moment, I start avoiding Rober. I also try to lock my cat inside of my home.

The weekend arrives. It is my performance day.

The park is alive with the festive atmosphere of the art show. Vibrant colors, delicious smells, and the distant strumming of a guitar fill the air. As I step onto the stage, adjusting my microphone and scanning the crowd, my gaze locks on to a familiar pair—Rober and Thunder. They're seated in the front, looking quite the comedic duo: Rober with a dashing hat and Thunder sporting a little bowtie, making them stand out amid the spectators.

Taking a deep breath, I mentally prepare for my performance, but there's a nagging thought. What if Thunder decides this is the perfect backdrop for his singing debut? My nervous energy, however, seems misplaced as I begin. Thunder sits still, his big brown eyes locked on to mine, with an expression that says, "Don't worry, I've got your back."

As the melodies flow, I get lost in the music, my voice harmonizing with the instruments. The performance feels magical. As the last note lingers in the air and the crowd erupts in applause, I can't help but smile, relieved that Thunder maintained his gentlemanly demeanor throughout.

Walking off stage, I'm greeted by Rober, his face beaming. "That was amazing, Lana!"

I grin. "Thanks for keeping Thunder... quiet."

Rober chuckles. "I told him it was a 'listening' concert. He's a good listener, especially when treats are involved." Hearing his name, Thunder offers a playful wave of his tail, looking up at me as if seeking approval.

I bend to pat him. "Thanks for behaving, big guy." Thunder responds by licking my hand, which makes me laugh.

Seizing the moment, Rober says, "You must be starving after that stellar performance. How about lunch? There's this fantastic food truck I've been wanting to try."

"I'd love to," I reply, my stomach growling in agreement.

A tantalizing aroma of grilled sandwiches fills the air as we walk towards the food truck. We each get a sandwich, and Rober, the gentleman, finds us a shaded spot under a tree. Thunder sprawls out beside us, clearly enjoying the moment as much as we are.

Taking a bite of my sandwich, I mumble, "This is delicious."

Rober grins. "Told you. Nothing but the best for the star of the day."

We chat and laugh, and there's a lightness between us that wasn't there before. Maybe it's the music, or perhaps it's Thunder's newfound respect for my singing, but things feel different.

Rober, gazing intently, says, "I meant it, you know. You were incredible today. There's something about your voice—it's captivating."

I blush. "Thank you, Rober. That means a lot coming from you."

We share a moment, a mix of lingering eye contact and unsaid words, a delicate dance of emotions unfolding between us. Sensing the change in the atmosphere, Thunder lets out a tiny, comedic "woof," breaking our trance.

We both burst into laughter, the tension dissipating. Rober raises his sandwich. "To new beginnings?"

I tap my sandwich against his, adding, "And to Thunder, the most behaved dog at a concert."

The festival, filled with art and melodies, also hosts the budding rhythm of two hearts, tentatively finding their harmony.

After the festival performance, my life returns to my regular routine, but I have different feelings.

Every morning, predictably, Thunder is at my window. Each time I practice, this robust dog tries to harmonize with me. But it becomes something I anticipate with warmth. Our impromptu duets, once an interruption, now feel comforting. As I warm up to Thunder, my feelings for Rober also deepen.

One evening, as I return from a tiring rehearsal, Rober is standing outside his door. He quickly puts a finger to his lips, signaling me to be quiet, and points towards the bushes near my backyard.

I tiptoe closer, and my heart just melts. There they are, Thunder and Whiskers, supposed adversaries, curled up together in peaceful slumber. It's a scene straight out of a fairy tale.

Turning to Rober, eyes wide with delight, he whispers, "Looks like they're setting an example for us."

This newfound secret of our pets' unexpected bond brings us even closer. Evening coffees on the patio become our thing. I sit on his swing chair, discussing anything and everything. However, Rober remains a mystery in many ways. Any talk about his past, and he retreats. He's a firefighter—that much he shares. But there are shadows he's not ready to illuminate.

Sitting together one evening, I finally venture, "Rober, why do you never talk about your past?"

He hesitates, then says, "Some stories, Lana, they're better left untold. At least for now."

I nod, respecting his privacy. Before returning home, I look at his eyes, "Whenever you're ready to share, I'm here."

He gazes at me, eyes brimming with gratitude. "Thank you, Lana." Under the starlit sky, Rober looks into my eyes, stands up, walks to me slowly, and hugs me tightly.

It is our first hug. There's warmth, there's understanding, and two hearts are drawing closer.

I return home, the warmth of Rober's embrace still lingering. I'm lost in thought, replaying the comforting feel of his hug, when the jarring ringtone of my phone interrupts my daydream. Hesitantly, I pick up.

"Miss me?" The tone is smug, unmistakably Alex's. A shiver runs down my spine.

"Alex?"

"I've got a contract here, Lana. I can make you a star." He oozes confidence, but I sense the menace beneath his words.

"It's over. Stay away from me."

He chuckles darkly. "It's not over. You belong with me, Lana. With my guidance, you'll rise. Without it, you'll fade."

The pit in my stomach deepens. Alex needs to understand boundaries. "I don't need your 'guidance,' Alex. I've moved on. So should you."

The line goes dead.

A rush of adrenaline propels me to action. I hurriedly go around the house, locking all exterior doors and windows. Memories of our toxic relationship flash, and I feel trapped again. I know he can turn up unannounced, and I shudder at the thought.

That night is a nightmare for me.

Every creak and rustle outside send my heart racing as I anticipate his next move. I find it hard to shut my eyes, haunted by the day's events. The weight of fear threatens to pull me under, and the cold emptiness of the night seems almost unbearable.

As I'm about to give in to the overpowering dread, I feel a gentle nudge on my bed. Looking down, I see Whiskers, his large, round eyes full of concern. He hops up beside me, purring softly. He nudges his head against my hand, urging me to pet him. I pull him close, his soft fur providing some comfort.

Like a rhythmic lullaby, his consistent purring begins to soothe my jagged nerves. Whiskers, sensing my distress, snuggles closer, curling up beside me. His warmth and the gentle rise and fall of his breathing become my anchor to the present.

As the night wears on, the bond between us, the unspoken understanding, only grows. Whiskers doesn't leave my side, reminding me that amid all the chaos, there's still purity and love. His presence, steady and comforting, helps me brave the night, and I find solace in his quiet company.

The following day, I still cannot get rid of the fearful feeling. I need to tell someone, and

Rober instantly comes to mind. He's been my pillar of late, understanding and supportive. He needs to know about this.

The day is booked with my work. In the evening, as I'm returning from grocery shopping, a forceful grip catches my wrist in the dim light of my garage. I freeze, recognizing Alex's brooding silhouette.

"Lana," he murmurs, his voice low and threatening. "Thought I could surprise you."

Terrified, I attempt to muster every ounce of courage. "Let go of me, Alex!"

He smirks, squeezing my wrist even tighter. "You can't avoid me forever. I'm here to remind you where you truly belong."

"You're mistaken. I don't belong to anyone, especially not you!" My voice shakes with anger.

Without warning, a rapid sequence of events unfolds. From the shadows, a guttural growl precedes the lightning speed of Thunder's advance. The usually gentle giant now resembles a trained Army dog, lunging at Alex with unparalleled ferocity.

Alex, caught off guard, barely manages to side-step the first attack. But Thunder is relentless, snapping his jaws and cornering him against the garage wall.

"Get this beast off me!" Alex yells, panicked, but his arrogance is still unmistakably present.

Almost on cue, Rober emerges, his demeanor cold and determined, clearly showcasing his trained military background. "On your knees," he commands, advancing with an almost deadly grace.

Alex attempts a quick retort, but the combined threat of Rober and Thunder renders him momentarily speechless. Seizing the moment, Rober lunges, skillfully taking down Alex and pinning him to the ground, with Thunder growling beside them, ready to strike.

"Call the police," Rober tells me.

Soon, sirens wail in the distance, growing closer.

Two officers arrive swiftly, handcuffing a struggling Alex.

"You'll pay for this!" he spits venomously, his eyes darting between me and Rober with raw hatred.

One of the officers, clearly familiar with Alex's notorious reputation, remarks, "Looks like we finally got something solid on you."

As they lead him away, the tension that has filled the garage dissipates. I turn to Rober, overwhelmed with gratitude. "I can't thank you enough," I say, my voice shaky.

With a slight smirk, Rober replies, "All in a day's work. And Thunder deserves some credit too."

Sensing the shift in the atmosphere, Thunder trots over, wagging his tail, looking as if he hasn't just taken on a dangerous man.

Rober extends his hand, pulling me into a comforting embrace. "Promise me you'll be careful," he murmurs.

"I will," I reply, "especially with you and Thunder around."

The bond between us is palpable, solidified by danger and mutual respect.

***

The atmosphere in the dining room is thick with an unspoken understanding. The warm golden glow from the chandelier softens the room's edges, making it feel intimate and cozy. The gentle clinking of cutlery against plates is the only sound interrupting the comfortable silence.

After a few moments, Rober takes a deep breath, signaling he's ready to share something significant. "Lana," he begins, his voice lower than usual, "there's something about my past I've never really spoken about."

I look up, intrigued. His usually playful eyes now hold a depth of pain and remembrance. "Before the firefighting... I was a military dog trainer," he admits. I can see the memories playing out in his eyes as he continues, "Alice, she was my partner, my companion. Together, we navigated the treacherous terrains of Afghanistan. My bond with her was unlike anything I've ever felt."

The room is silent except for the faint chirping of crickets outside.

"We faced many perils together, evading land-mines, ambushes, and hostile forces. Alice was more than just a dog. She was a soldier, my protector." He chokes up a bit, and I see him fighting back tears. "One fateful day, an ambush... she saved me, lunging at an enemy, taking a fatal shot meant for me."

I can't help the gasp that escapes my lips.

Rober's voice cracks as he continues, "Alice was a hero. She died so I could live. And Thunder...." He takes a deep breath. "Thunder is her offspring, her legacy. Every time I look at him, I see Alice's brave eyes, her unwavering loyalty. That's why I spoil him; it's my way of honoring Alice's memory."

Tears well up in my eyes as I process his heart-wrenching story. I move closer, laying a comforting hand on his. Without a word, I kneel beside Thunder, who has quietly observed us. I wrap my arms around the massive dog, feeling the warmth and heartbeat of this living connection to Rober's past.

"I promise," I whisper to Thunder, my voice thick with emotion, "I'll treat you like my child too, with all the love and care you deserve."

Rober watches, his eyes shining with a mixture of pain, gratitude, and a love deepening with each shared moment.

***

A few months later, the sun casts a warm orange hue, painting the sky with strokes of pink and gold. The scent of blooming roses fills the air, and the gentle chirping of the birds serenades us, making this moment seem almost surreal.

Setting up the camera on a tripod, I ensure it perfectly captures the dreamy evening sky. Whiskers is being his mischievous self, and I laugh, trying to make him sit still for the photo. On the other hand, Thunder sits obediently next to Rober, a true testament to his disciplined lineage.

With a twinkle in his eye, Rober declares, "All right, everyone. Let's say 'forever' on three!"

As the camera captures our smiles, Robert turns to me, his eyes reflecting the golden light. He's holding a small velvet box. My heart skips a beat.

"Lana," he says, trembling slightly with emotion, "you remember when we first met, right? Thunder howling, Whiskers causing chaos? Since then, every day with you has been something special. Whatever I've been through before doesn't compare to the thought of not having you by my side."

He opens the box, revealing a stunning diamond ring that catches the last rays of the setting sun. "Every day with you feels like a song, a melody I never want to end. Lana, will you marry me and make our song last forever?"

Tears blur my vision, every emotion bubbling up. "Yes," I reply, voice choked with emotion, "a thousand times, yes."

Sensing the gravity of the moment, Whiskers rubs against our legs with a contented purr. Thunder gives an affectionate bark. And as we lean in for a kiss, the camera's timer captures

this perfect moment—a promise of endless to-
morrows.

My Next Door Neighbor

Bang! Bang! The door shakes as Mr. Harlan, the landlord, pounds on it. His voice, rough like gravel, pierces through the thin walls of my small living room. "Lena! Open up! I know you're in there!"

I'm frozen, clutching the frayed hem of my apron. The room, cramped and cluttered with secondhand furniture, feels smaller with each knock. This is my world: stains on the carpet, a small TV blaring cartoons, and toys scattered around. I hear Tommy, my five-month-old boy, sniffling in the corner.

"Mommy, is the man mad?" Emily, my four-year-old, asks, her eyes wide and scared. I kneel, brushing her hair with my fingers, trying to smile.

"It's okay, sweetie. Go play with Tommy," I whisper, but my voice trembles.

Finally, I gather the courage to open the door.

Mr. Harlan stands there, his bulky frame blocking the sunlight. He's not a man who smiles since I signed the lease agreement. His face always set in a scowl, his green eyes sharp and unyielding.

"Lena, you're two months behind on rent. This can't go on," he barks, his voice echoing in the small hallway.

"I know, Mr. Harlan, I'm really trying to—" I start, but my voice is shaky, betraying my anxiety.

"Trying isn't paying, Lena. I've got bills too. I can't let you stay here for free." His tone is harsh, and I flinch.

But I do not hate him. He could have kicked me out last month if he only cared about his landlord's business. He must pay his home loan mortgage, property insurance, and taxes for his apartment.

Behind me, Tommy starts to wail, his cries mingling with the sound of a car honking outside. The noise of the big city, usually a background hum, feels overwhelming now.

"Please, I just need a little more time," I plead, my hands clasped together as if praying. "I've been looking for extra work, and I'm expecting some money soon."

Mr. Harlan sighs, his impatience evident. "I've heard that before. You've got until the end of the week, Lena. That's it. If you can't pay, I'll have to evict you."

My heart sinks. End of the week? That's just four days away.

I nod, unable to speak, fighting back tears.

Mr. Harlan turns and walks away, his steps heavy and final.

I close the door. Emily looks up at me, her small face filled with worry. "Are we going to have to leave, Mommy?"

I force a smile, though inside, I feel like crumbling. "No, baby, we're not going anywhere. Mommy will figure it out." I'm more likely to convince myself than her.

I look around the room at the sofa with a broken spring and the tiny water painting with a broken frame. All the valuable belongings were already traded for money. However, this is our home; no matter how shabby, it is our shelter. And the thought of losing it tightens my chest.

Tommy's cries grow louder. I scoop him up, bouncing him gently.

I need to be strong for them. I need to find a way. But as I rock my little boy, whispering soothing words, I can't help but wonder, how?

After Tommy falls asleep, I start housework. Dragging the trash bag, I step out into the chilly winter evening air. My mind is still reeling from Mr. Harlan's ultimatum.

Lost in thought, I almost bump into Andrew, my next-door neighbor. He's leaning against his doorframe, dressed in a faded leather that somehow adds to his "bad boy" charm.

He's handsome and doesn't try too hard, with a gentle edge to his rugged looks.

"Hey, Lena. Rough day?" His voice is smooth, with a hint of concern.

I force a smile, brushing a loose strand of hair behind my ear. "Just the usual," I keep it light, not wanting to dump my troubles on him.

He nods, his dark brown eyes thoughtful. "I overheard a bit. I'm sorry you're going through that."

There's a sincerity in his voice that takes me by surprise. In the big city, people usually care little about others' problems.

"Thanks, Andrew," I lift the trash bag, but it's heavier than I thought.

"Here, let me help with that." Before I can protest, Andrew takes the bag from me. His hands, rough and robust, like a prizefighter, do not match his software engineer job.

We walk to the dumpster, and the silence is smooth and comfortable in a strange way.

"If you ever need someone to watch the kids for a bit, I'm usually around," Andrew says casually as we walk back.

I'm taken aback. "Oh, I couldn't ask you to do that. You must be busy with work and all."

He chuckles, a sound that's warm and easy. "One of the perks of working from home. As an individual contractor, I've got a flexible schedule. And I don't mind, really."

I hesitate, torn. The offer is tempting, especially with my job hunt and the need for extra hours. "I'll think about it, Andrew. Thank you."

We reach our doors, and Andrew waves and smiles. "Anytime, Lena."

His offer echoes as I tuck Emily into bed that night. It's hard to trust someone with my kids, but there's something about Andrew that just feels right.

The following day, I find a note under my door: If you ever need me to babysit, just knock. -Andrew

It's the push I need. Later that day, I knock on his door, my heart racing. Andrew opens it, a warm smile on his face.

"Hey, Lena. Need that favor?"

I nod, feeling a mix of relief and nervousness. "Tomorrow morning, just for a couple of hours. I have a job interview."

"No problem." His encouragement feels genuine.

The following morning, I leave Emily and Tommy with Andrew, their giggles fading as I head down the hallway. As I walk to the interview, for the first time in a long while, I feel a glimmer of hope.

After the job interview, I rush home to pick up my kids. Then, I bake an apple pie to thank Andrew for his help. It's a small gesture, but it feels important to show my appreciation. The aroma of cinnamon and apples fills my cramped kitchen, offering a brief escape from my worries.

I carry the warm pie to Andrew's apartment, feeling nervous and excited.

Andrew opens the door with a surprised smile. "For me?" he asks playfully, his eyes lighting up.

"Yeah, just a little thank you for helping with Emily and Tommy," I reply, handing him the pie.

He invites me in, and I can't help but notice how his place contrasts with mine—tidy and modern with a personal charm.

"Thank you, but Tommy and Emily are waiting on some pie, too," I make an excuse. I'm so embarrassed to invite anyone to my own home. I'm a professional interior designer for goodness' sake.

I hurry back to my apartment, my heart racing with anticipation. The job interview went well, and I'm eager to check my email for updates. I switch on my computer, but it stubbornly refuses to boot up. I try again, frustration mounting. It's just another thing in a long list of things going wrong.

"Mom, is the computer broken?" Emily asks, peering over my shoulder with curious eyes. In the hard times, she is more mature than her age.

"I don't know, sweetie. Let me see if Andrew can help," I reply, trying to mask my worry.

I knock on Andrew's door, hoping he's home. He opens it with a smile that's both comforting and disarming. "Hey, Lena. Everything okay?"

"My computer's acting up. I'm waiting for an email about the job interview and...." I trail off, feeling a bit helpless.

"Let me take a look," he says, his tone light but reassuring.

In my apartment, Andrew examines the computer with a practiced eye. He clicks a few keys, his brow furrowed in concentration. "Looks like it just needs a little update and a reboot. I'll fix it."

As he works, I find myself watching him. There's a sense of calm about him, a quietly compelling confidence.

"You're really good at this," I remark.

He chuckles without looking up. "Well, it's part of my job. Can't let a computer beat me."

I laugh, the tension easing from my shoulders. "I used to be good at my job too, before... everything changed."

He looks up, his eyes gentle and understanding, encouraging me to keep talking. So, I do. I share my love for interior design and the business I built from scratch.

But I don't go into the part about how everything fell apart, about my husband leaving me for another woman. At the same time, I was pregnant with our son. It's a wound still too raw, and I'm not ready to expose that pain.

Andrew nods, listening intently. "Have you considered applying for assistance? It might ease the burden a bit."

I take a deep breath, feeling a mix of pride and vulnerability. "I've thought about it, sure. But I want to make it on my own first. I need to know that I can do this," I say, my voice steady despite the storm of emotions.

Andrew finishes with the computer and turns to face me, his expression one of genuine admiration. "You're courageous, Lena. Not everyone would keep pushing forward the way you do. It's impressive."

His words, so heartfelt, stir something profound inside me. I remember when sweetness and warmth were part of my everyday life, but those days are long gone. I'm no longer used to this kind of kindness, this acknowledgment of my struggles. It's a comforting and overwhelming feeling, a gentle reminder of a past I've had to leave behind.

"Thanks, Andrew. "I open the front door for him.

He smiles. "Anytime, Lena. And remember, if you ever need help or just someone to talk to, I'm next door."

Andrew leaves, and I realize how much his support means to me. Andrew sees my struggles and still believes in me. It is like a beacon in the darkness.

The morning light filters through the thin curtains, casting a soft glow on the piles of bills cluttering my kitchen table. Among them is a notice for a second job interview, but it's scheduled for ten days from now.

Today marks the end of the deadline Mr. Harlan, the landlord, gave me for the rent. It will be too late to save my situation even if I'm lucky enough to get the job.

Pay, or leave, by today.

A sharp knock on the door jolts me back to reality.

It's Mr. Harlan, the landlord, his expression grim. "Lena, I'm sorry, but I have no choice. I need to put an eviction notice on your door."

Panic rises in my throat as I face Mr. Harlan. "Please, just give me a bit more time. An eviction will ruin my credit," I plead with him.

"Lady, you don't have any credit to speak of," he retorts, his tone dismissive.

Just then, Andrew exits his apartment, interrupting the tense moment. "Mr. Harlan, how much does Lena owe?" His voice is steady, exuding a quiet confidence.

I'm stunned, watching as Andrew speaks with the landlord. Before I can muster a word of protest, Andrew has paid the overdue rent and the additional penalty. Mr. Harlan, looking somewhat perplexed, finally leaves.

I turn to Andrew, a mix of emotions swirling within me. "Andrew, why did you do that? I can't accept this." My voice is a blend of gratitude and embarrassment. The thought of owing Andrew, not knowing when or how I'll be able to repay him, fills me with a deep sense of shame.

"You needed help, Lena. It's okay to accept it sometimes," he replies reassuringly.

But I can't shake off the feeling of helplessness. I start looking for additional work, but it's almost impossible with two kids to care for.

Andrew notices my obvious distress. "Lena, a builder friend, wants someone to decorate a model home. I think you'd be a great fit for it."

This opportunity feels like a lifeline thrown to me in stormy seas. I eagerly accept the job, dedicating all my energy and creativity. My design receives glowing praise, leading to an official contract with the builder.

When my first paycheck arrives, I don't hesitate. I go straight to Andrew with a portion of the money. "I need to pay you back, at least partial-ly, for now."

Andrew shakes his head, pushing my hand back. "Keep it, Lena. You earned it."

"No, Andrew. I can't keep owing you. Please," I say firmly.

After a moment, he accepts the money, under-standing the importance of this gesture to me. "Okay, Lena. You win."

As he closes the door, I stand in the hallway, feeling relief and newfound confidence.

Working with that first builder marked a turning point in my life. Eventually, I secured contracts with several builders. It's a breakthrough that even allows me to afford a babysitter when I need to go out for work.

As the first rays of light brighten my life again, Tommy's first birthday arrives, bringing a sense of new beginnings and hope.

I'm hanging streamers in the small living room, the morning sun casting a soft glow on the fad-ed wallpaper, when a knock at the door breaks my concentration. I open it to find Andrew, his arms laden with colorful balloons and a home-made cake.

"Happy birthday to Tommy," he declares, his smile reaching his eyes.

"Andrew, this... this is amazing," I stammer, overwhelmed by his thoughtfulness.

We work together, turning the living room into a little celebration haven. The balloons bob against the ceiling, and the cake, with its lop-sided icing, sits proudly on the table. Tommy's cute eyes widen in delight, and my heart fills with warmth.

As the kids play, Andrew and I find ourselves in the kitchen. He hands me a cup of coffee, our fingers brushing briefly. "You've done a great job with them, Lena," he says softly.

"Andrew, you were the one who opened the door for me. Now I'm working with multiple builders," I say, handing him the remaining money I owe him. A rush of gratitude fills me as I extend the envelope with a thank-you card to him.

This time, Andrew accepts the check without any argument, understanding the significance of this gesture.

We share a quiet moment inside the kitchen, the air between us charged with unspoken emotions. I find myself drawn to Andrew, our faces inches apart. My heart races, but fear grips me. I pull back, the memory of my past hurt flashing in my mind.

Andrew looks at me, understanding in his eyes. "It's okay, Lena," he says gently.

The rest of the day is a blur of laughter and birthday songs, but the moment in the kitchen lingers in my mind.

That night, lying in bed, I replay the almost-kiss. My heart aches with a mix of fear and longing. "I'm falling for him," I whisper into the darkness, the words both a confession and a realization.

I'm curious if he's awake, thinking about us. The thought makes my heart skip a beat.

The following day, I see Andrew in the hallway. "About yesterday...," I begin.

He smiles a little sadly. "No need to explain, Lena. I get it."

But I need him to know. "Andrew, I'm just... scared. I haven't felt this way in a long time."

He reaches out, taking my hand. "I'll be here, Lena. Whenever you're ready."

His touch is a promise, and I nod, my heart full of conflicting emotions—fear of being hurt yet hope for a new beginning.

As he walks away, I realize this is more than a fleeting attraction. It's deep, complicated, and genuine. But am I ready to take that leap again?

The newfound stability in my life feels like a warm embrace, a far cry from the chaos of the past. But just as I relax into this rhythm, life throws another curveball.

Andrew's been in a car accident!

My heart plummets as I hear this terrible news from a neighbor upstairs.

Dropping everything, I rush to the hospital, where I find Andrew with a broken leg and a few bruises, but thankfully, nothing life-threat-ening.

"Hey, Lena." He greets me with a weak but char-acteristic smile. "Looks like I won't be dancing for a while."

His attempt at humor in the face of pain is like him, and it warms and wrenches my heart. "You better stick to software for now," I reply, trying to keep the mood light.

When Andrew returns home, I help him with his daily needs. It feels natural to care for him, and a deep sense of connection grows between us.

Recalling Andrew's love for tranquil spaces, I decide to use my interior design skills to trans-form his bedroom into a more comfortable place for his recovery. I select soft-colored wall decorations, carefully crafting a serene sanctu-ary where he can rest and heal.

When Andrew sees the transformation, his eyes light up. "Lena, this is incredible. It feels like... home."

His words strike me in a way I didn't antici-pate, unexpectedly revealing my hidden desire, a longing I hadn't fully acknowledged until now.

But with this realization comes a familiar fear. The thought of opening my heart again, espe-cially when life is just starting to stabilize, is daunting. The scars from my past relationship are still hidden beneath the surface.

One evening, as I'm leaving his apartment, An-drew reaches out and takes my hand. "Lena, I can't thank you enough. You've been my rock through all this."

I look into his eyes, seeing the sincerity and something more that speaks of shared mo-ments and unspoken feelings.

"I wanted to be here for you, Andrew," I say soft-ly, my heart aching with a mixture of emotions.

As I walk back to my apartment, my mind is a whirlwind of thoughts. The care I feel for An-drew is undeniable, but so is the fear of getting hurt again. It's a tug-of-war between wanting to leap into the possibilities of a new relationship and holding back to protect my fragile heart.

I must face these feelings, confront my fears, and decide what I want.

But as I close the door behind me, I realize that the crisis isn't just about Andrew's accident. It's about what awakened in me—a longing for love, companionship, and the courage to trust again.

As I help Andrew with his daily walk, a routine that has become a comforting part of our days, I feel closeness far beyond neighborly or friendly concern. His progress is slow but steady, a testament to his resilience.

Today, as we walk around the living room, Andrew's foot catches on the edge of the rug. He stumbles, and I instinctively reach out to catch him. Our bodies press close in the brief, panicked moment, and I can feel his heartbeat against mine.

"Whoa, that was close," Andrew breathes, steadying himself. His arm is still around my waist, and I'm acutely aware of how right it feels.

At that moment, all the emotions I've been holding back come rushing to the surface. "Andrew, I'm scared," I blurt out, the words tumbling from my lips before I can stop them.

He looks at me, concerned about me etching his features. "What's wrong, Lena?"

"It's just... I'm afraid of what's happening between us. I've been hurt before, and I don't know if I can go through that again," I confess, my voice trembling slightly.

Andrew's expression softens, and he gently takes my hand. "Lena, I understand. I've seen what you've been through and would never want to add to your pain."

His words are like a balm, soothing the raw edges of my fears. "I care about you, Andrew. More than I thought I would. But I'm just so afraid of getting hurt."

He nods, his eyes never leaving mine. "I care about you too, Lena. You and the kids. You've brought so much happiness into my life. I want to be there for you in whatever way you need."

The sincerity in his voice is unmistakable, piercing through the walls I've built around my heart.

"I want that too, but I need to take it slow. Can you understand that?" I ask, hoping he can sense the depth of my feelings despite my fear.

"Of course, Lena," he reassures me, and I feel a weight lift off my shoulders.

As we resume our walk, I feel a newfound sense of hope. The emotional revelation has brought us closer. For the first time, I'm not facing challenges alone.

Our understanding has blossomed into something beautiful, something that slowly and cautiously begins to look like dating.

Andrew and I start spending more time together, each moment filled with the tender exploration of a new and profoundly familiar relationship.

As Andrew's leg heals and my interior design business flourishes, I find myself overcoming the financial burdens that once seemed insurmountable. With each successful project, my credit rebuilds, and alongside it, my confidence grows.

One evening, Andrew suggests we go out to a nightclub. "It's time to see if this leg can handle a dance floor," he says with a twinkle in his eye.

The club is vibrant and alive, the pulsating music filling the air. As we step onto the dance floor, I feel excited. The lights flicker like stars, casting a magical glow over the dancers.

Andrew takes my hand, leading me into the rhythm of the music.

At first, we're both a bit awkward, mindful of his healing leg, but soon we find our flow. The music envelops us, and I find myself lost in the moment, in the feel of his hand in mine, his arm around my waist.

We dance close, the beat of the music matching the beat of our hearts. In the swirl of lights and sound, it feels like we're the only two people in the world. Andrew's smile is infectious, and I can't help but laugh, the sound mingling with the music.

As the song slows down, he pulls me closer, and we sway gently in each other's arms. I rest my head on his shoulder, feeling a sense of peace and contentment I hadn't thought possible. The music surrounds us, a soft cocoon in the bustling nightclub.

"This feels right, Lena," Andrew whispers, his breath warm against my ear.

"I never knew dancing could feel like this," I reply, barely above the music.

We stay like that for an eternity, wrapped in the melody and each other's embrace. The fears and doubts that once clouded my heart seem to melt away in his arms. I realize this is more than just a dance; it's a step towards a new life we're building together.

As we leave the nightclub, hand in hand, the cool night air feels refreshing against my skin. The city lights twinkle like distant stars, and I feel a deep sense of gratitude. For the first time in a long time, I'm not just surviving; I'm thriving in love and life.

***

A year has passed since Andrew and I started our journey together. Our love has grown, rooted in understanding and shared experiences, blossoming into something beautiful.

It's a crisp autumn evening, and Andrew has planned a picnic in the park. The leaves are a kaleidoscope of colors, painting a perfect backdrop. As we sit on a blanket, surrounded by the glow of lanterns he's hung from the trees, the world feels like it's ours alone.

"Lena, I have something I want to say," Andrew begins, his voice a mixture of nervousness and certainty.

He takes my hand, his eyes locking with mine. "This past year has been the best of my life. You've shown me what it means to love and be loved, to share life's burdens and joys. I can't imagine my life without you and the kids."

He reaches into his pocket and pulls out a small velvet box. My heart skips a beat as he opens it, revealing a simple yet elegant ring. "Lena, will you marry me?"

Tears well up in my eyes as joy overflows in my heart. "Yes, Andrew. Yes, I will marry you."

The proposal is simple, yet it's the most romantic moment of my life. Our embrace under the starlit sky seals our promise to each other.

Our wedding was small and intimate a few months later, just like we wanted. Close friends and family surround us as we exchange vows, the love and support palpable. Emily and Tommy stand by us, their faces alight with happiness.

As the celebration winds down, Andrew takes my hand, a mischievous glimmer in his eyes. "I have one more surprise for you," he says.

We drive through familiar streets until we pull up in front of a beautiful house, its windows glowing warmly in the evening light. My breath catches in my throat.

"I bought us a home, Lena. A place where we can make new memories without worrying about rent or instability. A place where we can grow old together," he says, his voice filled with emotion.

Tears stream down my face as I look at the house and then back at Andrew. This is more than just a house; it's a symbol of our new life, of the stability and love we've built together.

"Andrew, this is... I don't even have words. Thank you," I say, embracing him tightly.

As we stand there, in the embrace of each other, looking at our new home, I swear I will decorate our home with love.

Fake Identity True Love

Friends to Lovers Sweet Romance Short Stories Collection

Eva Stone

Contents

The Mysterious Homeless Man

I am going to the library on Saturday afternoon to do more research for my graduate school assignment. As I pass by a fast-food restaurant, the rain suddenly becomes heavy. Raindrops as big as grapes fall heavily on the red brick walkway. I seek refuge from the relentless rain when I run to the restaurant. I find a homeless man standing on the corner near the entry door.

Everyone rushes by, oblivious to the lone figure huddled against the elements. His presence tugs at my heart, a vivid contrast to the bustling indifference around us.

"Hello there," I say, turning to him. "Would you like a meal?"

Despite his unkempt appearance, the man before me meets my gaze, and I see intelligence sparkling in his eyes. He is tall, and his spirit radiates with humor and wit. "Well, I'd be a fool to turn down an offer like that." He chuckles, his voice carrying warmth and mischief.

"Come in, please."

"No. No one wants to see me inside. I can wait here."

I run into the fast-food restaurant, and the aromas of greasy fries and sizzling burgers fill the air. I stand in the line and realize I forgot to ask the homeless man what he wants. So, I walk out and head to him.

"Sir, what do you want?"

The water falling from the roofline forms a water screen between us. My jeans are wet up to my calf.

This time, this man does not smile. He looks at my eyes and says, "Anything you give me."

"I want to give you something you like. Chicken or beef?"

"Anything you like."

I return to the restaurant. By the time I walk out, I bring two warm burgers; one is a chicken burger, and another one is a beef burger. I bid him farewell and go to the library, immersing myself in books and knowledge. Hours pass in the quiet solitude of the library. The storm outside cannot bother me.

When I finally decide to head home, the night has draped itself in darkness. As I enter the rain-soaked streets, I am surprised to find the homeless man sitting outside the fast-food restaurant. It will be cold tonight, and he must be soaked from the earlier storms.

I approach him once more. "You're still here," I start to worry for him.

He nods, his eyes mirroring the rain-soaked pavement. "It's where I stay," he replies with a hint of resignation.

Without hesitation, I make a heartfelt offer. "Would you like to come with me? I have a place where you can stay for the night, and I can prepare a simple dinner."

His face lights up, and his gratitude shines through. "That's very kind of you," he says, his voice brimming with sincerity. "I'd be honored to accept your offer. But I do not want to bother your family."

"I live alone. My roommate has her private bedroom." He is a thoughtful man.

Together, we leave the stormy streets behind and find our way to my modest abode, where warmth and companionship replace the cold and loneliness of the outside world.

"Sit down, please." I share a living room and kitchen with my roommate. I point at the creamy couch—it's mine.

He glances at the spotless couch, then comes to my tiny dining table near the kitchen and sits on the dining chair. He does not want to get my couch dirty.

I cook a simple dinner. We have a few moments of eye contact. I have never brought any stranger into my room, but I'm doing the right thing to help this man.

I bring salad and sandwiches to the table.

"May I?" He looks at his hands and asks.

"Follow me, please." I lead him to my bathroom. He washes his hands twice and does not miss his fingernails.

We have dinner quietly. Under the soft glow of the dining light, I notice he is a good-looking guy, and his fingernails look neater than mine.

I say gently. "I'm Nancy. May I know your name?"

With a quick wit and a hint of humor in his eyes, the homeless man replies, "You can call me PG."

"PG?"

"Short for 'poor guy'."

We share a moment of laughter as the rain continues to pour. At this point, Cindy, my roommate, returns from work.

"Good rain," she says as she walks in. She has a car, and she is still dry.

"Sorry, I did not know you had a guest." She peers her head from the entry of the living room, then back to her room. Curly red hair almost obscures half her face, but I can still see her making a face to me as she notices PG.

I started cleaning the kitchen and washing the dishes. PG sits on the chair calmly.

I hope he can stand up and say goodbye to me, but he has not and possibly will not. It's still raining. What should I do next? Should I ask him to leave? I may bring trouble to myself.

Despite our little connection during our meal, I feel uncomfortable letting him stay in the living room. My roommate may not like that idea. But she will not mind if I let PG sleep in my room.

So, I make a generous offer. "PG, would you like to stay here tonight? I can spend the night with my roommate."

PG nods. Gratitude washes over his face as he accepts my offer. I put a new bath towel in the bathroom and pick up my blue sleeping bag from the closet.

"Good night, PG."

"Good night, Nancy."

A few seconds later, I'm inside Cindy's room. We have been roommates for two years. We are as close as sisters.

"Is he your relative?" Cindy looks down from her bed. There are hundreds of question marks on her face. She is usually not that curious.

"No. I met him on the street." I slip into my sleeping bag and feel the floor is so hard.

"You are damn brave; you could have invited danger to our home." Cindy jumps down and locks the bedroom door angrily.

I do not blame her. The night passes slowly, with my thoughts often drifting back to the stranger named PG. I'm curious if he's comfortable in my bedroom. Is he warm and dry now? I hope he's okay.

The following morning, I knocked on my door with trepidation and curiosity. No response.

As I step inside, I'm met with a sight that utterly astonishes me. My typically messy home has been transformed into a place of pristine cleanliness. It's as though a fairy with a penchant for tidiness has visited overnight.

PG did not touch my bed.

I marvel at the orderliness of my surroundings, my heart swelling with gratitude and disbelief. On my glass end table, I discover a beautifully crafted thank-you note. It's a work of art, a testament to PG's thoughtfulness and appreciation for my kindness.

The note reads:

Dear Nancy, Thank you for your generosity and compassion. Your kindness has touched my heart, and I wanted to express my gratitude in the best way I know how. Sincerely, PG.

Tears well up in my eyes as I read those heartfelt words. In offering PG shelter for the night, I realize I received a gift far more significant than I expected—a reminder that despite life's storms, there is room for unexpected connections, kindness, and the beauty of human compassion.

PG may have called himself a "poor guy," but in my eyes, he was the wealthiest soul I had ever met. This extraordinary encounter served as a testament to the power of kindness and the beauty of shared humanity.

The next few days, I always look for PG when I pass by the restaurant. But I will never see him again. He seems to have disappeared from the city, from my life too.

Weeks later, I'm walking down the same busy street, and there he is again, PG, sitting outside the fast-food joint. The streetlights' soft glow dimly lights the road, and the previous week's rain has given way to a chilly breeze. The restaurant's bright neon sign flickers, casting a warm light on the damp pavement.

I decide to seize the moment and approach PG. "Hey again, PG!" I'm so happy to find him again.

He looks up, his eyes crinkling at the corners as he smiles back. "Hey," he replies, his voice carrying a quiet warmth that contrasts with the chill in the air.

We sit down together on the sidewalk, and I notice a few disapproving glances from people passing by. Their expressions aren't cheerful, but I ignore them and focus on the conversation with PG.

"How about dinner tonight? My treat."

PG hesitates for a moment, then nods appreciatively. "That sounds good. Thanks."

We chat about various topics—books, movies, favorite local spots—all in a short but friendly exchange. PG's replies may be concise but laced with intelligence and depth.

I ask him, "What's your favorite book?"

He leans in as if sharing a secret and says, "One Hundred Years of Solitude by Gabriel García Márquez. It's like a journey through time and memory."

His response catches me off guard, and I smile, genuinely impressed. "I love that one too," I admit. "Magical realism at its finest."

PG nods, his eyes lighting up. "Exactly! It's like stepping into a dream."

As the night deepens, our conversation flows easily, and I am more drawn to PG. Despite his few words, something is captivating about the way he speaks. He's a fantastic person, and his quiet respectfulness adds to his appeal.

I've seen PG as extraordinary proof that sometimes the most exciting people are the ones you least expect to meet.

Months have passed, and winter has firmly gripped the city. The days are growing colder, and I follow my usual routine, often walking by that familiar fast-food restaurant. But I last saw PG a long time ago. I start worrying about him.

It's a snowy evening, and the world is draped in a soft, white veil. The street is calm, with the only sounds being the muffled footsteps of passersby and the occasional car gliding by. The frosted windows of the restaurant cast a warm and inviting glow onto the chilly pavement outside.

Approaching my apartment building, I spot PG huddled in a corner, his body trembling from the cold. Concern propels me forward, and I hurry over to him.

"PG, it's freezing out here," I exclaim, the frosty air stinging my cheeks.

He looks up, a weary but grateful smile on his face. "You're telling me," He replies with a hint of humor, his breath forming tiny clouds in the frigid air.

"PG, it's getting late and so cold outside. Why don't you stay in my apartment tonight?"

PG looks at me, hesitating.

"Come with me, please." I want to bring PG to my apartment.

"No, but thank you."

"How about having a hot meal?" I keep trying.

"I do not want to bother you again," PG is hard-headed.

"I thought we were friends. But you are so distant, PG."

PG's eyes reflect gratitude but also determination. "Nancy, I appreciate it, but I can't impose on you like that. I'll find a place to stay."

I respect his choice but want to ensure he's safe and warm. So, I gather all the cash I have, about $55, and hand it to him. "Please, take this. Get yourself a warm jacket and find shelter for the night."

PG accepts the money, his eyes conveying appreciation. "Thank you, Nancy," he says, his voice sincere. "You've been incredibly kind."

I watch him disappear into the snowy night. The mixture of emotions inside me deepens. At this moment, amidst the falling snowflakes. PG is homeless, but he is a very respectful person.

After the new year, my article is published in a famous magazine. And then, I surprisingly receive an invitation to attend a publishing conference. I'm so excited about it.

The event is in a grand convention center with authors, publishers, and literary enthusiasts. The lobby buzzes with excitement as participants exchange ideas and discuss their latest projects.

As I browse the conference agenda, I focus on a keynote speaker who resembles PG. The speaker's name is Paul Gibson. The mere thought sends a shiver down my spine and my heart races. It can't be him, can it?

When the time comes for this mysterious speaker to take the stage, I find myself on edge, my nerves tingling with anticipation. As he begins to speak, my suspicions intensify. It's PG's voice, unmistakable and hauntingly familiar.

Does PG have a twin brother? Until this moment, I realize I know nothing about PG.

During the lunch break, I go to the dining hall, a bustling room filled with round tables and animated conversations. I stand there, lost in a sea of faces, unsure what to do next. That's when I see him.

PG enters the hall with a group of well-dressed and important-looking people. He moves with a confident stride, his presence commanding the attention of those around him. My heart leaps into my throat, and I feel a rush of emotions—surprise, disbelief, an overwhelming desire to reconnect, and a little anger.

He approaches, our eyes locking, and he calls out my name. "Nancy!"

I stand there, stunned and speechless for a moment. Then, the anger and sense of betrayal surge forward, and I finally find my voice, though it trembles with emotion. "PG! Is that you? How could you...?" I can't speak anymore.

"Nancy, I'm so sorry. It just... happened."

My frustration simmers as I look at his eyes. What I want to say is: "Just happened? You left me hanging, wondering what happened to you. I thought you were homeless, struggling to survive!" But I bite my lip and don't let these words out in front of others.

PG looks at me with mixed emotion, his voice low and irresistible. "How about dinner tonight? My treat."

It was the words I spoke to him. He even copies my tone.

"That sounds good. Thanks."

We both repeated the exact words, but the roles have switched.

Then, he walks away with the others.

For the rest of the conference, I'm lost. I expect dinner to arrive.

The night has fallen, and the conference is finally over. I take my time dressing up for the dinner party, choosing an elegant outfit. I head to the dining hall and find my way to the table, where I wait for PG.

Moments later, he arrives, but he looks different. No name tag, no suit; instead, he's dressed in business casual attire. There's a sense of transformation about him, and I can't help but feel curious and slightly puzzled.

I beckon him to sit, and as we settle into our chairs, he explains, "Nancy, I have to tell you something. It's not easy."

I nod, my curiosity deepening as I encourage him to continue.

With a sigh, PG begins his story. "I'm not who I pretended to be," he admits, his gaze locked on mine. "I'm a billionaire. I was tired of being pursued for my wealth, and I wanted to find a genuine connection. I wanted to meet someone who cared about me for who I am, not for my money."

His confession surprises me, and I can hardly believe what I hear. "So, you're saying... all this time, you've been pretending to be homeless?"

PG smiles. "Not all the time. Most days, I still have to return to manage my business." A mixture of regret and hope is in his eyes. "Yes, Nancy. I disguised myself as a homeless man to find a true connection. And then, I met you."

I sit there, absorbing the weight of his words, grappling with the deception and the truth behind his actions. "But why didn't you tell me the truth earlier?" I ask, my voice filled with a sense of betrayal.

He reaches out, his hand gently covering mine. "I'm so sorry, Nancy. I didn't want to scare you away. I wanted to be sure you liked me for who I am. Even if I'm homeless, we can share something in common."

Emotions swirl within me, a mix of anger, disbelief, and an undeniable connection that has grown between us. "Do you... do you love me?" I finally ask, my voice shaking.

PG gazes at me with sincerity and vulnerability. "Yes, Nancy. I love you. I did plan for this, but my feelings for you are genuine."

"I'm not pretty. I'm just one of the most ordinary people."

"You are the one I've been searching for. You have a beautiful heart. I trust that you will never betray me, whether I'm rich or poor. You are the one I want to share my entire life with."

Tears well up in my eyes, and despite the web of lies, I realize that my feelings for him run deep. "I love you too, PG."

In that moment, our love transcends deception, and we embrace the connection that has grown between us, uncertain of the future but willing to face it together.

The soft, melodic strains of music fill the air as the evening transitions into party time. The room is aglow with warm, inviting light, and the atmosphere is electric with the promise of joy and celebration.

Amid the lively crowd, PG extends his hand toward me, his eyes locking on mine with a warm, inviting smile. "Nancy, would you care to dance with me?"

I take his hand without hesitation, and we move gracefully to the dance floor. PG's movements are effortless, and he leads with a confident grace that leaves me utterly enchanted.

His charisma radiates, making him even more handsome and captivating in my eyes.

As we sway to the rhythm of the music, it feels as though the world outside this moment doesn't exist. Our laughter mingles with the melodies, and I can't help but be drawn further into PG's magnetic presence.

"PG, it is our happy night."

"Nancy, it is the beginning of our happy life."

Chasing Shadows of the Heart

I'm on a busy downtown street taking photos for a travel magazine. I've got my camera up, scanning for a good shot when I see her. She stands out from the crowd, catching my eye like something special.

I'm trying to get a great photo, and she's different. She looks right at me, strong and intense. Then, clear and firm, she says, "Stop. I do not want to be in your picture." Her voice is full of annoyance but also something like a challenge.

I put my camera down and meet her intense look. Her eyes are this amazing hazel, full of all these emotions. I can see she's mad, but it's not just that. She's interesting, more than just her anger.

This throws me off.

"Sorry," I say, giving her a guilty smile and show-ing I mean no harm. "I didn't mean to crash into your privacy like that."

She tells me to delete the picture immediately.

Walking over, I give her my business card with both hands, trying to smooth things over.

She gives me this half-smile that lets me know she's less mad now. "So, you're Alex, the pho-tographer," she says, looking closer at me.

Her tone gives away a hint of hope, so I take a shot, "Can I keep the photo? It's the best one I took today."

But she's firm. "No. You can snap anything else around here. There's plenty to tell on this street, but I'm not one of those stories." Even as she speaks sharply, a twinkle in her eye sug-gests she's partly in jest.

I get the message; the photo has to go. "You know, moments like this are what it's all about,"

I tell her, keeping it light and nodding towards the busy scene around us. "Life in its pure form. Old buildings and new ones side by side, like the past and future mingled together."

She looks at me, her annoyance fading as fast as it appeared. "I guess you have a point," she admits, and I can see her relax a bit.

The air between us changes, becoming lighter and filled with a mutual curiosity. She's got stories hidden deep in those hazel eyes, and I'm drawn to them, wanting to peel back the layers of her initial resistance.

The city moves indifferently around us. Still, this little friction has sparked something, a connection neither of us expected.

"What's your name?" I ask.

She hesitates, then, with a slight pause, says, "You can call me Sophia."

It fits her perfectly.

"Sophia, how about you join me for dinner?" I ask, hoping to extend this unexpected encounter.

She sizes me up, weighing her options, then declines, "No."

"Not dinner then, just a drink for happy hour. I promise, no pressure."

Then, that enigmatic smile lights up her face, and she agrees with a nod. Leaning in, her eyes twinkle with a hint of trouble. "I'm in for dinner, but on one condition."

Curious, I lift an eyebrow. "Oh? And what's that?"

With a mischievous grin, she lays down her rule. "I pick the place."

I laugh, realizing she's got a mind of her own. "Deal. You call the shots tonight."

Sophia takes me to this cozy Thai place a couple of blocks away. Its welcoming, bright yellow doors and elephant statue greet us. The smell of spices hits me, promising a meal to remember.

Now, the challenge is deciding what to order. I know nothing about Thai food.

"How do you feel about spicy food, Alex? Their red curry is legendary."

She's got this look like she's plotting something fun. I hesitate, then blurt out, "Sure." The truth is, my relationship with spicy food is more miss than hit, but I'm not about to show weakness.

Her smile widens, "Trust me, you don't want to miss this. Let's get you that red curry."

Before I know it, she's ordered for me, and I'm bracing myself for impact. When the curry arrives, I'm mentally preparing for an adventure.

As I take the first bite, her eyes are glued to me, filled with anticipation. Instantly, I'm a mess. Sweat beads on my forehead, and my eyes water as if I'm cutting onions.

Sophia can barely contain her laughter. "You good?"

I'm fighting for composure, my voice strained. "Absolutely, just enjoying the ride."

Her laughter fills the restaurant, reminding me of simpler times. Despite the heat, this moment of shared joy over my culinary misstep brings us closer.

The Thai restaurant glows warmly around us, our laughter blending into the cozy atmosphere. Despite the initial challenge posed by the spicy dish, the evening unfolds into a beautiful adventure.

As we talk more, finding common ground in our love for the arts, it feels like we're moving closer, both physically and metaphorically. The night deepens, and we almost forget the world outside, lost in our conversation and the connection that seems to grow stronger by the minute.

But then, a commotion interrupts our bubble. We look at each other, puzzled, and then Sophia's face changes; she knows she needs to leave. "I'm sorry, Alex," she tells me regretfully. "I have to go."

I try to keep it light, masking my disappointment. "No worries. Sometimes, you gotta do what you gotta do."

After a brief goodbye, she's off, vanishing into the night as quickly as she came into my life. Left in the quiet after her departure, I can't help but feel a mix of sadness and hope. Our brief connection was unexpectedly deep; now, I'm left wishing for another chance to see her.

And then, as I sit there, it dawns on me—I never got her phone number.

Feeling regret and hope, I pay the bill and return to the night. The cool air hits me, reminding me that this evening with Sophia might be the beginning of something special. But in a city this big, finding her again feels like looking for a needle in a haystack.

I can't shake off the memory of our time together – her laugh, her eyes sparkled, and that undeniable connection. I'm determined to see her again, but all I have to go on is a handful of photos and the vivid impression she's left on me.

Back home, I pore over my camera's pictures, searching for any trace of her. I've already deleted that confrontational snapshot, but there's a chance she's somewhere in the others, caught accidentally in a frame.

As I sift through the images, time stretches out. I'm looking for that unique smile that's been etched into my mind. The endless parade of faces and places begins to blur, leaving me feeling lost.

But then, I see her. In the backdrop of a photo, there is a figure that makes my heart skip. Zooming in, I can hardly believe it – Sophia is walking out of a Cafe. I quickly save this precious clue.

With a burst of excitement, I know my next step. I have to return to that street, the place where everything started.

With Sophia's photo as my guide, I dive back into the downtown crowd, heart thumping with the hope of finding her again. She's sparked something in me I just can't shake off. I'm outside a quaint café, the ninth stop in my relentless search.

Crossing the threshold, the scent of coffee wraps around me, a comforting embrace. Conversation murmurs fill the space, lending it an intimate vibe. This café feels like a secret haven in the city's hustle, a spot ripe for confessions and tales waiting to be told.

Approaching the counter, I notice a red-haired lady with warm, welcoming eyes. From her name tag, I know her name is Elena. She's busy preparing drinks for the customers.

I take a deep breath and step forward, determined to find any information that could lead me to Sophia. "Excuse me, I'm looking for someone, and I heard she's been here before. Her name is Sophia." Then I show her Sophia's photo.

Elena pauses in her task and looks at the photo thoughtfully. "Sophia, you say? She's not a regular here, but I remember her pretty face. She came in a few times, always alone, and did not talk to anyone."

My heart skips a beat, and I lean in closer, eager for details. "Do you know anything about Sophia? Any way I could reach her?"

Elena nods, her eyes holding a hint of curiosity. "She was a bit of a mystery. She was always lost in thought as if she carried the world's weight. She had an artistic air, like a painter searching for inspiration."

I feel a pang of longing. "Is there anything else you remember that could help me find her?"

Elena smiles, a knowing twinkle in her eye. "Well, bookstore, maybe? She carried a bag of new books once. There is a bookshop just around the corner. Maybe you'll have better luck finding her there."

Gratitude wells up inside me as I thank Elena for her information. With renewed hope, I exit the café, the scent of coffee lingering in the air as I head toward the bookshop, my next destination in this pursuit of the enigmatic Sophia.

With Elena's cryptic hint about the bookshop, I find myself standing in front of the quaint little store around the corner. As I step inside, the smell of books and the soft creaking of wooden floors greet me.

As I browse the shelves, my mind races with thoughts of Sophia. I wonder what secrets lie hidden beneath her enigmatic exterior. Elena's description of Sophia as an artist searching for inspiration keeps playing in my mind.

Just as I'm about to leave, I overhear a conversation at the counter. An elderly customer is raving about the live music performances at a nearby concert hall, mentioning a talented musician named Sophia.

My heart skips a beat as I connect the dots.

Sophia—a musician?

I approach the elderly customer who mentioned Sophia, and my curiosity is piqued.

"Excuse me, I overheard you talking about a musician named Sophia. Can you tell me more about her?"

The elderly customer smiles with joy, "Of course! Sophia is an incredible musician. She's in her late twenties, with long, flowing dark hair and a captivating stage presence."

I eagerly ask, "Do you know when and where her next performance is?"

The elderly customer checks his phone slowly and then looks at me. "Her next show is tomorrow night at seven at the Hilton Concert Hall. It's an experience you won't want to miss!"

I sigh gratefully. "Thank you so much for the information! I appreciate it."

As I gather the details, excitement bubbles within me. Sophia, I will find you tomorrow.

The following day, before 7:00 p.m., the Hilton Concert Hall in the heart of downtown comes alive with anticipation.

I'm standing at the big front door, feeling super excited, and my heart is beating fast. I'm here because of how strongly I feel about Sophia and buzzing with energy.

As the doors open, I hear the buzz of people talking and see the gentle light filling up the room. So many people are around, all looking forward to hearing Sophia's music.

The crowd falls into a hushed reverence as the lights dim and the stage comes alive. And then, Sophia appears—a vision in the spotlight, the enigmatic musician I've been searching for, now stands before us.

Holding her guitar, Sophia starts to play, and her voice, captivating as ever, fills the room. Her music is more than just sounds; it's a peek into who she is. She sings about love, yearning, and what it means to be human.

I'm totally drawn in by the beauty of her tunes and the honest feelings in her singing. Every song feels like she's sharing a secret with me, letting me see a part of her heart. It's like she's singing just for me.

When she finishes her last song, everyone claps loudly. Sophia's smile is bright and genuine as she says thanks and steps back from the mic.

I can't wait any more. My heart pushes me through the crowd until I stand right before her. She looks surprised to see me there.

"Sophia," my voice filled with awe and admiration, "your music is incredible."

She turns to me, her gaze holding a mix of curiosity and vulnerability. "You found me."

I smile, my determination paying off. "I had to. After all, you're the missing piece of the puzzle."

Sophia's gaze softens, and she leans closer as if drawn by an invisible force. "What do you want, Alex?"

I take a step closer, my heart laid bare. "I want to know you, Sophia. The real you, the artist, the musician, the woman behind the mystery."

She stares at me, her gaze piercing into my eyes as if trying to glimpse into my heart. "This goes beyond my expectations, but I do want to get to know you better, too," she says softly, a hint of vulnerability in her words.

In the following weeks, I met with Sophia a few times. I notice that she's avoiding any conversation about her personal life. Questions about her background or dreams are met with a gentle but evasive smile, deepening the mystery surrounding her.

I start feeling frustrated because I want to know more about her and understand her. I try to get her to share more with me, but she's not ready to open up. This starts causing problems between us, turning our smooth connection into one with bumps and misunderstandings.

One evening, after yet another elusive response from her about her personal life, I can't hold back my frustration any longer. "Sophia, why are you keeping so much hidden? Is it so wrong for me to want to know you better?"

She sighs, her eyes filling with a mix of sorrow and determination. "Alex, you have to understand... I'm not like other people. I have my reasons for being guarded."

The tension between us rises as our differences come to the forefront. I, an open book, wear my heart on my sleeve while Sophia, the enigmatic musician, guards her emotions fiercely.

"The more I care about you," I confess, my voice tinged with desperation, "the more you become a mystery to me. I just want to be a part of your world."

Sophia looks away, her expression conflicted. "Alex, you have no idea what you're asking for."

The fight leaves a heavy silence between us as if we're being pushed apart by the things we can't agree on. We're both stubborn and full of love, but our own worries and doubts are getting in the way.

The days after our fight are tense. It seems like we're both trying to avoid making it worse, but it just makes everything feel more awkward.

I can't stand feeling so far from her anymore, so one night, I decide it's time to talk and try to overcome the barriers she's put up around her.

"Sophia," I say gently, "we can't go on like this. You've become a mystery I can't unravel, tearing us apart."

She sighs, and I can see sadness and resignation in her eyes. "I didn't want to burden you with my past, Alex. It's a painful part of my life I've tried to leave behind."

My heart aches at the vulnerability in her voice. "You don't have to carry it alone, Sophia. We can face it together."

She takes a deep breath, her fingers trembling slightly. "Okay, Alex. It's time you knew the truth." Sophia's voice quivers as she reveals the painful story she's kept hidden for so long. "It all happened on a night I'll never forget. I was at a party, and I lost track of time. My parents were on their way to pick me up. They never made it."

As Sophia opens up, her voice trembles with guilt and sorrow. She recounts the tragic accident that claimed her parents' lives, her eyes glistening with unshed tears. "I was too caught up in my happiness that night and didn't go home when I should have. If I had been more responsible, they might still be alive."

I gently squeeze her hand, offering my support and understanding as she shares her painful past. "Sophia, it's not your fault," I say softly. "You were just a young girl, and accidents happen. Your parents wouldn't want you to carry this burden forever."

She looks at me, her eyes searching for solace. "I know, but it's haunted me for so long. I've never forgiven myself for what happened."

I pull her into a comforting embrace, holding her close. "You don't have to carry this guilt alone, Sophia. We'll face it together, and I'll be here for you every step of the way."

She looks into my eyes, and suddenly, the walls between us disappear. I realize that something important has changed in our relationship. But I need to recognize that Sophia still has another secret, one that is dangerous and uncertain. This secret will challenge our love and trust, leading us on a path with many surprises and unexpected turns.

Sophia and I continue to grow closer as the days turn into weeks.

One evening, under a sky filled with stars, we sit on a park bench, the world around us fading into the background. The cool breeze rustles the leaves, and the gentle sounds of the night seem to envelop us.

"I've always dreamt of traveling the world," I confess, my gaze fixed on the stars above. "Capturing the beauty of different cultures through my lens."

Sophia smiles, her eyes reflecting the moonlight. "That sounds incredible, Alex. And I'd love to be a part of your adventures."

Her words warm my heart, and I turn to her, my hand finding hers. "And what about you, Sophia? What are your dreams?"

She hesitates for a moment as if contemplating her answer. "I dream of sharing my music with the world," she finally says, her voice soft but determined. "I want to touch people's hearts and make them feel something."

I'm captivated by her passion and sincerity. "You already do that every time you play."

Our eyes meet, and at that moment, I realize that something profound has shifted between us. It's not just a connection anymore; it's deep and unconditional love.

Our bond deepens as the weeks become months, and we fall in love. Our personalities, once so different, complement each other perfectly. My openness balances her guardedness, and her sensitivity grounds my adventurous spirit.

We revel in the beauty of our shared moments—the sunsets we watch together, the late-night conversations that stretch into dawn, and how our hearts beat in harmony when we're close.

One evening, as we sit on the rooftop of a quiet café, I take her hand and look into her eyes. "Sophia," I say, my voice trembling with emotion, "Did I ever tell you I love you?"

Tears glisten in her eyes as she smiles, a smile that lights up my world. "I love you too, Alex."

While Sophia and I enjoy our growing love, a scary threat creeps into our lives. It's like a dark storm cloud on the horizon, disturbing our newfound peace.

One night, as we take a moonlit stroll through a park, an eerie sensation crawls up my spine—a feeling of being watched, hunted even. I grasp Sophia's hand tightly, my heart pounding in my chest.

"Sophia," I whisper, my voice trembling, "do you sense it too? Something's not right."

"What happened?"

"I feel we are followed."

Sophia's eyes widen in alarm, mirroring my unease. "Alex, it's as though my past has caught up with us."

"Your past?" I inquire, my curiosity mixed with concern.

"I was a runaway bride," she admits, her voice laced with vulnerability.

My heart aches at the confession, and I can't help but wonder about the untold story behind those words. "What happened?"

Sophia bites her lip and shakes her head, leaving me in the dark about the details of her past. However, I can sense the weight of her unspoken words, and I know there are still layers of her history that she's not ready to reveal.

We become more afraid as days turn into anxious nights. We see shadows moving in the corners of our eyes, and faceless dangers seem to be hiding nearby. It feels like someone is relentlessly pursuing us.

Who's behind it?

Why are they so determined to catch us?

What will come our way?

I start searching for Sophia on the internet. One fateful night, my restless curiosity leads me to an old, obscure newspaper article buried deep within the internet archives. The headline sends shivers down my spine: "Bride's Mysterious Disappearance on Wedding Day."

The photograph accompanying the article reveals a hauntingly familiar face—the missing bride, none other than Sophia.

I confront her with my discovery, my voice heavy with concern. "Sophia, is this you?"

Tears brim in her eyes as she nods, a shudder of fear running through her. "Yes, Alex. It's me. I ran away to escape a life I never wanted, but he is still hunting me."

I pull her into a comforting embrace, determined to protect her from the looming threat. "Tell me, Sophia. What happened? Why is he still after you?"

She takes a deep breath, her voice trembling as she unravels the painful past. "I was very lonely after my parents passed away. I was so young when I fell in love with him, Alex. I didn't know who he really was until it was too late. He's a criminal, involved in things I can't even speak of."

I listen intently, my heart aching for her. "And the wedding?"

She looks down, her voice barely above a whisper. "I was supposed to marry him. But as I stood in that white dress, I realized I couldn't go through with it. I couldn't tie myself to a life of darkness."

The pieces of the enigmatic puzzle finally fall into place—her evasiveness, constant movement, and aversion to being photographed—all connected to a past she's been desperately trying to escape.

I hold her tighter, understanding the gravity of her decision. "You did what you had to do, Sophia. But we'll face this together. I won't let him hurt you." I prepare to confront the shadows that haunt Sophia's past.

We sit in the dimly lit sanctuary of our living room, faces bathed in the soft glow of candlelight, and she begins to speak.

"My ex," she says, her voice quivering with fear and determination, "was not just an ordinary man, Alex. He was deeply involved in a criminal world—a drug dealer."

Her words hang heavily in the air, and I feel a shiver run down my spine. I can see the pain etched into the lines of her face as she continues.

"Our relationship began as something beautiful, but as I got to know him better, I discovered the darkness that consumed him. He wanted me to be a part of his dangerous world and share his secrets and crimes. When I refused, it turned into a nightmare. He was violent."

As I listen to her story, the room seems to close in. I can't imagine the terror she must have endured, the constant fear of being hunted down by a ruthless criminal.

Sophia's eyes glisten with unshed tears as she meets my gaze. "I had to run away, Alex. It was the only way to escape his grasp, to protect myself and those I love."

Her confession fills me with a profound sense of compassion and love. I take her trembling hand, squeezing it gently in a silent promise of support.

"We'll face this together, Sophia," I say, my voice unwavering. "We'll ensure that he can never harm you again."

I understand our love will face a tough challenge with her past and the danger looming. But in this difficult time, our connection will become even stronger. It will be like a strong fortress of love and strength, ready to withstand any problems.

A few days after Sophia shared her secret with me, I walk her home after her performance. The night is cloaked in darkness, and we find ourselves cornered in a dimly lit alley, the walls closing in around us. Sophia clings to my arm, fear etched across her face, but her eyes have a glimmer of determination.

The man from her past steps into the flickering pool of light, a sinister smile on his lips. "Well, well, well, Sophia. Thought you could run forever?"

My voice is steady, unwavering. "You won't harm her," I say firmly, placing myself between Sophia and her menacing pursuer.

He chuckles, the sound dripping with malice. "And who's going to stop me, lover boy?"

But Sophia is no longer the terrified woman who once fled from him. She steps forward, her voice quivering but filled with resolve. "I won't let you control my life anymore. It's over."

The tension in the air is palpable as the confrontation escalates. He, Sophia's ex, unleashes a torrent of threats and accusations, each word a weapon aimed at her heart.

"You thought you could escape me, Sophia?" he sneers, his voice dripping with venom. "You thought you could run away and start a new life?"

Sophia's eyes blaze with defiance as she stands her ground. "Yes, I did. And I won't let you destroy that life."

He scoffs, his anger intensifying. "You don't understand what you've gotten yourself into, Sophia. You don't know the depths of my reach."

I watch, my anger simmering, as he taunts her.

But Sophia remains resolute, her voice unwavering. "I may not know everything, but I won't let you control me anymore."

Their conversation is a battleground filled with emotional landmines and painful memories.

Despite the danger, Sophia refuses to back down, and it becomes clear that this confrontation is a turning point in her battle to break free from her past.

I intervene, my words laced with conviction. "Sophia's made her choice, and it's not with you. It's with me."

The man's face contorts with rage, his eyes narrowing into a furious glare. "You think you can take her from me?" he hisses, venom dripping from every word.

In the tense standoff, I stand firm, my voice steady. "I'm not here to take anyone from you. I'm here to protect Sophia from you."

He scoffs, his anger fueling his aggression. "You don't know what you've gotten yourself into."

As he takes a menacing step forward, Sophia, trembling but determined, pulls out her phone and dials 911. "I'm calling the police," she says, her fingers shaking as she holds the phone to her ear.

The man's eyes fill with rage and fear. He strikes me hard in the face, and a struggle breaks out as we try to protect ourselves. He is much stronger than me, but I must keep my line to protect Sophia.

Amid the chaos, sirens wail in the distance, growing louder with each passing second.

The sound of approaching police cars sends a shock of adrenaline through us. We continue to fend off the man's relentless attacks, our hearts pounding as we await the arrival of the authorities.

When the police finally arrive, the alley is chaotic and violent. With sirens blaring and lights flashing, officers rush to our aid, pulling the man away and restraining him. Sophia, her voice quivering, tells them about the threats and the danger we faced.

I feel relief as the handcuffs click shut, and they take the man into custody. I'm exhausted.

Sophia removes her scarf, using it to clean the blood from my face. Each touch is gentle, a soothing caress against the aftermath of the confrontation. I wince as she tends to my injuries, her concern evident in her eyes.

"Thank you," I whisper.

Sophia hugs me tightly. It is the first time she hugs me in front of others.

With Sophia's ex behind bars for many years, the darkness that had haunted her past is finally behind us, or, at least, will be left behind for quite a long time. Once hidden behind layers of fear and secrecy, Sophia's sunshine nature shines brightly around me.

One sunny afternoon, we walk in the park. The atmosphere is filled with warmth and hope.

I take Sophia's hand, leading her to a picturesque spot by a tranquil pond. The soft breeze rustles the leaves, and the world pauses as if holding its breath in anticipation.

"Sophia," my voice filled with love and conviction, "from the moment I first saw you, you captured my heart. And now, I want to spend the rest of my life with you." I drop to one knee, producing a small velvet box from my pocket. I open it to reveal a glistening ring that symbolizes my love and commitment. "Sophia," I continue, my eyes locked on to hers, "will you marry me? Will you be mine forever?"

Tears shimmer in her eyes as she smiles, her voice filled with emotion. "Yes, Alex. Yes."

I slip the ring onto her finger, and as our lips meet in a tender and passionate kiss, the world around us fades insignificantly.

In that kiss, we lock in a future together, our hearts beating like a vow of love. The park around us seems to light up, echoing our joy, transforming the world from a place of doubt into our blank canvas. Here, we'll sketch a life rich in love, joy, and a steadfast belief in the power of love to overcome everything.

Holding Sophia's hand, I look into her eyes, pouring my soul without saying a word. "Sophia," my whisper carries every ounce of my love, "our path together is the most beautiful journey. You are everything to me, the truest desire of my heart."

Sophia's eyes glisten with tears, and her smile speaks volumes. My heart overflows as I say, "In your eyes, I've found where I belong. Your laughter brings me happiness, and your love gives my life meaning."

Then, soft and enchanting, Sophia's voice weaves into mine, "Alex, you're my sanctuary, my peace, my endless love. With you, I've discovered a love that breaks all barriers and is endlessly deep and true."

With another kiss, we step into our forever, the world around us disappearing. We stand in the power of our love, an unbreakable bond ready to face whatever comes, together in every dawn and dusk that awaits us.

The Mystery Postcards

I'm Jake, a young mailman in my early twenties. Each morning, I set out on my trusty mail route through the winding streets of our quaint little town. The town itself paints a charming picture with its narrow lanes lined by cozy cottages, their colorful gardens bursting with vibrant blooms.

I enjoy driving on the rolling hills and watching sunlight filter through the canopy of ancient oak trees that seem to arch over the road, casting dappled shadows on the pavement.

I wind my way past the corner bakery, where the scent of freshly baked bread mingles with the morning air. The townsfolk, friendly and familiar, wave as I pass by. Mrs. Johnson waters her petunias on the porch, and Mr. Adams sits on his porch swing, sipping his coffee.

The town feels like a snapshot of simpler times, where everyone knows each other's name. The only thing that can make a difference to my peaceful daily life is a change in the weather.

Something crucial is absent from my life, and I'm eager to open a new chapter.

One of my old coworkers is retired, and I'm assigned to another side of the town to take over his position. The first morning brings an unexpected twist. I turn a corner onto Elm Street, where an old, abandoned house stands like a forgotten relic of the past. Overgrown vines creep up its weathered facade, and the windows, cloaked in dust, haven't witnessed life in years.

Curiosity piqued, I slow down my mail car, lingering at this forgotten place. Then, something peculiar catches my eye—a stack of unaddressed postcards lies haphazardly in the mailbox by the crumbling gate. These aren't ordinary letters, the words flowing as naturally as the river that meanders through our town. The words on the postcards touch my heart so profoundly; they feel like a warm embrace on a cold winter's day. It's like a wake-up call, making me realize that what I've been missing in my peaceful life is high spirits.

There's a mystique about them, an air of secrecy that pulls me in. Moreover, there's no sender's address on any of them. These postcards seem to have been left here, waiting for someone to stumble upon them to discover their hidden messages.

Without a second thought, I channel my inner Sherlock Holmes and become a detective extraordinaire. I slip on my gloves and yank those mysterious letters out of the mailbox. I hope to return them to the sender.

I need to find the sender. After diligent research through a detective friend, I traced the letters back to an author with a pen named Emily and her PO box. Emily is somewhat of a recluse, rarely seen in public. Her books, though, were celebrated for their lyrical prose and emotional depth.

I return all the postcards to Emily.

One evening, as the sun dips below the horizon and the world is bathed in twilight, I sit down at my tiny desk, a blank sheet of paper before me. Inspired by the words I've found; I decided to reach out to Emily. I do not dare to reveal my identity. I create a pseudonym: "Sam."

I write a letter to Emily. I tell Emily about my discovery of her postcards, how her words have captured my heart, and how I feel a strange connection to the sentiments in her writing. I sign it "Sam the Seeker."

Weeks passed, and I'm still waiting for a response from Emily.

I eagerly check my mailbox each day. Then, one afternoon, nestled among the bills and flyers, I find a letter addressed to "Sam the Seeker." The familiar, elegant script reveals that it's from Emily.

My heart races as I tear open the envelope and read her response.

Her words are every bit as enchanting as those in the unaddressed letters. She thanks me for my letter.

And so, some correspondence begins between us, all while we remain unaware of each other's true identities. Our letters flow back and forth. Emily's letters are like windows into her soul, filled with sensitivity and sharp insights. My letters take on a playful tone, infused with easygoing humor, as I share stories from my daily life. I have never been so open with anyone; our communication knows no limitations as if we are painting the canvas of our hearts with the vibrant colors of our shared experiences.

As our letters continue, a sense of longing and anticipation grows within me. I find myself thinking of Emily more often than not, wondering what she looks like, what her laughter sounds like, and what it would be like to meet the enigmatic author behind the letters that have captured my heart.

***

One quiet evening, I sit at my desk, the soft glow of a desk lamp illuminating the letter before me. The entire message can be summarized in three words: "Can we meet?"

Time suddenly becomes agonizingly slow as I wait for Emily's response with bated breath. One day passes, then a week, and eventually, two weeks.... The weight of my confession and the uncertainty of her reaction hang over me like a storm cloud. I wonder if I've been too forward, too eager to unravel the mystery that has bound us together.

Then, one crisp autumn afternoon, a letter from Emily arrives. She's already in town and provides the meeting location and time.

We meet in a quiet corner of our town, under the canopy of oak trees that line the park by the river. The anticipation of our meeting fills my days with a sense of euphoria. I imagine how she might look, and her voice might sound when I finally face her.

The day of our meeting arrives, and as I stand beneath the familiar oak trees, my heart races with excitement and nervousness. I watch as a figure approaches, which seems to shimmer with the same enchantment that drew me to her letters.

Emily stands before me, her eyes meeting mine with curiosity and warmth. Her smile is as radiant as the sun breaking through the leaves. As we exchange our first words in person, it feels like the natural continuation of a conversation that has been ongoing for months.

"Hey," I say excitedly.

"Hi" is her response, and her voice is soft and calm.

Emily has deep blue eyes that seem to hold the secrets of the ocean depths, and her long, soft hair frames her face with a gentle cascade. Her complexion is pale white, perhaps from spending much of her time indoors, lost in her writing. She wears a simple yet comfortable white top and a long cream skirt. As the wind rustles her clothes and hair, she effortlessly blends with the natural surroundings, a vision of grace and beauty.

As we stroll along the riverbank, our hands brush against each other, igniting a spark of electricity that leaves no doubt in my mind—we are meant to be together.

The sun hangs low on the horizon, casting a warm, golden hue over the tranquil waters of the lake. Emily and I walk in comfortable silence for a while, the soft rustling of leaves and the distant chirping of birds providing the backdrop to our moment.

Eventually, Emily breaks the silence with a thoughtful sigh. "You know," she begins, her voice soft and contemplative, "the owner of that abandoned house I keep sending postcards to was a talented writer I admired since I was young."

I turn to her, curious to hear more.

Her eyes are distant as she recalls memories of the past. "I loved him secretly, but I never dared to tell him my feelings."

Emily turns and looks at me, "He took his own life before I could express my love for him. I am filled with regret. If I had braved enough, perhaps the story could have been rewritten."

My heart aches for her, and I squeeze her hand gently in understanding. "I'm so sorry, Emily," I offer, my voice filled with empathy.

She smiles faintly, her eyes glistening with unshed tears. "Thank you," she says, her voice barely above a whisper. "I miss him so much."

"So, you send him all the postcards?" I inquire.

Emily nods and replies, "Yes. I want him to receive my postcards on his birthday, every holiday, or whenever I miss him."

It dawns on me that all the postcards let her release her emotions. Emily continues to explain, "I hope he can read them in heaven, so I use postcards instead of sealing them into envelopes."

Her story profoundly touches me, and my admiration for her grows with each word she shares.

"Emily," I begin, my voice filled with respect, "your dedication to his memory and beautiful words are truly remarkable."

She looks at me with gratitude shining in her eyes. "Thank you," she says, her voice tinged with emotion. "Since I started talking to you, I feel much better. You understand me well; I thought you should be at least a middle-aged man."

"I'm going to be a middle-aged man, Emily," I assure her. "I respect you and admire your words."

Emily's eyes meet mine, and at that moment, as we continue to walk along the lake, it feels like our souls have intertwined, bound by the shared stories we carry and the unspoken understanding of what it means to love, to grieve, and to find solace in each other's company.

The town that once seemed so ordinary has transformed into a place of magic and wonder, where love has bloomed unexpectedly, like a wildflower in a hidden meadow.

Those postcards, once abandoned and forgotten, have become the thread that weaves our hearts together. We both can feel it through silent gazes.

Emily rents a log cabin near the river in town, where she writes her novel, enjoying the beautiful view of the lake. This allows me to meet her in the following days. She always travels around, staying in beautiful places for a few days before moving on to the next. I think this is her romantic lifestyle.

One sunny afternoon, as I finish my usual rounds, I am drawn to the bustling town square. People mill about, sipping coffee at outdoor cafés and browsing the quaint shops that line the cobbled streets.

And then, as if guided by fate, I see her, Emily.

Emily sits at a small, sunlit table outside a café, her head buried in a book. Her dark hair cascades over her shoulder, and her eyes sparkle with a deep, hidden intensity. She looks like an enchanting stranger, and for a moment, I don't recognize her as my pen pal.

I approach her table and ask if the empty chair across from her is taken. She looks up, her eyes widening in surprise, but she graciously invites me to join her.

As I settle into the chair, I smile. "What are you reading?"

She glances down at the book on the table, her lips curving into a warm smile. "It's a classic, Pride and Prejudice. I've always loved the wit and charm of Jane Austen's writing."

I nod, feeling a sense of connection. "I'm a fan of Austen too. Have you read Sense and Sensibility?"

Emily's eyes light up. "Yes, I have! It's a beautiful novel. Austen had a unique way of exploring the complexities of human nature and relationships. I hope I can visit her hometown someday."

"Emily, travel can open our minds, allowing us to see the world from different cultures and perspectives."

She responds, "Not always. Travel can also enable me to hide from my world."

Her reply catches me off guard. I wonder why she feels the need to hide from her world.

"Where will you go next?" I ask, attempting to cover my surprise.

"Paris," Emily confesses with a wistful smile. "The city of love and art."

I can't resist the opportunity. "Well, maybe someday, we could go together. Explore the cobblestone streets, sip coffee at sidewalk cafés, and visit the Louvre."

"As my bodyguard?" she asks with a playful tone.

"Lifetime." I lay my hands on her shoulder.

It is the first time I have given my commitment to Emily.

"Thank you, Sam."

Sam! Sam is not my real name.

I must tell Emily the truth. Will our story take an unexpected turn, or will it crumble under the weight of this revelation? I'll see.

"Emily, I'm not Sam, my name is Jake."

"Jake," she hesitantly murmurs, her voice without surprise, "Jack Anderson."

"How do you know my full name?" Her knowledge takes me aback.

"This is a small town; a mailman is a public friend."

"Sorry, Emily, I didn't use my true identity when writing to you. But all my feelings for you are real."

"I know." Emily nods slowly, her gaze steady. "I believe you, Jake."

Relief washes over me, and I smile reassuringly. "I'm glad to hear that."

"It's just... it's been bothering me, and I wanted to discuss it with you." Emily's expression becomes a mixture of skepticism and curiosity. "You like my words, but maybe not who I am."

"What makes you say so?"

"My real name is Alyssa Smith. I'm thirty years old—possibly too old for you. I have a kidney problem, and the doctor said I can only live for another five years unless I replace my kidney."

My heart sinks, shock and sorrow gripping me as I learn of Alyssa's kidney problem and her potentially short time left.

"Alyssa, I will try my best to help you recover. I will share everything with you."

In the days following Alyssa's revelation about her identity and physical condition, I began searching online to find the best doctors who specialize in her condition. I'm determined to do everything to help her.

One chilly evening, we sit in front of her cozy fireplace inside the little cabin, the flickering flames casting dancing shadows across the room. The warmth of the fire mirrors the growing connection between us as we face the challenges ahead.

I turn to Alyssa, my voice filled with sincerity. "Alyssa, I've been researching, and I think you must visit the best-specialized doctor to determine whether your kidney needs to be replaced. We need to make sure you receive the best treatment possible."

"Agreed."

"I can give you all my money, and I can sell my car if you need more."

She looks at me, her eyes reflecting gratitude and vulnerability. "Jake, I appreciate your concern and willingness to support me, but I don't want you to empty your account or sell your car for this. I can take care of myself."

I pause for a moment, touched by her independence and strength. "Alyssa, I want to be there for you in every way possible. It's not about the money; it's about us facing this together. Your health and well-being mean the world to me."

She smiles, her expression softening. "Thank you, Jake. You light the hope in my life. I promise to consider all the options and make the best decisions for my health. I'll no longer ignore it."

As the fire crackles and the room fills with warmth, we hold each other's gaze, knowing that our love has grown stronger through these challenges. I stand up and walk to her. I hug her tightly. We'll face whatever lies ahead.

A week after Thanksgiving snowflakes gently fall from the sky, creating a serene winter wonderland as I continue my mailman's routine. The world around me is blanketed in white, with the snow covering ancient oak trees that seem to arch over the road and the cozy cottages along the way. Residents have already decorated their houses for Christmas, but my thoughts are a thousand miles away, centered on Alyssa.

Alyssa is visiting her doctor today, and unfortunately, I'm bound by my task. I can't be with her during this crucial moment, and it gnaws at me as I navigate the snow-covered streets, delivering letters and parcels.

Then, as I'm on my route, my phone rings. It's from Alyssa. I pull over to the side of the road, my heart pounding in my chest, and answer it.

"Jake," her voice trembling with emotion.

I cannot breathe.

"It's good news. The best gift for Christmas."

I can hardly believe my ears. My grip on the steering wheel tightens, and I struggle to find my voice. "What is it, Alyssa? Please tell me."

She takes a deep breath before speaking, her words carrying a weight that lifts a heavy burden from my shoulders. "I don't need a kidney replacement, Jake. The doctor says my condition is treatable, and I can recover."

Tears well up in my eyes as her words sink in, and I can feel a lump forming in my throat. The weight pressing my chest for weeks suddenly lifts, and relief washes over me.

I lay my head on the steering wheel, overcome with emotion. The snow continues to fall outside, blanketing the world in a peaceful hush. Alyssa's voice on the phone is a lifeline, a beacon of hope, and a promise of a brighter future.

Finally, I find my voice, "Alyssa, I can't express how grateful I am to hear this. It's the best news I could have hoped for."

Alyssa's laughter rings through the phone, a beautiful sound that warms my heart even on a cold winter day. "Jake, we're in this together, and I have hope now. Christmas is going to be a wonderful celebration this year."

I wipe away tears of joy as I sit in the car, overwhelmed by the magnitude of this moment. "You're right, Alyssa," I reply, my voice filled with conviction. "Christmas is going to be the most beautiful celebration, and the best gift of all is having you by my side."

"Jack, I want to invite you to my home. We'll share our first Christmas."

As the snow continues to fall outside, I'm filled with a deep sense of gratitude and love. The world may be covered in white, but at that moment, my heart is bathed in warmth and hope. I accept Alyssa's invitation to spend our first Christmas together at her home in another town.

As I arrive at Alyssa's home, I'm taken aback by its grandeur. It's a huge, expensive house with large windows that stretch from the floor to the twenty-foot ceiling. The rooms are adorned with beautiful Christmas decorations that fill the space with warmth and holiday cheer. It's a sight to behold, and I feel awe and a touch of apprehension.

Alyssa notices my reaction and smiles warmly. "Surprised?" Her eyes twinkle.

I nod, feeling a bit overwhelmed. "I am, Alyssa. Your home is incredible."

She chuckles softly. "I know it might be different from what you're used to, but remember, it's just a house. What matters most is who you're with, not where you are."

I appreciate her reassurance, but I express my uncertainty. "I'm unsure if I can get used to this life, Alyssa. I come from a low-middle-class background, and this is... well, it's a different world."

Alyssa steps closer, her arms wrapping around me in a comforting embrace. She whispers in my ear, her words filled with sincerity, "Jake, remember this—anything that can be accounted for may not be the most valuable thing. The most precious things are often the ones you cannot put a price on. The most valuable thing in my life is you. I was depressed and lonely for a long time, and you have changed my life."

"But, Alyssa, I must be honest about my financial situation. I have only $4,500 in my bank account, and I live in a one-bedroom apartment."

Alyssa responds, "I can share my financial situation too. I make at least $530,000 monthly from my published novels, and I have multiple million dollars in my account."

I've never known anyone personally with such wealth, and for the first time, I feel we may not be a good match. But Alyssa gently reassures me, "Jake, money can't buy happiness. Financial wealth doesn't equate to spiritual richness. Your kindness and beautiful soul are what I need."

Alyssa looks around her grand house and then into my eyes. "For me, living in this house or the log cabin near the lake doesn't make a big difference. This huge house makes me feel isolated at night. Romantic desires don't drive my travels; they're an escape from my small, isolated world."

Her words touch my heart, and I fall deeper in love with her. We smile, and in that moment, my doubts seem to melt away.

As the evening unfolds, we enjoy a romantic dinner by candlelight, savoring each other's company and the delicious food Alyssa has prepared.

After dinner, we cozy by the roaring fireplace, the crackling flames casting a soft, golden glow over the room. Alyssa's hand finds mine, and there, in the warm flickering light, she begins to talk about the letters I sent to her under my fake name, Sam. She shares how she felt when she first read those letters, and her words create an intimate atmosphere that draws us closer.

As the night progresses, our conversation turns quieter and more tender. We gaze into each other's eyes, our feelings laid bare. Then, we share our first night.

"Jake," Emily begins, her voice soft and affectionate, "I can't help but feel like we're living a real-life fairy tale."

"It's just a good start," I reply with confidence. I'll make myself a better man.

Two Builders

In the bright stage lights, I feel like I'm glowing. I stand there, saying lines perfectly, like I've practiced a million times. "I love you," I tell my co-star, sounding so sure. But deep down, I feel lost. Those words aren't mine; they're just lines from a script.

The crowd is like a dark ocean, clapping and cheering. I look out at them, wishing for a real connection, something that's not just acting.

When the show ends and the sound of applause fills the air, I don't feel overwhelmed; I feel lonelier than ever. There's a massive gap between me and the real world, much more than the distance from the stage to the last row of the audience.

I sneak off to my dressing room, away from everyone saying, "Great job."

The door clicks shut, leaving me alone in the quiet. The room is beautiful, but it feels so empty. I stare at my reflection, all dressed up and smiling, but the smile doesn't reach my heart. It's just like the pretend love I show on stage. How can I keep wearing this fake smile in my life, away from the bright lights and applause?

My phone buzzes, a message from a friend: Drinks tonight?

I glance at it, then at my reflection. The woman in the mirror looks back, her eyes asking, For what? Another night of hollow laughter and fleeting glances?

I change into my regular clothes, leaving behind the famous Emma. The city at night feels less bright; it sounds quieter. I wish for someone who wants to talk to the real me, not the actress. Someone who looks past fame and sees a girl who wants a simple, cozy kind of love.

It's early spring. The city feels alive as I walk, but inside, I feel empty. I will find a man who loves me for who I am, not for my face or fame, who can share the same umbrella with me in the storm.

I call my best friend, Lily; I must meet her at Café Lumière.

I enter the cozy embrace of the café, a world away from the glaring stage lights. Across from me sits Lily, my best friend since our sandbox days, her green eyes reflecting the soft glow of the hanging Edison bulbs.

The café buzzes with life, a soothing contrast to my solitary thoughts.

"You seemed a million miles away on stage tonight," Lily says, concern and curiosity lacing her voice.

I stir my coffee, watching the ripples settle. "Maybe I was," I admit. "Lily, I'm tired of the façade. The applause, the glamour... it's empty."

Lily leans in, her expression earnest. "What you need is someone real. Someone who loves Emma, not the Emma on billboards," she jokes.

I shake my head, a hint of sadness in my tone. "They're drawn to my face, not my soul," I reply. That's the heart of my problem.

"We all have to deal with it. It's like the flu for us," Lily says with a sigh, showing sympathy and weariness. "What do you want to do about it?"

I nod, my mind racing with a budding plan. "What if I try something different, like finding someone online and going on blind dates... but with a twist?" I pause, watching Lily closely for her reaction.

Lily's eyebrows shoot up, a mix of curiosity and confusion in her eyes. "A twist?" she echoes, intrigued but not quite understanding.

"I'll wear makeup, something subtle but notice-able. A birthmark, perhaps, on my forehead."

Lily's eyes widen. "To scare off the shallow ones?"

"Exactly," I say, the plan taking shape. "If some-one can look past it, maybe I'll find a real con-nection."

Lily's laughter fills the space between us, warm and encouraging. "That's brilliant, Emma! It's like your own undercover love mission."

We plot and plan, our conversation a mix of excitement and nerves. I feel a spark, a sense of adventure I haven't felt in years. The waitress refills our cups, her smile an unwitting accomplice to our scheme.

"So, the birthmark," Lily says, her tone severe yet playful. "How big are we talking?"

I touch my forehead, imagining it. "Big enough to be noticed, small enough to be intriguing."

"And if someone sees past it?" she asks.

"Then maybe they can see me," I say, my words a mix of hope and uncertainty.

Our plans laid, we part ways, the night air crisp against my skin.

I park my car inside the garage and walk back home, each step a dance between doubt and determination.

I stand before my mirror that night, tracing an imaginary line on my forehead. For the first time in a long while, I see not just Emma, the actress, but Emma, the dreamer, the hopeful romantic. And with that vision, I drift into sleep, a smile playing on my lips.

Tomorrow, a new act begins.

The next day, I created a profile on an online dating website, using a fake name and an AI photo for a bit of anonymity.

Two weeks pass, and I finally arrange my first blind date—a meeting with Alex, a small business owner. His profile, peppered with photos of him in various entrepreneurial endeavors, boasts a penchant for "deep conversations and meaningful connections." The claim piques my interest, raising the bar for our upcoming encounter.

The clink of fine dinnerware sets the scene as I meet Alex, his eyes momentarily snagging on the birthmark before regaining his composure. "You look... different than I imagined."

I meet his gaze steadily, unfazed. "Appearances can be deceiving," I say with a poised smile.

Disappointment flickers across Alex's face, but I don't let it rattle me. As we order, his cell phone rings. "Excuse me. This is important." He leans back, absorbed in his call, his voice sharp and commanding.

As he launches into a self-aggrandizing monologue about his latest business deal, I listen, my expression composed. "It's all about leveraging your assets," he declares, more to himself than to me.

I interject, aiming to find common ground. "What about outside of work? Any hobbies?"

He barely pauses. "My job is my passion. Why bother with anything else?" His gaze drifts over my shoulder, disinterested.

Curious, I glance back to see a blonde woman laughing with friends. Turning back to Alex, I make my decision. I place money for my meal on the table, my movements deliberate.

"Are you leaving?" Alex finally looks at me, surprised.

"Yes," I reply, my tone calm but firm. "I value my time too much to misspend it." With that, I stand and walk away, my head held high.

The second date is with Darren, an engineer, a seemingly kindhearted soul.

Darren greets me with a smile that somersaults spotting my forehead. "Oh, is that... new?"

"Fresh out of the box," I quip, eager to see where this rabbit hole goes.

"How new? Looks suspiciously like a birthmark." Darren's eyes are glued to my forehead as if it might reveal the universe's secrets.

Over coffee, Darren transforms from Mr. Nice Guy into Captain Fix-It. "You know, laser treatment is almost like magic for birthmarks," he explains, his eyes twinkling with the fervor of a late-night infomercial host.

I try a detour. "So, engineering, huh? Do you build bridges or just cross them?"

He gives a half nod, already rerouting back to the main agenda. "Yeah, bridges, buildings... but let's circle back to your... unique situation. I'm a problem-solver, you see."

"I'm more of a beauty-spot enthusiast," I jest, gesturing to my forehead.

He perks up. "Great to hear! And speaking of beauty, I know a fantastic doctor...."

"No need," I interject. "I'm pretty fond of God's little freebies. This one came without a receipt."

As I escape, feeling more like a fixer-upper than a date, Darren's voice follows me. "Just think about it! I'll text you some top-tier clinics!"

"Thank you," I respond, friendly. Darren is a nice guy, but not my type.

My third date is with Brian, a novel writer in his thirties with striking good looks. He meets me at the bookstore café, his eyes flickering to my forehead with a hint of curiosity.

"Interesting choice for a date," he comments.

"I thought it'd be nice to surround ourselves with stories," I reply, hopeful for a literary connection.

Our conversation initially dances around literature, finding a comfortable rhythm. But as the evening unfolds, Brian's focus wavers, increasingly captured by his phone.

"Sorry," he apologizes without looking up, "just checking the progress of my new book's release."

"That's exciting, congratulations on the publication."

Brian shrugs, a hint of frustration in his tone. "It's okay. Spent fifty bucks on Facebook ads this morning and barely broke even. The world of readers is a mystery," he says, his eyes narrowing in thought.

His nervous energy is palpable.

Seeking lighter territory, I ask, "What's your favorite book?"

Brian offers a distracted nod, his attention stolen by the TV screen behind me. "Oh, lots of them," he murmurs, barely engaging.

I feel disappointed as I realize my competition is a football game. "Maybe we should wrap up for tonight," I suggest gently.

"Sure, sure," he replies, his eyes still glued to the screen. "We should do this again, right?"

I smile, knowing it's just a formality. As I walk away, Brian's gaze remains fixated on the TV.

Outside, the wind plays with my hair, and a wry smile tugs at my lips despite the sting of letdown.

Three blind dates, three unique experiences—it feels like I've just wrapped up an episode of a reality show. It's time to put a full stop to this chapter of my dating life.

I text Lily about my decision.

The following day dawns with a gray overcast, mirroring my mood. I fly back to my hometown; I want to spend a few days with my mom, who understands me the most.

I find solace in the familiar comforts of my childhood home. The aroma of freshly brewed coffee and cinnamon fills the kitchen where my mother, a beacon of warmth and wisdom, moves with a grace that belies her years.

"Rough dates?" she inquires, handing me a steaming mug.

I nod, sinking into a chair. "It's like navigating a minefield of egos and indifference."

She sits across from me, her eyes soft yet piercing. "Emma, you're looking for something real in a world that often isn't. It's brave, but not without its challenges."

I sigh, staring into my coffee. "Maybe I'm chasing a fantasy, Mom. Maybe what I'm looking for doesn't exist."

"Doesn't exist?" She chuckles lightly. "Your father and I found it. It's not a fantasy, Emma. It's just rare."

"But how do you know when to keep going or when to just... stop?" The question hangs in the air, heavy with doubt.

She reaches across the table, her hand covering mine. "You keep going until it feels right to stop. You're strong, Emma. Stronger than you give yourself credit for."

I think of the birthmark, a façade that brought only shallow encounters. "But what if I'm wrong? What if all I find are more disappointments?"

"Then you learn from them." Mom's voice is firm yet kind. "Every disappointment teaches you more about what you truly want. And what you don't."

I ponder her words, a lifeline in a sea of uncertainty. "But it's hard, Mom. It's so hard feeling invisible."

"You're not invisible," she insists. "Not to the people who matter. You're a light, Emma. And the right person will see that. They'll see you, not the actress or birthmark, but you."

Her conviction is a balm to my bruised hope. "What if I never find them?"

She smiles, a blend of nostalgia and confidence. "Then they'll find you. Love has a way of surprising us, often when we least expect it."

I finish my coffee, feeling a renewed sense of purpose. My mother's belief in love for me reignites a spark I thought had dimmed.

I stand up, hugging her tightly. "Thanks, Mom. I needed this."

"Anytime, my dear. And remember, the right person will see your heart, not just your face."

A few days later, I left the warmth of my childhood home and flew back to LA. The sky has cleared, and with it, so has my resolve.

After returning to LA, I settle back into my routine. Life continues as usual until one day, an unexpected opportunity knocks: a notice to audition for a famous movie director. But, as luck would have it, my audition coincides with a brewing storm.

I find myself driving through the storm, anxiety knotting my stomach. Glancing at my watch, I remind myself this meeting is crucial—a potentially career-defining moment. Determined to be punctual, I weave my car through the city's busy streets.

As I make my way, I enter a newly developed city area. It starkly contrasts the familiar urban landscape—a raw, incomplete world of half-built structures, where the earthy smell of wet soil mingles with the scent of construction materials. The storm intensifies, adding a dramatic backdrop to the already daunting journey.

My GPS starts to falter, confused by the new and uncharted roads.

"Not now," I mutter, eyes scanning for any familiar landmark.

Then, disaster strikes—a loud pop, and my car lurches. A nail, hidden amidst construction debris, has punctured my tire. I pull over, the car coming to rest in a muddy field, far from the neat, orderly streets I'm used to.

As I step out, the heavens open up, unleashing a torrent of rain. I wrestle with the jack and spare tire, but the rain is relentless, turning the ground into a treacherous sea of mud. My hands slip on the wet tools, frustration mounting with each failed attempt.

"You look like you could use some help!" a voice calls out through the downpour. I look up, squinting through the rain, to see a man approaching. He's robust, and his solid build indicates his physically demanding job. Despite the storm, there's a kindness in his eyes and a certain rugged handsomeness about him.

"I'm Steven," he says, his voice strong over the roar of the rain, extending a hand already streaked with mud.

"Emma," I reply, attempting a smile that feels more like a grimace. "I'm in a bit of a rush. I have an important meeting and can't afford to be late."

"No worries, Emma. Let's get this sorted quickly." His confidence is infectious.

Steven takes over. His movements are efficient and skilled, even in the pouring rain. The storm has turned my hair into a dripping mess, and my face is streaked with rain and mud, masking any trace of the carefully made-up professional I was this morning.

"Thank you, I... I don't know what I'd do without your help," I say, watching him work, feeling helpless.

He flashes a quick, reassuring smile. "Not a big deal."

I chuckle, the sound muffled by the rain. "It's a big help to me."

The tire is replaced, and Steven doesn't leave me stranded. He walks me back to my car, his boots squelching in the mud. "I'll guide you out of here," he offers. "This place is a labyrinth if you're unfamiliar with it."

We drive slowly, the rain still pouring but less fiercely now. The sun peeks through the clouds, casting a warm, golden light on the sodden earth.

"There, you should be able to make it from here," Steven says, pointing out a familiar road.

"I can't thank you enough, Steven," I say, realizing I don't want this to be the last time I see him.

"Do you... would you mind if I got your contact information?" I ask, fumbling for my phone.

He grins. "Sure thing, Emma. Here, let me type it in for you."

I take one last look in the rearview mirror as I drive away. Steven is still there, watching as he disappears into the fading rain. Despite the chaos of the day and my disheveled appearance, his kindness, and my unexpected resilience leave me feeling surprisingly uplifted.

Pulling up to the meeting venue, I pause for a much-needed respite. I glance at myself in the rearview mirror, taking stock of my appearance. I try to tame my hair with careful movements, now a wild testament to the storm I've just braved. I use a tissue to gently wipe away the mud streaks on my cheeks, inadvertently removing the last traces of my makeup. I take a deep, steadying breath, looking at my reflection—raw, unadorned, yet resolute. "This is me," I think, a quiet resolve building within. "Take it or leave it."

As I enter the audition room, the director, a woman with a stern face and piercing eyes, initially looks taken aback. Her assistant quickly hands me a one-page script. "You have two minutes to prepare," she states crisply.

I scan the script, simultaneously visualizing my performance. Inwardly, I steel myself against the distraction of hundreds of other competitors in the waiting room, pushing aside thoughts of my disheveled appearance.

Standing in the center of the room, I begin. As I delve into the character, I sense the director's demeanor shift. The sharpness in her eyes softens, replaced by what seems like grudging respect.

After my performance, she extended a firm handshake, her initial surprise now morphed into a subtle nod of approval. "Impressive confidence," she comments. "You're the first actress to come to an audition without makeup." The edges of her lips curl into a faint smile, acknowledging my unconventional choice.

Stepping out of the building, a sense of relief washes over me. Successful or not, today's experience is about more than just an audition. I've navigated through a storm and emerged with a newfound inner strength.

My phone vibrates with an incoming message, snapping me back to reality. It's just a few simple words from Steven: Can you find your way back? His considerate and timely message brings a warm smile to my face.

Waiting at a red light, I hastily reply: Of course. Thanks. My fingers fly over the screen, sending the message into the digital void.

But as the light shifts to green and I start to drive away, a twinge of regret washes over me.

In my rush to respond, I realize I've just let slip a perfect chance to see him again.

The city around me buzzes with life, but my mind is still partly back in that muddy field, with the rain pouring down and Steven's steady presence.

As I start the drive home, I expect to meet Steven again.

In the following weeks, I received exhilarating news: I'd been chosen as the lead actress in a movie. Eager to share my gratitude in person, I decide it's time to see Steven again.

Sitting in my quiet living room, the box of chocolates beside me, I hesitate momentarily before picking up my phone. My fingers hover over Steven's contact, the one he entered in the storm. I tap the call button.

"Hey, Steven, it's Emma," I say when he answers, my voice steadier than I feel. "I wanted to properly thank you for your help. Could we meet at that coffee shop near the construction site where you're working?"

There's a brief pause, and his warm voice fills my ear. "Sure, Emma, that sounds great. When were you thinking?"

"How about this afternoon, roughly after thirty minutes?" I suggest, hoping it's not too soon.

"That works for me. See you then, Emma."

As I end the call, I'm on my way.

I push open the door to the coffee shop, a box of chocolates tucked under my arm. The bell above the door chimes as I scan the room. I spot him near the window, his robust frame hunched over a small table, engrossed in his phone.

"Hey, Steven," I call out as I approach. He looks up, and his face breaks into a smile, his eyes lighting up in recognition.

"Emma, right? The damsel in distress from the construction field?" he teases, standing to greet me.

I laugh, setting the box on the table. "Guilty as charged. I brought these as a thank-you. You were a lifesaver."

He accepts the box. "Wow, this is too much, but thank you." His tone is genuine. He gestures for me to sit down.

As we settle into our seats, I order a coffee, and he gets a black tea.

"So, how did the meeting go after all that?" he asks, leaning forward, genuinely interested.

"It went well. I arrived right on time," I reply, chuckling at the memory.

I find myself studying him, the lines of his face, the way his eyes crinkle when he laughs. He's ruggedly handsome, and the kindness about him is endearing. But there's something I need to know.

"So, Steven, you are the builder, "I begin, a little hesitant. "Is there a Mrs. Builder in your life?"

"No."

"Maybe a girlfriend?"

"No."

"Why?" I keep digging.

He looks surprised momentarily, then laughs, a deep, hearty sound. "No, no Mrs. Builder. And no girlfriend either. My work keeps me pretty busy."

I feel a flutter of relief mixed with excitement. "I can imagine. It must be fulfilling, creating something lasting."

"Yeah, it is," he agrees, his eyes meeting mine. "What about you? Anyone waiting for you to come home?"

"No, just me," I reply, feeling a warmth spread through me at the thought that maybe, just maybe, there's a possibility here.

"Unbelievable," Steven says with a smile, his eyes twinkling with humor and admiration. "A girl like you... must have admirers lining up."

I meet his gaze, a playful yet determined glint in my own. "I prefer to be the one making the selections," I reply, my tone lighthearted but confident.

"What do you make for a living?"

"I'm a manager of a Walmart."

As we part ways, Steven hesitates for a moment. "Would you... maybe want to grab dinner sometime?" he asks, a hopeful note in his voice.

I smile, feeling a rush of happiness. "I'd like that." I am already looking forward to seeing him again.

Stepping out of the coffee shop, I know this is the beginning of something promising with Steven.

A month later, as autumn paints the city in hues of amber and rust, our relationship blossoms with a newfound lightness.

On a brisk evening, Steven invites me to his cozy apartment with a view of the city skyline. He cooks dinner, each dish a testament to his attention to detail and care. We dine to the backdrop of soft jazz, the city lights twinkling like distant stars.

After dinner, he pulls out an old photo album. It's a window into his past, each picture a story. He points to a young boy with a makeshift hard hat. "I, age seven, 'supervising' my dad's garage project."

I laugh, touched by the glimpse into his child-hood.

Then he grows quiet, turning to a photo of a younger him with a woman, their arms wrapped around each other. "That's Sara," he says, his voice a whisper. "We were engaged."

The air shifts, heavy with unspoken words. "What happened?" I ask gently.

He closes the album, his eyes meeting mine. "She passed away in a car accident just months before the wedding."

The pain in his voice is palpable, a wound still fresh despite the years. "I'm so sorry, Steven," I say, my heart aching for his loss.

He nods thoughtfully. "We all have scars. The differences lie in their size and depth."

I gently take his hand, feeling a connection deeper than words. "And in how we choose to heal them," I add softly, meeting his gaze.

That night, as I lie in his arms, enveloped in the comforting rhythm of his heartbeat, a profound realization washes over me. In the whispers of the night, it becomes clear just how deeply we've come to love each other.

Autumn's embrace turns to winter's chill, and with it comes an evening that feels ripe with unspoken words. Steven and I sit in his living room, a fire crackling in the hearth, casting a warm glow over us.

I've just returned from my movie shoot, and the experience is still vivid. Before leaving, I told Steven I needed to go away for months of training. But the truth is, it was a lie.

As the weight of my dishonesty settles in, I'm overwhelmed with guilt.

The need to make things right, to confess and apologize, presses urgently against my con-science. I know I can't let this lie stand between us—it's not the foundation I want for whatever might bloom between Steven and me.

Steven looks at me, a question in his eyes. "You've been quiet tonight. What's on your mind, Emma?"

I draw a deep breath, the weight of my se-cret pressing against my chest. "Steven, there's something I need to tell you. Something about me that I've kept hidden."

He leans forward, his expression open, encouraging. "You can tell me anything, Emma."

I pause, gathering the courage. "It's about my life... my career. I'm not just Emma. I'm Emma Delaney, the actress."

The words hang in the air, a fragile confession. Steven's expression shifts, a mixture of surprise and confusion.

"The Emma Delaney?" he asks, disbelief coloring his tone.

I nod, my heart racing. "Yes. I kept it hidden because I wanted someone to see me, the real me, not the actress or the celebrity."

Steven sits back, processing the revelation, his silence like a widening gulf between us.

"Emma, why didn't you tell me sooner?" His voice is soft but holds an undercurrent of hurt.

"I was scared," I whisper. "Scared that you'd see me differently, that our connection would change."

He looks into the fire, contemplation etched on his face. "I understand why you did it, but it feels like you didn't trust me."

The truth of his words stings. "I do trust you, Steven. More than anyone. It's just that... this world I'm in, finding something real is hard. What we have it's the most genuine thing I've experienced."

He turns to me, his eyes searching mine. "Emma, I've fallen for you, for the woman I've come to know. Your world and fame don't change how I feel."

Relief washes over me, a wave of gratitude and love. "I'm so sorry, Steven. I never wanted to hurt you."

He takes my hand, his grip firm yet gentle. "I get it, Emma. And I'm not going anywhere. But let's promise each other no more secrets."

I nod, a promise sealed in our entwined hands. "No more secrets," I echo.

We sit quietly, warmed by the fire. It's like the steady flame inside us. Telling Steven the truth has opened my heart, and his understanding shows me a love that's more than just being famous or rich.

Outside, the winter wind keeps blowing, but inside, we feel peaceful. Here, by the fire, it's just Steven and me, our hearts together, sharing a solid love because we're honest and trust each other.

Spring is here. Steven and I relax in his small, cozy garden on a sunny Sunday afternoon. It feels like we're a world away from the busy life I'm used to. Here, in this simple moment, we find our little paradise.

We sit on an old bench, holding hands and watching the sunlight play through the leaves. The gentle breeze brings the smell of flowers, filling the air with calmness and new beginnings.

"I always dreamed of this," I say softly, resting my head on his shoulder. "Finding peace in simple things."

Steven laughs, a deep sound that's comforting. "Life's strange like that. The best parts are often hidden in the simplest moments."

I look up at him, my heart full. "With you, Steven, every moment is special."

He kisses my forehead softly. "You've taught me that love is found not in big gestures but in these quiet times together."

The engagement ring on my finger sparkles in the sunlight, a symbol of our love.

Printed in Great Britain
by Amazon

53703991R00238